DONNYBOY

DONNYBOY

A biographical novel by

RON PHILLIPS

LEAWOOD PRODUCTIONS, INC.

Library of Congress Control Number: 2010918116

Copyright ©2011 Ron Phillips

Cover Design by Simplissimus

Illustrations by Roger Beerworth

First Leawood Productions trade paperback printing, January 2011

Leawood Productions, Inc. 1676 Foothill Road, Ojai, CA 93023

For more information, contact:

Leawood Productions, Inc. 1676 Foothill Road, Ojai, CA 93023

DONNYBOYBOOK.COM

ISBN 978-1456538675

Printed in USA

To Mom and Dad,
without whom there wouldn't be a Donnyboy.

ACKNOWLEDGEMENTS

To Linda Phillips, for encouraging and believing in me and keeping me honest for over 40 years. To my writer's group— Pat Hattmann, Patric Peake, LaNette Donough, Anne Boydston, and Cindy Mullins—who kept Donnyboy's voice on pitch. And to Kenyon Phillips, whose unshaking belief in *Donnyboy* and peerless editorial skills elevated this book to a higher plane. Thanks, guys.

SYNOPSIS

In a small South Dakota town at the end of WWII, a fearless
stray dog and a principled German Prisoner of War embolden
Donald "Donnyboy" Cook, an insecure 13-year-old, to stand up
against the bullies who terrorize him and the intolerance
choking his community. Along the way, Donnyboy overcomes
his loneliness and isolation by making friends with several
colorful classmates and falling in love with the smartest,
prettiest and most competitive girl in his grade.

THE CHARACTERS

DONALD "DONNYBOY" COOK

ERIC STIENDLER

PETE FLAVORIAN

BILLY ROGERS

JANE COOK

AL COOK

ALICE CODY

CLEO SAMPSON

BO FOLEY

LESTER LEACH

CHAPLIN

Based on true events.

CHAPTER 1

WEDNESDAY, JANUARY 31, 1945

The view through the windshield was dismal. Stark, frost-covered fields, unbroken except for an occasional silo.

Even with the heater going full blast in our Buick Century, we wore coats. The seat was especially cold. I pressed my nose to the side window, opened my mouth and puffed. A circle of fog spread on the glass. I drew a question mark in the fog. It bled tears.

I didn't know what was in store for me in our new town. Based on the ones we'd lived in before, I dreaded it.

We left Peoria at six o'clock this morning. Mom packed food to eat along the way. I had no appetite. Except for some bathroom stops, Dad drove straight through. The Burma-Shave signs started to repeat themselves.

A futuristic-looking chrome clock on the dashboard read three forty-five. We'd made good time in spite of the U-Haul trailer hitched to the back of the Buick. Too good. The closer we got, the edgier I felt.

"Can you turn on the radio, Dad?"

"Sure, Donnyboy." Dad took a gloved hand off the steering wheel and flicked the switch.

Mom sat next to Dad in the front seat. "Not too loud," she cautioned. The radio announcer's voice crackled over the car speakers.

"...the Allies announced today US Ninth Army units have almost reached the swollen Roer River—the last major obstacle in their march toward Dusseldorf and the Rhine. And then on to Berlin."

Dad grunted in satisfaction. "They're breathing right down Hitler's neck."

Mom looked up from her *Collier's* magazine and smiled. Suddenly her eyes widened. "Look!"

I raised Chaplin's heavy head off my lap and sat up. He continued snoring as his head plopped on the seat next to me.

Outside, a green and white weathered sign read:

FARMINGTON, S.D.
POPULATION 5,113

"Counting the dogs," Dad snickered.

Mom swatted him with her magazine. "Al!" She turned around to face me. "Farmington will be a perfect place for us to settle down."

I wondered how she could be so sure since she'd never been here before. But I hoped she was right.

Outside my window, empty fields gave way to a maze of white-boarded pens connected to a string of red barns. The pens were empty. "What's all that?" I asked.

"Stockyards." Dad answered.

"Where are the animals?"

"Probably slaughtered."

My stomach clenched. "They do that here?"

Mom sighed. "Don't pay any attention to your father, Donnyboy."

We passed a gigantic red and white radio tower that stretched so high I had to squash my face against the window to see the top. Near the tower sat a squat, square building. Neon letters across its flat roof read:

WXAX
WORLD'S TALLEST RADIO TOWER

Mom crinkled her nose. "Surely that's not the Senator's radio station?"

Dad laughed. "It's the engineering shack. The studio's in town. You'll see."

The way he said it tickled my curiosity. Dad had been to Farmington once before. Senator Garney, the owner of the station, flew him up in his private airplane.

We entered the outskirts of town. A tourist court with miniature log cabins and a Flying Red Horse filling station faced each other on either side of the highway. Occasional houses appeared with skeletons of cars randomly parked in unkempt yards.

The highway became Center Street, and suddenly sidewalks surfaced. We passed the naked limbs of towering trees reaching out to touch one another as the street widened. Elegant houses replaced the shacks. They were two or three stories high, with wide porches and deep yards. Some had spike-fenced widow's walks on their roofs.

Compared to the homes in the towns we'd lived in, these looked old-fashioned but statelier.

"Keep an eye out for Pearl Street," Dad said.

A couple blocks later, Mom pointed. "There." Dad turned right. Pearl wasn't quite as grand as the other streets, but it was close.

"The address is 612," Mom said, reading from the Senator's telegram. "Even numbers are on the right."

The houses sat so far from the street that I had to strain to see their numbers. I started to read one aloud when a siren interrupted me, its wail especially grating on this peaceful block.

Through the windshield I saw a camouflaged Army Jeep with blinking red lights rolling toward us. The Jeep led a convoy of slow-moving Army trucks with their headlights on. It reminded me of a funeral procession.

A tall GI with Sergeant stripes and a cocky grin sat next to the Jeep driver. He motioned for Dad to pull over.

"What's this all about?" Mom asked uneasily.

Dad stopped at the curb. "Beats me."

I hunched forward for a better look. Chaplin awoke and scrambled up on his haunches beside me. His head almost touched the headliner. Chaplin was tall for a dog. I was short for a 13-year-old.

The Sergeant gave us a half salute as the Jeep passed. Even though it was freezing, the cloth sides of the trucks were rolled up. An MP sat in the front of each truck, leaning nonchalantly on a rifle. Two rows of soldiers sat facing each other along the sides of each truck.

The soldiers looked glum. Their fatigues were grey instead of green, with no stripes or patches. Each one wore a black armband with *POW* printed in white.

Mom gasped.

I tensed. "How come it says 'pow' on their arms?"

"It's not a word," Dad answered. "It's initials. Stands for Prisoner of War."

I was frightened but fascinated at the same time. "You mean they're *Nazis*?"

Dad shook his head. "Not every German's a Nazi. But they're German soldiers for sure."

"What are they doing here?" Mom asked in a worried tone.

"No idea," Dad answered. "But relax, you two. They're probably just passing through."

I scrunched down in my seat, but I couldn't keep my eyes off the prisoners. I edged back up.

The lead Jeep must have stopped at Center Street, because the trucks slowed to a halt. One stopped right across from our car, and that's when I saw him.

He sat in a row of prisoners with their backs to us. He was twisted around and staring into space, like you do when you're thinking more than looking. He was smaller than the other prisoners, and probably no more than eighteen or nineteen years old. He had sandy hair, hazel eyes and boyish features that were sharpening into an adult face.

"Hey, Eric!" the guard growled. "Turn around." The truck jerked forward, and Eric's head dropped. Our eyes met for an instant. His were forlorn, as though he had some great, unbearable grief locked deep inside of him.

Just like me.

CHAPTER 2

THURSDAY, FEBRUARY 1, 1945

We had the entire second floor of a roomy white house with a front porch and a deep front yard. My folks' bedroom and bath were in the back. A short hallway led to a kitchen big enough to eat in. The dining room and living room were off the kitchen. My bedroom was under the steep front roof of the house. It had a small bathroom.

Our private entrance was up a short flight of stairs at the rear of the house. It certainly beat most apartments we'd lived in, even though the dark wood in the living room made it seem a bit gloomy.

We always rented furnished places because we moved around so much. The only things we took with us were dishes, clothes, bed stuff, my bunk bed, Dad's rifle and shotgun, our RCA console radio, and my small record player. These all fit in a small U-Haul trailer. Mom insisted on getting me a bunk bed last year in case a friend wanted to stay overnight. It hadn't happened yet.

Once the boxes were unpacked and my bed set up, Dad went to the station to say hello. I sat down in the kitchen with a cup of hot chocolate while Mom shredded Velveeta onto a tuna and noodle casserole for dinner. "Where are the folks who own this place?" I asked.

"San Diego. Their son's in a Navy hospital there."

"What's wrong with him?"

"A Kamikaze crashed into his ship. He may lose a leg."

I grimaced.

Dad came back from the station. While he seemed disappointed in the musicians he had to work with as well as Mr. Cody, the station manager, he had some big news. "You know those POWs we saw coming into town yesterday?"

"Uh-huh," I said. Ever since I'd seen that young prisoner, Eric, I couldn't get him out of my mind.

"The Army's set them up in a camp by the river, right next to the station."

Mom stopped in the middle of dishing out her casserole. "What on earth for?"

"Missouri River's been flooding all winter and gnawing away at the bank. The bridge from here to Nebraska will collapse if they don't shore it up."

The edges of Mom's mouth drooped. "What's that got to do with bringing dangerous enemies here?"

"Manpower shortage. Senator Garney came up with the idea to use POWs. Makes sense to me."

I got a funny feeling inside of me. I couldn't tell if it was excitement or fear.

CHAPTER 3

FRIDAY, FEBRUARY 2, 1945

Today would be yet another first day at a new school. The view out my bedroom window made me even more depressed. Thick, somber clouds swallowed the morning sun. A tree branch scratched against my window like a witch's fingernails. I sat on my bed and clipped on my tie. Chaplin sat beside me. I reached up and rubbed behind his ears. He drooled in ecstasy.

Mom's high heels clickety-clacked toward my room. I shoved Chaplin off the bed and smoothed his shape from the spread.

She threw open the door. Mom was just over five feet tall, and just under 100 pounds. But she was mighty. She gasped with surprise. "You are dressed. And your bed's made."

I nodded dourly.

Mom paused at my dresser, and glanced in the mirror. She unbuttoned her red suit jacket, pursed her lips, rebuttoned it. Everyone always said Mom was beautiful. She thought her nose was too big because she was Greek.

"Why are you moping?" she asked crossly.

"Look at me."

Mom was a big believer in "first impressions." She had picked out my clothes for today: camel sweater, yellow shirt, striped bow tie, long white socks, brown shoes, and brown short pants. No matter how hard I argued, she insisted that I wear them. I pleaded with Dad to at least let me wear long pants. As usual, he stayed out of it.

"They'll think I'm a freak," I whined.

Mom wouldn't give an inch. "They'll see you're from a fine home. Besides, you have cute legs."

She dragged me over to the dresser, drowned my hair in Lucky Tiger Tonic and scraped my head with my hairbrush in an effort to cement my cowlick down. It immediately popped back up. A sharp pain knifed my stomach. I doubled over wincing. Chaplin rushed over to me and licked my hands.

Mom looked alarmed. "You? You're not?

I took a deep breath. "Just a bad twinge." I stroked Chaplin's back.

Mom led me out into the living room. Chaplin stayed by my side. "Al, it's that time," she called out.

A long belch came from their bedroom.

Mom looked worried. "You didn't drink your milk again, did you?"

"Can't hear you, Jane."

Dad had a bad stomach. That's why he wasn't drafted. He's supposed to drink plenty of milk and not much coffee, but does just the opposite.

Mom lit a Chesterfield with a silver Ronson lighter shaped like a genie's lamp. I slumped down in the living room chair hoping Dad would never come out.

He did, though, looking uncomfortable in a fancy black and white cowboy outfit. He got it when his musical group, the Indiana Outlaws, made a movie with Gene Autry last year.

Dad was handsome in a slick sort of way. He had a pencil mustache like Errol Flynn, and parted his hair in the middle like Ronald Colman. He was so thin that other musicians called him "Slim." Mom hated that name.

I was surprised by Dad's getup. Radio station studios were usually stuffy little rooms with microphones and music stands and maybe a piano. The walls and ceilings were covered in soundproof tan tiles with hundreds of holes in them. Hardly the kind of place that called for stage clothes.

"How come you're all dressed up?" I asked.

"Cody," Dad said, making a face. "Studio A here is huge, with big glass windows so people can look in. Farmers come to town to watch the radio shows. Cody says we need to give 'em a show." Dad shrugged into a black suede coat with fringes on its sleeves.

Mom slung what looked like a dead fox over her shoulders and snapped its mouth onto its tail.

"Please, Mom. Can't I just wear some normal clothes?"

She let out an exasperated breath and swept out the back door. I put on my pea coat and trudged after her.

The outside air hit my lungs like ice water and made me feel dizzy. I leaned against the railing to keep from falling. My teeth chattered. The veins in my bare legs turned blue.

Mom called from the back yard. "Donnyboy, hurry."

"It's colder than the North Pole!" I stomped my feet to get the circulation going. "I don't like this place."

"Quit stalling."

I clutched the railing and edged down the stairs. Heights scared me, even little ones.

The streamlined green fenders and smiling chrome mouth of Dad's Buick Century backed into the gravel alley. It was a 1941, the last year they made cars for civilians. Dad all but licked it clean.

We drove down the alley past an immense vacant lot on our left. Dad switched on the radio. A man named Farmer Frank reported in a droning voice: "...*hogs generally steady. Good and choice barrows and gilts up fourteen seventy-five*..."

Mom flicked the radio off. Dad turned left on Pearl Street.

If Dad had his way, he would still be playing in Paul Whiteman's road band. But when I got old enough for school, Mom laid down the law: Dad had to quit life on the road and settle down, "or else."

"Or else" meant she'd move to Moline with me and live with her father—my Grandpa Jim—who never approved of Dad in the first place because he ran off with Mom and wasn't Greek.

Dad gave up the road and joined a Western group called the Indiana Outlaws at station WIBW in Topeka. Before long they became pretty famous and other radio stations wanted them. The group's leader, Clyde Clauser, would take the group from one station to another whenever anyone offered more money.

I'd gone to so many different schools by the time I was twelve that I couldn't even remember them all. That's when my "problem" started. And Mom gave Dad another "or else."

Dad quit the Outlaws and promised Mom we'd settle down for good. I'm sure he meant it, but it didn't hurt that he was sick and tired of playing the same old Western music. Senator Garney got in touch with Dad and offered him the program director's job at radio station WXAX. To sweeten the deal, he got Dad a recording contract with Columbia Records.

We turned onto Front Street. A wide park sloped down to the widest river I'd ever seen. The water looked like liquid dirt.

"What's that?" I asked.

"Missouri River," said Dad.

"How come it's so brown?" Mom wondered.

"Mud from the flooding," Dad replied.

I heard the *chug-chug-chug* of a tall contraption at the river's edge. A circle of men with *POW* stenciled on the backs of their slickers were guiding a huge black pole suspended by ropes. The machine puffed out steam and pounded the pole into the riverbank.

"The POWs!" I pointed, straining to see Eric. But we were too far away to distinguish faces.

Mom pointed at two white-belted MPs smoking and chatting. "Those guys certainly aren't watching the prisoners very closely."

"Germany's a bit of a swim from here," Dad chuckled.

Mom frowned. "Don't be flip."

Five blocks ahead, a two-story white bridge straddled the river. Its sides and tops were made of thick, crisscrossed girders, like something from a giant Erector set. "There's the bridge they brought the Germans over to save," said Dad.

All bridges gave me the wimwams, let alone one that could collapse at any second. "We don't have to cross it, do we?"

Dad shook his head and turned into a wide driveway. My jaw dropped. Mom gasped.

Dad laughed. "Welcome to Garney Castle. Station's on the top floor."

The front of the castle was a block long, four stories tall and had two round things on top like you see on Russian buildings. It was faced with corn ears painted a gaudy yellow, green and gold.

Mom giggled. "This isn't for real, is it?"

Dad nodded.

The windows were shaped like giant corn kernels. Each corner of the building sprouted a giant gold and green cornstalk. Dad slowed down at the front entrance. A sign above the front doors said:

GARNEY SEED CO.
CORNIEST COMPANY ON EARTH

Dad kept moving. "Aren't you going to get out?" Mom asked.

"Staff can't go in the front. Cody says we'd lose our 'mystique,' whatever that is. We've got an 'Artists' Entrance.'"

Mom looked impressed.

Dad pulled around the corner of the building and stopped. There were no doors on this side of the building.

"Why are you stopping here?" Mom asked tartly. "We'll be late for school."

Dad nodded at an old fire escape. "That's the Artists' Entrance." It zigzagged up four stories to a small door with a naked light bulb over it.

"You're kidding?" I blurted. Mom's eyebrows almost touched the veil on her red hat.

Dad opened the car door, grabbed his fiddle case and kissed Mom on the cheek. "See you here around one fifteen. Good luck, DB."

I watched in terror as he began to climb the stairs. They clanged, shuddered and shook, churning my stomach with every step Dad took. I covered my eyes, expecting the worst. The clanging stopped. I split my fingers and peered up. Dad waved from the top landing. He opened the door and disappeared inside.

Mom turned to me, her face grave. "Don't ever go near that thing, hear?"

I nodded. "Don't worry." But seeing Dad breeze up the stairs made me feel like a coward.

Mom braked hard in front of the school. She checked her hair in the rear view mirror, grabbed a large envelope and opened the door. "Let's go, Donnyboy."

I didn't move.

Mom ducked back into the car. "Quit stalling."

"I'm not going anywhere, 'til you promise."

"Promise what?"

"Not to call me Donnyboy in front of anyone. It's too babyish." Dad started calling me Donnyboy when I was a baby. I liked it, but only around my folks.

Mom shot me an annoyed look. "Okay. Let's go, *Donald*."

The school loomed like Frankenstein's castle, a dreary box of red stone streaked from years of rain. The black paved surface of the empty playground had a spider web of deep cracks.

We entered a long, dark hallway with classrooms on either side. A string of caged light bulbs cast a dull yellow glow on the scuffed grey concrete floor. The air smelled used. Steam swooshed from strings of radiators. It had to be 80 degrees. I whipped off my pea coat.

A big kid with tiny black eyes set too close together and two rat-like front teeth came out of the boys room. When he saw me, he stopped and broke out laughing. It sounded like an asthma attack.

My body slumped. Mom grabbed the back of my sweater and pulled me up. "Could you lead us to the principal's office?" she asked in an icy voice.

Rat Face pointed to a worn oak staircase. "Up there."

"Thank you," Mom replied, and pulled me toward the stairs.

"What happened to the rest of your pants?" Rat Face taunted, and shuffled toward a classroom.

I trudged up the stairs, trembling with humiliation. To make matters worse, my socks kept falling down.

"Hurry," Mom urged.

"Look what you got me into 'cause of these stupid clothes," I grumbled. "Just imagine what'll happen when the class sees me."

Mom set her jaw. "Did you say something to me, young man?"

I dropped my head and didn't answer. The second floor looked just as dreary as the first. We hurried to a door with the word *Principal* lettered on frosted glass.

Mom knocked. Nobody answered. She knocked louder. Nothing.

From inside came the clatter of someone pecking on a typewriter. Mom twisted the worn brass knob and the door swung open.

Inside, a fat blue-haired woman stuffed behind a desk struggled to type with two fingers. She wore tiny round spectacles. Over her shoulder was a closed door marked *Principal*.

Blue Hair either didn't see us or didn't want to. We walked up to her desk. Mom cleared her throat. Blue Hair looked up with a startled expression. Her eyes bugged when they shifted from Mom to me.

"I'm here to enroll my son."

Blue Hair seemed paralyzed by my appearance.

"I'd like to enroll my son," Mom repeated.

The woman blinked back to life. She ripped out the paper she'd been typing on and, after several tries, rolled in a form halfway straight. "Name?"

"Donald Lee Cook."

I noticed Blue Hair's lips moved as she typed. "Grade?"

"Eighth."

Blue Hair lifted her eyes suspiciously. "He's pretty small for eighth grade."

Mom handed her the large envelope. "His records are all here."

Blue Hair shrugged, pulled the form from her typewriter and swiveled to face the back office. "Mr. Chester, new stoodent."

"What?" A gruff voice replied.

"New stoodent. Eighth grade."

A chair screeched and the back door creaked open. A man peered out with stringy reddish-grey hair and a thick red mustache. He was tall and stocky. He wore a stained dress shirt and tie and a silver whistle around his neck.

Blue Hair gave Mom the envelope and form. Mr. Chester motioned warily for us to come into his office. "Don't usually get new kids this time of year." He paused. "Or anytime for that matter."

A shelf of sparkling sports trophies was the only bright spot in his office. The brown walls were dingy and bare except for a couple of light rectangles where diplomas probably once hung.

Chester pointed to two brown cracked leather chairs across from his desk. "Take a seat." He sat and hooked his thumbs into black and grey striped suspenders. "This principal thing, it's just temporary," he explained. "Real job's coach."

"And the regular principal?" Mom asked.

Chester chuckled. "Old Van Ness kinda went off the deep end last Christmas. School Board put me in charge 'til he's better. Or they come up with a replacement."

Mom introduced us and handed him the envelope and the form.

Principal-Coach Chester put on a pair of finger-smudged spectacles. He unwound the string on the flap of the envelope and shuffled through the pages.

When he finally looked up, he stared at me like I had two heads. "Eight different schools. In two years?"

My stomach lurched.

Mom smiled. "My husband's been with a popular musical group. It required a lot of relocation. Senator Garney has hired Mr. Cook in an important position at WXAX. We expect to make Farmington our home from now on."

Chester peered at me. "Don't suppose you're into sports?"

"I like to run," I said.

Chester grunted, placed his hands on his desk and stood. "I'll see he gets to his teacher."

"I'd love to meet her," Mom said.

Chester frowned. "Best you save that for another time. Don't want to make a hullabaloo with class on."

Mom started to protest.

Mr. Chester ignored her and pushed open his door. "Nice ta meet ya, Missus Cook."

Mom sighed. "What time is school out?"

"Three fifteen."

She patted my cheek. "Pick you up then, Donny–uh, Donald. Bottom of the steps." Mom marched out the door past Mr. Chester without a word.

The principal stared at me for what seemed like a lifetime. Sweat dribbled from my armpits. Out of nowhere, he lifted his whistle and blew. He walked out the door, waving for me to follow.

Three slabs of blackboard stretched across the front of the classroom. Above, a brown banner displayed the alphabet, each letter carefully printed in upper and lower case. A narrow oak rail held dusty erasers. A copy of the *Weekly Reader* was pinned to a tan corkboard on the right wall. A butcher paper chart stretched wide showing who in the class had bought how many war stamps. On the left wall, another corkboard held a poster with a happy family bundling waste paper and the words: *Get in the Scrap!*

"New student, Miss Morris," Chester declared as he led me up to the teacher's desk. The room smelled of stale steam and chalk dust.

The kids became deadly silent. My skin felt like ants were crawling all over it. I didn't dare look at anyone.

"Name's Cook. Donald Cook." He dropped my records onto the teacher's desk, turned and strode out the door.

Miss Morris's eyebrows arched. Then her mouth crept into a welcoming smile. She looked younger than any teacher I'd ever had—friendlier, too. She had large brown eyes, a rosy complexion, short chestnut hair, and a plump, sweet face.

Miss Morris stood and held out her hand. "Pleased to meet you, Donald," she said in a tinkling voice. "A new student is an unexpected pleasure here."

My hand trembled as she took it in hers. I sensed a room full of eyes staring at my short pants. Most of the boys wore rolled-up dungarees and thick wool shirts, while the girls sported solid color skirts and bulky knit sweaters or flowery rayon dresses. I saw a lot of Army boots. Even on one of the girls.

The kids looked bigger and older than me. No surprise. I was small for my age. Plus I'd skipped a grade—not that I was a Quiz Kid or anything. When we had moved to Wisconsin a couple years back, they'd put me in sixth grade instead of fifth by mistake. The schoolwork didn't seem any harder. I'd stayed a grade ahead ever since.

Miss Morris pointed to the cloakroom. "Hang up your coat. Then we'll get acquainted."

I moved toward the cloakroom, eyes straight ahead. After I'd entered, tittering broke out. I took two quick breaths and strolled past hooks filled with well-worn mackinaws, pea coats and mufflers. One coat stood out from the rest. It was dark blue with a wide cloth belt and fancy gold buttons. A shiny pink purse with a white Scottie dog dangled over the coat.

"Having problems?" Miss Morris called out.

"No, ma'am. Trying to find an empty hook." I finally spied one almost covered by the fancy coat. I slipped my pea coat onto it and scooted back to the classroom.

"I'm afraid all our desks are full," Miss Morris said, standing behind a chair sitting right next to her desk. "'Til we can round one up, you'll sit here."

My forehead broke out in a sweat. I wanted to get lost in a back row; instead, I was a bull's eye for attention.

A commotion broke out in the back of the room. A red-haired oaf banged through the classroom door. His bib overalls were caked with mud or, judging by the smell that quickly reached the front of the room, something worse.

"Bo Foley!" Miss Morris snapped.

He swaggered in and swiped a finger across his runny nose. "That's me." The ragged sleeve of his black jacket ended about four inches short of his tattered shirt cuff.

One of the boys slapped his desk and cried, "Yeah, Bo!" It was the rat-faced kid from the hall.

Miss Morris wagged a finger at him. "Shush Lester, or you'll be cooling your heels in Mr. Chester's office again."

Lester curled his lip, but shut up.

Miss Morris frowned at the redhead. "Well, Bo, guess it's time for a pow wow with your Pa."

"Great idea," a good-looking boy with a scar above his right eyebrow said from across the room. He slouched cockily in his desk with his hands laced behind his head. His biceps strained the sleeves of his grey T-shirt.

"Stay out of this, Billy," Miss Morris said with surprising pleasantness.

Bo glowered at Billy. Billy challenged Bo with narrowed eyes. Bo turned away and faced Miss Morris. "No need to bring in Pa." His voice sounded subdued.

"Then you'd better not be tardy again."

"Okay," Bo grumbled. Then he noticed me. "What's *that*?" he cackled.

My face flared up like a three-alarm fire.

"A new student," Miss Morris snapped. "Now hang up your coat and get to your seat."

On his way to the cloakroom, Bo paused next to a boy with a carefree smile and dark skin. The kid's clothes looked almost as out of place as mine. He wore a collarless black shirt with puffy sleeves. His pants billowed out and tied around his ankles just above bare feet and sandals.

Bo gave the kid a sharp jab on the arm.

The kid squawked.

Miss Morris looked up. "Pete? What's wrong?"

The brute glared at Pete. "Nothing," Pete groaned. "Musta hit my funny bone." In spite of his foreign-looking clothes, Pete sounded as American as any of the other kids. Bo smirked and ducked into the cloakroom.

Miss Morris started going over my records. The longer she read, the gloomier I felt. I pulled up my socks and stared at the floor.

When she finally looked up, her eyes were kind. "My, you've lived in more places than most of us will in a lifetime. What brings you to Farmington?"

"My Dad. He's the new program director for WXAX."

Miss Morris motioned toward a plump boy and a striking blonde girl. "Darrel and Alice's fathers work at the station, too."

Darrel smiled and waved. He had a burr haircut and a purple, amoeba-shaped birthmark on his neck.

Alice sat smack in front of me. Her piercing blue eyes dismissed me with an annoyed blink and shifted away. She had a perfect nose and a Cupid's bow mouth. Her clothes were perfect, too. She wore a fuzzy white sweater with a pink Scottie dog in the center. The only thing imperfect about her was her fingernails. Though she tried to hide them, they were bitten to the quick.

Miss Morris stood next to me. "Kids, this is Donald Cook." My introduction was met with a few giggles and rowdy responses from Bo and Lester. I wanted to crawl in a hole and disappear.

"Tell us where you're from, Donald."

"Peoria, Illinois," I whispered.

"Speak up," Miss Morris urged. "We won't bite you." Judging from the sneers I got from Bo and Lester, I wondered.

Miss Morris smiled. "We've just been studying the capitals of all 48 states." She turned to the class. "Who can tell me the capital of Illinois?"

A hand rocketed up in front of my face. "Chicago!" Alice said confidently.

Miss Morris tilted her head. "Are you sure about that?"

Alice's smile dropped. She began to swing her leg. "I think so."

Miss Morris turned to me. "Is that right, Donald?"

I felt squeezed. I knew she was wrong. But I didn't want to make Alice madder than she already seemed to be at me. "I'm not sure. We weren't there very long," I hedged.

"Come on, you know," Miss Morris insisted.

"Well, most people don't know it, but Springfield's the capital of Illinois. Abraham Lincoln was from there."

"Correct," Miss Morris nodded.

Several boys hooted at Alice. Her eyes blazed. Her leg jerked out so far it barely missed my shins.

The recess bell crackled through the air like an electric shock. Kids slammed books inside their desks and scurried for the cloakroom. Alice rose in a huff, making certain not to look at me.

"No running!" Miss Morris shouted. "And when recess is over, be sure all the balls are back in the barrels."

I remained seated, longing to be home with Chaplin.

Miss Morris set her hand gently on my shoulder. "Let's see if we can scare you up a desk."

"EEEK!" came a screech from the cloakroom. Alice burst out waving the pink purse that I'd noticed hanging over the fancy blue coat. The clasp was open.

"It's gone!" Alice cried as she approached us. She pointed at me. "He took it!"

"Hold on, Alice," Miss Morris tried to calm her. "What's gone?"

Alice pointed inside her purse. "My money. A dollar eighty-nine. It was there when I came to school."

"What makes you think Donald took it?" Miss Morris asked.

Alice shook her finger at me. "He went into the cloakroom after class started. Hung his coat right next to mine. Every day I bring money. It's never been taken before. Not 'til he came."

Miss Morris looked at the purse, then me. "Know anything about this, Donald?"

My stomach seized. "No," I sputtered. "I saw the purse. But I didn't touch it. Honest!"

Alice crowded closer. "He's got my money. I know it. Make him empty his pockets, Miss Morris."

"I can't do that."

"You have to!"

Miss Morris's eyes flitted in confusion. "Would you mind, Donald?"

As I slowly tugged my pockets inside out, a volcano erupted inside of me. My stomach spasmed violently, and a stinking stew of half-digested eggs and toast spewed up and out of my throat.

All over me.

All over Alice.

And all over my empty pockets.

Mr. Chester made me wait in the hall outside his office until Mom arrived. Kids kept passing by holding their noses. I felt like a freak. When Mom finally got there, I could feel her hurt and disappointment. Chester pulled her into his office. She didn't tell me what they talked about. But she sure acted morose afterwards.

I picked at my dinner and went to bed early. Dad and Mom were having a serious talk in the living room. I couldn't hear what they were saying, so I slid out of bed and tiptoed to the door. Chaplin started to follow me, so I made a sign for him to stay. He looked crushed, but eased back onto the bed. I put my ear to the keyhole.

"The whole thing's cockeyed," Dad said. "DB wouldn't steal."

"Of course not," Mom replied. "But Chester didn't believe me. Or didn't want to. I could tell he disliked Donnyboy the instant he saw him."

"I'm sure that outfit you had him in didn't help."

I wished he'd said so this morning.

"First impressions are important, Al. Donnyboy looked like he came from a fine family."

I heard Dad's Zippo lighter click open and spark.

Mom's voice grew forlorn. "Chester went over Donnyboy's records and saw that he's had this problem before. He said if it happened again, he might have to move Donnyboy to a special school."

"What kind of school?"

Mom broke down. "For kids with emotional problems."

Her words branded my brain with white-hot pain.

"Like hell he will," Dad snapped.

"Don't be so sure," Mom's voice trembled. "Donnyboy is getting worse."

"Then we'll move," Dad declared.

"No, we won't!" Mom nearly shouted. "All our moving around is what's caused this. He's scared of his own shadow. He needs roots."

I clenched my eyes shut, trying to squeeze away the pain of her truth. I heard Dad take a long drag on his cigarette. "OK. We'll give it some time. But DB's got to lick this one way or another."

A numbing silence spread into my bedroom and cloaked me with despair.

"My day wasn't so hot either," Dad muttered.

"What happened?"

"Cody's a prick."

"Why? The Senator went all out to hire you."

Dad laughed mirthlessly. "That's the problem. Senator Garney hired me behind Cody's back. I've also got a hunch he's paying me more than Cody."

Mom gasped.

"What?"

"I just put it together. The girl Donnyboy threw up on is Alice Cody."

CHAPTER 4

SATURDAY, FEBRUARY 3, 1945

C haplin nuzzled me awake. As I rubbed his tummy, all the grief from the day before came rushing back. I wanted to crawl under the covers and never come out.

"Donnyboy!" Mom called.

I didn't answer.

"Don't play games. I know you're up. I heard your toilet flush."

"What do you want?"

"Breakfast."

"I'm not hungry."

"Get in here. You have to eat. And your father needs to talk to you before he goes to work."

Reluctantly, I shuffled into the kitchen. Chaplin trailed behind me.

Mom and Dad sat at the breakfast table sipping coffee with pretend smiles. Threads of smoke streamed up from two cigarettes in an orange beanbag ashtray on the table. A glass of milk sat next to Dad's coffee. It hadn't been touched.

I sat down across from them. Chaplin plopped on the floor next to me, hoping for a handout.

"Morning, DB," Dad patted my shoulder.

"Where's your robe?" Mom asked. "It's chilly."

"My flannel PJs are warm enough."

Mom immediately went to my bedroom and returned with my robe. She insisted I put it on. She poured two Nabisco Shredded Wheat biscuits into my bowl and filled it to the brim with cream.

"Don't we have any milk? Cream makes me gag."

"You need cream to grow," she announced and swiveled her head to Dad.

He cleared his throat. "About what happened at school yesterday..."

My stomach clenched. "I don't want to talk about that."

Dad toyed with his Lucky Strike pack. "Sorry, but we have to, DB. The principal is making a big deal over it."

"I'm not going to any school for loonies."

Mom and Dad exchanged looks.

"I heard you talking." My eyes filled. "I'm not *crazy!*"

"Of course you're not," Mom grabbed my hand.

"And nobody's sending you anywhere you don't want to go," Dad said firmly.

My stomach relaxed but I still felt wary.

"We just want you to know what you're up against," Mom said. "So you won't throw up at school again."

My chest heaved. "It's not like I do it on purpose."

"We know. Just try extra hard not to." Dad clamped his handkerchief on my nose. "Blow."

I did, and every speck of hope drained out of me. My shoulders slumped. My head drooped. I felt doomed.

CHAPTER 5

SUNDAY, FEBRUARY 4, 1945

I didn't feel like reading. I didn't even feel like listening to my records. After Dad got home from his early morning show, Mom suggested we go to church—which surprised me because we almost never did. Dad said he was too tired, so we stayed home.

I decided to risk freezing to death so I could play outside with Chaplin. Mom made sure I had on enough clothes to survive a South Pole expedition, and Chaplin and I went into the backyard.

Chaplin adopted me on my second day of school in Peoria. I was standing on the sidelines at recess while the other boys were playing kickball and ignoring me. Suddenly, a big scrawny dog ambled onto the playground. His ribs actually stuck out, and his red fur was matted and filthy. He seemed eager to play.

The boys wanted none of that. They kicked the ball at him. Frail as he looked, the dog was nimble. The ball never hit him. Incensed, the boys started throwing rocks. The dog scampered behind me for protection.

The boys already disliked me because I was new and dressed funny. This clinched it.

"Move it, ya dandy," a fat, pimply-faced boy ordered.

I froze, weighing what to do. If I stayed put, they'd come after me. If I moved, they'd go after the poor dog. I pretended not to hear them.

The fat kid snarled. "You deef or somethin'?"

The dog nuzzled my hand. "I'll make sure he doesn't bother you," I whispered, grabbing the fur around his neck.

The fat kid whistled to one of his buddies, and before I knew it they were on me. The buddy got me in a bear hug. Tubby began slugging me.

The dog bared huge fangs. I heard a low, rattling growl, and *SNAP*! He latched onto the fat kid's trousers and shook so hard that the kid fell right on his butt. Wide-eyed and silent with shock, Tubby crawled away on his hands and knees. The buddy dashed after him.

I bent down to give the dog a grateful pet, but he'd vanished. I felt as if I'd lost a friend.

Walking home after school that day, I got a feeling someone was following me. I snuck a glance over my shoulder, tensing for another attack.

To my surprise, the stray dog pattered toward me with his head held high. He reminded me of the loveable tramp Charlie Chaplin always played in silent movies.

I slapped my leg. "Here, boy. Here, Chaplin. Come." He grinned, pranced over to me and followed me home.

Mom had a conniption when she saw him. But underneath her bluster, I knew she had a soft spot for anyone or anything that was helpless. When I told her what happened, Mom agreed he could stay. "But only until he gets some meat on his bones. Finding places to rent is tough enough during the War—and even tougher with a dog."

I ran to the store for some Strongheart dog food. Chaplin wolfed it down. Then I managed to lift and plop him into the bathtub. It took a whole can of Bon Ami to scrub off the ring he left and half an hour to mop up the bathroom floor and walls, but when he was dried off, he looked keen.

Chaplin's perkiness quickly won all of us over. Mom said he could stay, and he's been my only real friend ever since.

Chaplin danced down the back stairs while I took them one at a time. We picked a wide spot in the backyard and assumed our "Devil Dog" positions.

The ground had a silver crust from the frost. I got down on all fours, and it felt hard as a rock. Chaplin crouched facing me. I pawed the ground, bared my teeth and growled. Chaplin bared his and let out a rumbling roar. Like a shot, I sprang forward and wrestled Chaplin to the ground.

We rolled over and over. Finally, I managed to get on top, grabbed Chaplin's front legs and pinned them to the ground. He tossed his head and squirmed like a crazed snake. Cackling with glee, I shouted, "One, two, thr—darn!"

Chaplin slithered loose, knocked me over and straddled me. With a bloodcurdling growl, he pulled back his lips and bared his teeth. Saliva dripped from his fangs onto my cheek as he leaned in for the kill.

I squeezed my eyes shut, bracing for my doom. But instead of his teeth clamping down on my throat, Chaplin's thick, slobbery tongue slurped across my mouth.

"Eeewww!" I protested, wiping the slobber from my face. "Devil Dog!" Chaplin howled in delicious victory.

I lay on the ground and hugged Chaplin. The joy I felt was sobered by sadness. I realized how badly I wanted a friend.

After lunch I acted so restless that Mom insisted I go to the station with Dad. He pulled up in front of Garney Castle. "Go through the front doors, head to the rear and take the freight elevator up."

A beanpole of a teenager stood by the elevator stacking bags of seeds. He said he'd be happy to take me up. I think he appreciated the break. The elevator gate had wooden bars that stood as high as my head. The floor and inside walls were made of scuffed-up plywood. It had no roof, so when you looked up you could see the elevator's guts.

We bounced to a stop at the fourth floor. The teenager lifted the cage door and pointed down the hallway to Studio A.

I stepped into the hall and passed a line of windows. Outside, I saw a frozen field with piles of huge grey boulders. Beyond the field, an angry river crashed against the bank.

A handful of POWs chipped at boulders with pickaxes. I didn't see anyone guarding them.

Eric wasn't there. I moved down a couple of windows and looked out again. This time I spied him. He was straining to push a wheelbarrow overflowing with rocks. A brutish-looking prisoner stuck out his pickaxe and caught Eric's leg. He stumbled and slammed his head on the edge of the wheelbarrow. The wheelbarrow fell over, spilling rocks every which way.

Eric rolled to and fro on the ground with a hand clamped to his forehead. Blood streamed from his hand. The big guy laughed, and two nearby prisoners joined in. Eric struggled to his knees, looked up at them and spit.

The other prisoners stopped laughing, balled their fists and surged toward him. A Jeep roared up with its horn blaring. The attackers stopped. An MP Sergeant leaped out of the Jeep. I recognized him as the guy who motioned us over when we drove into Farmington. The Sergeant pulled out a handkerchief and tied it around Eric's forehead. He pointed questioningly at the three POWs. Eric didn't appear to answer.

The Sergeant moved closer to the attackers. He shook his fist and shoved the big guy in the chest. The POW sneered and went back to hammering the boulders.

The Sergeant's driver led Eric to the Jeep and helped him into the front seat. The Sergeant hopped in the back and they drove off.

I leaned against the window, watching until Eric disappeared.

CHAPTER 6

MONDAY, FEBRUARY 5, 1945

I demanded that I be allowed to wear long pants and a plain flannel shirt to school. Mom preferred that I wear a nicer shirt, but didn't press it. I also insisted on walking to school. The closer I got, the more I became filled with dread.

"Hey, you. Hold up."

I looked over my shoulder and saw the dark-skinned boy from class running toward me. He wore gauzy black pants and a heavy black coat. In spite of the cold, his bare feet were in sandals. I slowed, keeping my guard up.

He puffed as he caught up to me. "You're Donald something, right? The new kid in class." He gave me a toothy smile, grabbed my hand and pumped it. "I'm Pete. Pete Flavorian." He slapped his knee. "Boy oh boy, when you puked on ole kissy Alice I thought I'd pee my pants laughing!"

"It didn't seem that funny to me."

"Hell, everybody knew Bo stole her money."

I felt betrayed. "Why didn't somebody speak up?"

"What? And get creamed by him and his buddy Lester?" He shook his head. "No thanks."

I picked up my pace, smoldering from injustice.

"Most people call me an A-rab," Pete said flippantly. "They're nuts. I'm Persian, Royal Persian. My Dad's a Prince. I'm his first born, so I am, too. If we'd stayed in Persia, I'd live in a palace—except I'd probably be dead."

I looked at him, flabbergasted.

Pete leaned in confidentially. "Just before I was born, a cousin stormed the palace and tried to kill my pop. We escaped just in the nick of time."

"How come you came to Farmington?" I asked.

Pete sniffed. "Know a better place to hide?" He glanced around secretively and reached into the top of his shirt. He pulled out a gold medallion on a thin yellow chain. In the middle of the round medallion was a lion on a throne and what looked like hieroglyphics.

He cradled it like it was valuable. For all I knew, it could have come from a box of Cracker Jacks.

Pete stood up proudly. "This is our royal escutcheon. Pop gave it to me for safekeeping, in case anything happened to him. They'd have to cut my head off to get it. After the War's over, we're going back to reclaim our throne."

I saw Pete in a new light. He did look regal. Dark wavy hair, almond eyes, full lips, and a long, straight nose.

"Heard them talking about your pop on the radio this morning." Pete said. "Sounds like he's got a hit record."

"I don't know about that. It just came out. We've got our fingers crossed. Does your father have to work?"

Pete slumped. "We had to flee at the last minute and leave our treasure in Persia."

I pictured a cave full of jewels guarded by a giant spider like in the movie *The Thief of Bagdad*.

Pete perked up. "But he's got a great job here."

"What?

"Cooks at the Paris Café."

"Oh," I said fighting to keep a straight face. "Hey, can I ask you something?"

"Sure."

"Is Principal Chester nasty to everyone or is it just me?"

"Everyone, unless you're an athlete like Billy Rogers. Only thing Chester cares about is sports."

I nodded. "He acted kind of mysterious about the last principal."

Pete snickered. "Last Christmas Van Ness went off his nut. Stood in his front window with his arms outstretched loaded with Christmas lights and decorations. They sent him to the State Hospital up in Vermillion."

"Sounds sad."

"Just goes to show want kids can do to you."

I knew only too well.

We approached the school steps. My anxiety came rushing back. Bo and Lester stood at the head of the stairs. They were too busy grandstanding for a couple of girls to notice Pete and me. One girl was tall and had an unusually large chest. Her pudgy friend giggled nonstop.

The tall girl stood with one hip thrust out. She was good-looking, though I thought she could do with a few less coats of makeup. She cracked her gum, which had the same effect on me as fingernails on a chalkboard.

Bo shoved Lester into her. "Catch, Cleo!"

Cleo hurled Lester back. Her short jacket popped open to reveal a skin-tight hot-pink sweater. Her short purple skirt poofed up, and I caught a glimpse of her pink underpants. Cleo grabbed her chunky friend's arm and led her toward the entrance. "C'mon, Peggy."

Bo spotted us. "Look. It's the barfer and the A-rab!"

Lester rubbed his hands together in glee.

Pete spun around and made a beeline for the stairs on the other side of the building.

My mind raced. If I followed Pete, I'd be pegged a coward for sure. If I went up the stairs, I'd be at Bo and Lester's mercy.

Bo started down the stairs after me, Lester hot on his heels. The bell rang. Bo froze. Miss Morris's threat must have sunk into his thick skull. He gave Lester a frustrated look and jerked his thumb for them to leave.

After they were a safe distance away, I sped up the stairs and lost myself in a crush of kids pushing and shoving to get inside the doors. Just to be safe, I let everyone enter before me. When I headed through the door, something incredibly soft yet firm squeezed against my chest. Startled, I jumped back.

Cleo sidestepped past me, lifted an eyebrow and gave her gum a resounding crack.

Fortunately, Miss Morris had a desk for me. Unfortunately, it was in the front row right across from Alice. She swiveled in her seat to avoid looking at me.

Miss Morris stood. "As you all probably know, Alice reported some money missing from her purse Friday. It might have been lost. It might have been stolen." Her eyes rested on Bo. "We'll probably never know."

Miss Morris walked over to me. "Either way, it's a shame. And all the moreso because Donald got blamed without any proof." She touched my shoulder. "I think Alice and I owe him a big apology. Sorry, Donald."

Miss Morris faced Alice, who crossed her arms and clenched her jaw.

"You saw he didn't have your money," Miss Morris admonished.

"I guess, but...well, sorry." She said without conviction.

Miss Morris gave her a disapproving glance before announcing: "Everyone take out your Geography books."

I lifted my hand. "Pardon, Miss Morris."

"Yes?"

My heart thumped. "Even though I didn't take Alice's money, I did, uh, upset her."

The class giggled. Bo and Lester howled.

Miss Morris clapped her hands for quiet.

My face flushed. I reached into my pocket and set a handful of coins on Alice's desk. "Here's a dollar eighty-nine. I believe that's what went missing. I took it out of my savings."

Alice's haughtiness collapsed into confusion. She pushed the money away.

I shoved it back.

Alice gnawed at a barely visible fingernail and looked at Miss Morris for a way out. Miss Morris looked back sternly. Painfully Alice cupped the coins in her hand, slipped them in the pocket of her black and white tartan skirt, and muttered, "Thanks."

A raspy voice shattered the quiet. "Way to go, Cookie."

My head swung to Billy. Everything about him oozed confidence. The only blemish on his face was a small deep scar like a comma between his bright green eyes. He stared at Bo like a taunting rooster. "Maybe the lunkhead who took her money will pay you back."

Bo dropped his eyes from Billy's and glowered at me.

At lunch Pete told me about Billy. His folks split up and left him with his Grandma years ago. They lived in a small house by the railroad station. His Grandma worked two jobs, so Billy had pretty much raised himself. He was brazenly reckless, and the only kid in class who stood up to Bo and Lester.

From where I sat in the schoolyard, I saw Billy walk across the monkey bars standing on his hands. When he reached the end, he somersaulted in the air and landed perfectly on his feet. Pete rushed over to congratulate Billy, but the daredevil ignored him and swaggered from girl to girl gathering compliments.

Bo and Lester tried to strike up a kick ball game with some of the boys. Nobody took them up on it. Bo elbowed Lester, mumbled something and nodded at me. Lester jutted out his lower lip and nodded back.

I threw up my hands in helplessness. Clearly, Bo was going to take out his anger at Billy on me.

After lunch, Miss Morris announced, "Our next section in English is Composition. Bob Lyle, a friend of mine who is a reporter for the *Dakotan*, suggested we start a class newspaper. What do you think, kids? All in favor raise your hand." As a lonely kid who loved to escape into books, I dreamed about being a writer one day. I joined more than half the class in lifting my arm.

"I'll be editor," Alice declared.

"That's very gracious, Alice," Miss Morris said stiffly, "but before we take volunteers, let's talk about the different jobs we need to fill."

Alice frowned and crossed her arms.

Miss Morris listed the jobs on the blackboard. She gave a brief summary of what each entailed. Pete volunteered for circulation, Peggy for mimeographing. Cleo said she'd write a column. It took a little cajoling, but Billy agreed to write about sports.

I wanted to volunteer as a reporter but didn't want to draw any more attention to myself. The boy with the birthmark raised his hand. "I'll be a reporter," he announced with a friendly smile.

"Thanks, Darrel."

His name struck a bell. Mom had told me that he lived a block away, and that his dad was chief engineer at WXAX. Darrel's mother had invited Mom to join her Bridge club.

Miss Morris scanned the room. "Now about editor. Who besides Alice would like to be considered?"

Alice tapped her fingers on her desk and sulked.

No hands went up. "Come on," Miss Morris urged. Her eyes stopped at me. "Donald?"

I almost choked in surprise. "Me?"

"It would be a great way to get to know the class. And vice versa."

Alice's eyes shot knives at me.

I gulped. "Thanks for asking, but Alice would be much better than me."

Alice looked shocked.

"Why not work together? Co-editors?" Miss Morris suggested. "It's a big enough job for two. Right, Alice?"

Alice attacked another fingernail. "I don't see why—"

"Perfect," Miss Morris cut her off. "Okay by you, Donald?"

If I said yes, Alice would make my life hell; she might even make me throw up again. If I said no, the first teacher who had ever seemed to believe in me would probably write me off.

"What do you say, Donald?" Miss Morris pressed impatiently.

My mind raced. "Well, could I have a little time to think it over?"

She considered it for a moment, then nodded. "There's no school tomorrow because of teachers' meetings, so why don't you and Alice meet with me fifteen minutes before school on Wednesday to let me know what you decide?"

Heading home, I racked my brain trying to decide what to do. Aside from my nervousness about having to put up with Alice, I had no idea what an editor did. Still, Miss Morris seemed convinced I could handle it. And it felt good being asked. I even had an idea for a story, though it might ruffle a lot of feathers.

I kept wavering back and forth until I turned onto Pearl Street, where I walked smack into trouble.

Bo and Lester stood at the curb beside a bucket of sharp, fist-sized clinkers. They were having the time of their lives throwing them at five raggedy red-haired boys and girls who were obviously Bo's kin. I started to back out of there when I saw Lester hit a tiny little girl in the back of her neck. She shrieked and blood oozed from her wound.

"Bull's eye!" Lester hooted. Bo stopped throwing and looked confused. "C'mon, keep 'em flyin'!" Lester goaded. Bo hesitated a moment, let out a forced laugh and resumed firing.

I couldn't believe anyone would hurt their own brother and sister. Especially since I'd give my eye teeth to have one. Without thinking, I yelled, "Stop!"

Lester stopped in mid-throw, and his mouth stretched into a sinister smirk. "Lookit. It's the barfer."

Bo spun around. "Hey kid, barf for us."

Lester grabbed a clinker. "Maybe he needs a little help." He reared back and heaved one straight at me. I ducked and ran across the street for home. *Thwack!* The jagged ash tore through my red and black mackinaw and slashed my back. Lester danced with glee.

Bo threw one that slammed into my wrist and burst in a puff of powder. Lester followed with a jagged piece that slashed my knee. I lost my balance. A searing pain shot up my leg as I tumbled and twisted my ankle.

Bo and Lester cheered and moved toward me, arms cocked.

I struggled not to cry. "Lay off, guys. I never did anything to you."

Bo sneered. "Bullcrap. Ya got smartass Billy to taunt me in front a' everybody."

"And you dress like you're better than everybody else," Lester spit. He wound up and hurled one at point-blank range. The sharp ash nailed me on the temple. A stinging white flash exploded inside my head. I reached up and felt blood pulsing from the wound.

Lester bent over laughing.

Without warning, a rank paste of half-digested cheese, bread, apple, and cookies surged up from my stomach and out of my mouth.

"He's barfin'!" Lester screeched in delight.

They each grabbed a handful of cinders and moved in for the kill.

I heard a terrifying growl and the jangle of dog tags. I flipped over and saw Chaplin racing straight for Bo and Lester, his lips curled, fangs bared.

Lester took off running.

"Throw somethin' at him," Bo shouted, but his brothers and sisters had fled with Lester. Eyes wide with fright, Bo fired at Chaplin as fast as he could. A cinder glanced off Chaplin's back. Another struck his right paw and make Chaplin whimper. Another gashed his head. Chaplin howled in pain but kept right on after Bo.

"Mad dawg! Mad dawg!" Bo spun around to escape but he'd waited too long. With a ferocious growl, Chaplin leaped onto Bo's back and slammed him to the cement. In a split second, his bared teeth were inches from Bo's neck.

"Hey, kid, help! Help!" Bo blubbered.

I just stood there. All the anger and humiliation inside me wanted to let Chaplin attack. Chaplin opened his mouth and leaned in. Streams of saliva pooled on Bo's neck. Bo sobbed so hard his body went into spasms. "Pleeze, git 'im off me. *Pleeze.*"

Chaplin looked at me for a sign. All I'd have to do was nod, and he'd rip right into the bully. A puddle spread from Bo's pants onto the sidewalk. It disgusted me. Then I realized I'd looked almost as pathetic only minutes before. "Wait," I told Chaplin and hobbled over to where he had Bo pinned to the ground.

I grabbed Chaplin's collar and tugged. "Come." Chaplin resisted. I yanked his again collar. He gave Bo a final growl and backed off. Blood seeped from Chaplin's back, head and right front paw.

"Good boy." I reached down and kneaded Chaplin's ears as I limped toward our house. In spite of his wounds, Chaplin pranced beside me with his head and tail high. Seeing him like that changed something inside me. I forced myself to stand up straight and put full my weight on my hurt foot. Every step sent an electric shock up my leg, but I didn't waver. When we reached our front yard, I stopped and glanced back.

Bo stood in the middle of the street. Tears and snot streamed down his filthy face. He raised his fist and blubbered, "Jest wait. Ah'll git ya, gawdamit! You an yer gawdam dawg!"

"Oh, my Lord!" Mom clapped a hand to her mouth as we walked into the kitchen. She dropped her wooden spoon in the skillet, wiped her hands on her apron and rushed to me.

"What happened? A car hit you?"

"No. Nothing like that." I gave her the whole story.

Chaplin held up his bloody paw.

Mom groaned. "Oh, Chaplin, too." She looked bewildered. "Why would those boys do such a thing? You didn't provoke them, did you?"

"Thanks a lot, Mom." I tugged Chaplin's collar. "Let's go, fella."

Mom stuck out her arm and stopped me. "I didn't mean it that way. It's just I can't imagine anybody hurting you for no reason."

"Bullies don't need reasons."

She leaned in and hugged me. "You're right." She sniffed, and moved away from me with a sour face.

My face flushed with shame. "Sorry."

Mom closed her eyes and rubbed her forehead in despair. "Oh, Donnyboy."

"At least it didn't happen at school," I said gamely. "Chester doesn't need to know."

"Well, get out of those things and I'll run you a bath. Chaplin needs one, too. Then I'll tackle those cuts with iodine."

I shuddered at the thought. Iodine stung like the dickens, and Mom usually drowned a cut in it.

Steam clouds filled the bathroom and coated the medicine cabinet mirror. I'd stripped down to my underwear. I tested the water with my finger and yanked it right out. "It's boiling."

Mom cranked off the faucets. "You need it extra hot to sterilize those cuts. Be sure and use plenty of Lifebuoy soap, too." Chaplin plopped on the pink chenille bath mat and licked his paw. She kneeled down to pet him. "I'm calling the police."

"Don't!" I recoiled. "That'd just make things worse."

"What do you mean? Those fools could have blinded you."

"But they didn't. And if Bo and Lester get in Dutch with the cops, they'll go after me worse than ever." I looked at her pleadingly. "Please. I know what I've got to do."

Mom's face dropped. "You're not going to fight them?"

"No!" I groaned as if she should know better. "Now will you please leave so I can take my bath?"

"Hop in the tub."

I didn't move.

"Donnyboy," Mom put her hands on her hips.

"Mom, I'm thirteen."

"Oh." She picked up my clothes sheepishly and went out the door.

I decided it would be easier for Chaplin and I to bathe at the same time. He squirmed and pawed but I finally got him up to the lip of the tub, shoved him in and jumped in after him. The hot water felt like a blowtorch on my cuts.

Washing Chaplin was next to impossible. He wiggled and thrashed constantly, spraying the walls and floor with soapy water. Even the toilet paper got soaked.

It took every towel in the bathroom to dry us off and mop up the floor and walls. I put on my PJ bottoms and called Mom in for my iodine torture. In spite of my howls, Mom slathered three coats of the stinging iodine on even my tiniest scratch. Seeing my agony, Chaplin scrambled out the door and buried himself under my bed.

"I called Mr. Chester," Mom said as I sipped hot chocolate. My stomach cinched.

"Mom."

"Don't worry, I didn't say anything about your problem. I just told him what Bo and Lester did."

"What did he say?"

Mom gave a snort. "Nothing. He said since it happened off school property, he couldn't do anything about it."

"Good. Let's just drop it."

"Well, they shouldn't get away with it." Mom scowled and started dinner.

Dad was playing a personal appearance in Gregory, so we ate by ourselves. Mom made macaroni and cheese, one of my favorites. Then I went to bed.

After Mom shut my bedroom door, Chaplin jumped up and put his head on the pillow beside me. In spite of his cuts, he acted perfectly content. I started thinking about Miss Morris's offer to be co-editor of the paper, and what I should do. After the run-in with Bo and Lester this afternoon, there wasn't any question about it.

CHAPTER 7

TUESDAY, FEBRUARY 6, 1945

After breakfast, Chaplin and I played "Devil Dog" in the backyard. As we lay on the icy ground panting and exhausted, a beautiful voice lilted into the yard.

"When the lights go on again
All over the world.
And the ships will sail again,
All over the world."

I shoved Chaplin out of the way and sat up. A short, scrawny kid around my age swaggered into the yard singing. He finished his lyric, flicked away a cigarette and took a swig from a bottle of Pabst Blue Ribbon Beer.

"Acton's my name, singing's my game," he oozed in a honeyed voice. He had a burr haircut, yellow teeth, brown hair, and a lot of freckles. His eyes glistened with confidence, but I noticed a black and blue blotch under one of them.

"Hi," I replied hesitantly as I stood. "I'm Donald Cook." I patted Chaplin's head. "This is Chaplin." Chaplin walked over and gave the kid a sniff. His tail started wagging.

"Pleased to meet you both," the kid said grandly as he walked over to me. "First name's David." He stretched out his hand from beneath the sleeve of an Eisenhower Army jacket at least three sizes too big for him. Military patches filled almost every inch of the jacket. David reached into a breast pocket, pulled out a pack of Raleighs and shook it. "Smoke?"

"Uh, no thanks."

David held out the Pabst bottle, "I'd offer you some, but she's a goner." He slung the empty bottle over his shoulder towards the trashcan. He looked me up and down. "Pete told me about you. Said you were quite the dresser."

I groaned. "Oh, those short pants."

David looked serious. "No kidding. Pete said you looked keen. 'Course, we know how he dresses."

"Well, thank you," I replied, not sure if he was putting me on or not.

David pointed to the gash on my temple. "Hope the other guy looks worse."

"Afraid not." I pointed to his black eye. "How about you?"

He shrugged. "Ran into a doorknob."

"Oh."

I searched for something to say. "Live around here?"

"Naw, other side of Center. Maw and I bunk at Ben's place for now. He's bartender at the Dakota where Maw waitresses. House is tiny but

I can always find a place to flop. Who knows how long we'll be there anyway."

"You go to Farmington Elementary?" I asked.

He rapped his head with his knuckles. "Nope. Mine's the School of Hard Knocks. 'Sides, singin's my future, not schoolin'."

"You sure have a great voice."

He hitched up heavy wool Army pants. "Even got me a job singing at the Dakota every night. Get good tips. And these." He pointed to the patches on his jacket. "Soldiers give 'em to me. Got lots of enemy souvenirs, too."

"What kind?"

He rattled them off on his fingers. "Kraut helmet. Nazi flag. Jap knife. All kinds of swag. But this," he took out a small white box from his breast pocket, "this beats 'em all. Take a gander."

"What is it?" I asked suspiciously.

"Take a peek," his eyes teased.

I took the box and lifted the lid. Inside was a plain square of white cotton. I paused.

"Look underneath," he urged.

I lifted the cotton. Nested in another cotton square was a shriveled piece of yellow folded flesh. Its stench soured the air.

"Ugh." I dropped the box. Chaplin jumped in front of me and growled. David roared.

"Is that what I think it is?" I sputtered.

"Jap ear," David glowed. He bent down and put the ear back in its coffin.

I stared at him, disgusted yet entranced.

The upstairs door creaked open. Dad backed out carrying his fiddle case. "Running to the station, DB. Want to come along?"

"No, thanks. I'll stay here."

"Suit yourself." He ambled down the steps and noticed David. "Who's your friend?"

"David Acton. You should hear him sing. He's incredible."

"Is that so?" Dad walked over to David and held out his hand.

David gave Dad a saucy salute and shook Dad's hand. "Heard your new record. It's tops."

"Well, thanks, David," Dad started for the garage.

David hurried after him. "I was wondering, could I sing for you sometime? You name it, I'll be there."

Dad stopped and looked at him invitingly. "Most afternoons I'm home after two. Come by sometime and we'll set something up."

David grinned. "I will."

"Get the garage doors, will you, Donnyboy?"

I cringed when he said my name. But David didn't react at all. David helped me with the doors. After Dad left, he gave my arm a pat. "I gotta be goin', too, Donnyboy. Nice meeting you."

The way he said it sounded natural and friendly. He shook out a Raleigh and flicked a fingernail across the top of a kitchen match. It sputtered and burst into flame. He took a deep drag and blew out the match. As he sauntered away down the alley, he broke into song:

"Singin' his Cow Cow Boogie
In the strangest way.
Comma ti yi yi yeah
Comma ti yippity yi yeah."

The idea struck me after lunch. Mom had gone with Darrel Hays's mother to fold bandages at the Red Cross. The heavy scent of oil filled the living room. Dad sat in the overstuffed chair listening to the news and pushing an oilcloth through the barrel of his .22-caliber rifle. A 12-gauge shotgun nestled in an alligator skin case on the floor beside him.

Dad didn't hunt all that much. But like all the things he owned, he kept his guns in tiptop shape. I went hunting with him twice but hated it. I felt sorry for the ducks and pheasants. The last time I went, I spent the whole time sitting in the car.

Mom didn't like having guns in the house. So Dad hid them in their bedroom and only cleaned them when she was gone.

"How's that gash feel?" Dad asked sympathetically.

"Throbs a little, but not bad. I just want to forget the whole thing."

"If you say so, but those guys need to get what's coming to them."

After a long pause, I sat on the floor next to him. "Dad, could I ask a favor?"

"Depends," he teased.

"We're starting a class newspaper. Miss Morris has asked me to be co-editor."

"Hey, congratulations."

"I haven't decided if I'll do it or not. I'd have to work with Alice Cody." Dad chuckled.

"Anyway, I've decided I'd at least like to write a story. But I need your help."

"How?"

I told him.

Dad looked shocked. "You're kidding."

"I know it sounds nutty, but I think it could be really important."

Dad shook his head. "I don't have the clout to set up something like that."

"I know. But I bet the Senator does. You could ask him. He really likes you."

Dad set down his cleaning rod. "I'm not sure it's a good idea. For one thing, your mother would have a conniption."

I clenched his arm. "Dad. I hardly slept last night thinking about what's happened to me." My eyes welled up. "I'm scared all the time. Scared of being scared. No wonder I haven't got any friends. No wonder kids pick on me. I can't live like this. You can't imagine how alone I feel."

Dad's face softened. "You might be surprised."

I looked at him curiously. "What do you mean?"

He leaned his rifle against the chair. "It's a long story. Maybe some other time." He blotted my eyes with his handkerchief. "But, you're right. Sometimes you have to go out on a limb to get where you want to go."

"Then you'll ask the Senator for me?"

Dad paused. "Okay. But with a hitch."

I bit my lip.

"He'll be back from Washington tomorrow. I'll see if he'll meet with you. But you'll have to ask him yourself to do what you want him to do."

I blanched. "But—"

"If you want to change, it means taking some risks."

His words hit me with a jolt. "Okay," my voice trembled. "But don't tell Mom, all right? No sense in getting her riled up until we know if it's going to happen."

Dad thought about it a moment, then nodded.

A new sensation joined the fear in the pit of my stomach. Excitement.

CHAPTER 8

WEDNESDAY, FEBRUARY 7, 1945

Alice stood in front of Miss Morris's desk, impatiently slapping a sheath of papers against the black Scottie dog on her white sweater.

I apologized, although I was only two minutes late.

Miss Morris smiled hopefully. "Have you made up your mind?"

I nodded. "I'm not sure I know what a co-editor does, but I'd like to give it a try. Especially if I can write, too."

Miss Morris clapped her hands. "Of course you can. As far as the other duties, we'll all learn as we go along." She looked at Alice. "Right, Alice?"

Alice sighed mournfully.

I took off my stocking cap and headed for the cloakroom.

"How'd you get that gash on your head?" Miss Morris asked with concern.

"I, uh, fell." Which, technically, I had.

"Can we talk about the newspaper?" Alice cut in. "Time's running out. And I want to show you something."

I ran into the cloakroom and back.

Alice unfolded six Big Chief tablet pages. They were taped to form a newspaper page. She pointed to the top. "Here's the masthead." Perfectly formed capital letters spelled out *THE FLASH*. To the right was a lightning bolt and what looked like the guy in the Prince Valiant comic strip blowing a long trumpet.

"Now, I didn't have time to write anything," Alice non-apologized, "but I made headlines for all the different kinds of stories I think we should have." She pointed to *Outstanding Achievers*. "In every issue, we'll feature a top student. This is just a 'for instance,' of course." Beneath the headline, Alice had pasted a glamorous color photograph of herself.

Miss Morris frowned. "I'm not sure the mimeograph can handle pictures."

A shadow of disapproval crossed Alice's face, but she quickly continued. "Here's the heading for Billy's sport stories: 'Go Team, Go!' And in 'Doing Our Part,' we'll list everyone who's bought War Stamps—and how many."

I glanced at the War Stamps sales chart pinned to the wall. The bar after Alice's name stretched to the very end of the craft paper.

"Of course, this is just off the top of my head," Alice said with false modesty. "With more time, I can come up with lots more ideas." She smiled expectantly. "What do you think?"

I looked at Miss Morris. Miss Morris looked at me.

"Well?" A fingernail flew to Alice's mouth.

Miss Morris took a sip of water and looked at Alice sincerely. "As usual, Alice, you've put your heart and soul into this and given us excellent things to chew on. But we also need to listen to other ideas." She turned to me. "Donald, do you have any suggestions?"

My throat went dry.

Alice tapped her black and white saddle shoes.

"Donald." Miss Morris said.

"Gee. Alice's ideas really bowl me over. I just had one idea but it may not work out."

Alice smiled victoriously.

"Tell us about it," Miss Morris prompted.

I took a deep breath. "It's just a story. It kind of falls under 'Outstanding Achievers,' but with a twist."

"What kind of twist?" Alice furrowed her eyebrows.

"It's not about a student. It's about somebody in town most folks don't know, but he could have a real influence on us."

"Who?" Alice crossed her arms.

Sweat eked from every pore. "I can't say just yet. I haven't talked to him, and I may not be able to."

"This is supposed to be a *class* newspaper," Alice reminded me. "I don't see what some mystery man has to do with our class."

Miss Morris ignored her. "How soon will you know about this fellow?"

"In a few days, I hope."

"According to your schedule, Miss Morris, all the stories need to be in by next Monday."

Miss Morris nodded.

"What happens if his 'mystery man' says no?" Alice prodded.

Miss Morris looked at me encouragingly. "Have you a backup, Donald?"

"Oh yes," I blurted without thinking.

"Who?" Alice demanded.

My mind raced. "Uh, Pete. Pete Flavorian."

Alice threw up her hands. "You're kidding!"

"He says he's a Persian Prince."

Alice stomped her foot. "He's *demented!*"

Miss Morris spoke up soothingly. "Pete is his second choice, Alice. And you have to admit, Pete is quite colorful."

"Not in my book," Alice grumbled.

After the Pledge of Allegiance, Blue Hair came in, whispered something to Miss Morris, and motioned for Lester and Bo to come forward. The bullies glanced at each other and obeyed. Billy chortled. The class buzzed. After a hushed conversation, Bo and Lester followed Blue Hair. As they exited the room, Lester curled his lip at me.

Miss Morris announced I would be co-editor of the paper with Alice. To my surprise, many of the kids clapped. Everyone liked Alice's layout, although her photograph earned several giggles. Miss Morris asked Cleo if she had come up with an idea for her column. Cleo nodded enthusiastically. "Yeah. It's called, 'The Vacuum Cleaner: We Pick Up All The Dirt.'" That one brought down the house.

Just before lunch, Bo and Lester returned to the classroom looking surly. While they kept their eyes off me, I could feel their hate.

The temperature outside had plummeted to zero, so everyone ate in the gym. I sat in the bleachers far away from the bullies but kept my eye on them. They were busy stealing food from smaller kids.

Now that I had committed to working on the paper, I worried that the Senator might not see me. My Velveeta sandwich dangled unwanted in my hand.

Pete plopped beside me, and I handed him the sandwich.

"What happened to your head?"

I nodded at Bo and Lester. "The numskulls used me for target practice."

He grinned. "So that's why Chester called 'em to his office."

I shrugged. "I don't know why. He told Mom he couldn't do anything 'cause it happened off school property. Maybe he got a guilty conscience."

"They're sure steaming."

"Tell me about it."

Pete peered into my lunch bag and took out my cookies. "David said he met you."

"Uh-huh. Yesterday."

"When I'm on the throne, I'll make David my official Court Singer."

"He sure can sing. Say, do you know how he got that black eye?"

Pete reached further into my lunch sack. "Ben probably slugged him."

"The guy he and his mom live with?"

"Yeah. You never know when he'll go haywire. He beats up Blossom, David's mom, all the time. David wears baggy clothes so his bruises won't show."

"Why do they put up with it?" I asked indignantly.

Pete shook his head. "Blossom's got a lot of miles on her. Probably doesn't have another place to go. Either that, or she's sorry for Ben."

"Why?"

"He lost half his face fighting in North Africa."

Chaplin and I bounded through the back door. "It's fr-fr-freezing!" I stuttered.

Mom called from the kitchen. "Come get some hot soup."

I bit down on the ends of my mittens and pulled my hands free. "Dad home yet?"

"On his way. Said he had to meet with the Senator."

My neck tingled.

Even though Mom used cream instead of water in the Campbell's Tomato soup to "put more meat on my bones," I sipped it eagerly.

"Any problems with Bo and Lester?" Mom sat across from me and lit a cigarette.

"Not really. Chester called them into his office and must have bawled them out about ambushing me. They glared at me all day but kept their distance."

Mom perked up. "Well, maybe that principal is good for something after all."

The back door opened and I heard feet stomp on the foot mat.

"Dad?" I called out.

"Yeah. Hey DB, can you come here a minute?"

I bolted to him.

CHAPTER 9

THURSDAY, FEBRUARY 8, 1945

School let out at three fifteen. The Senator told Dad he'd meet me in his office at three thirty sharp. I ran all the way to Garney Castle and entered the dark-paneled reception room panting. A stout woman with dyed red hair sat behind a wide desk calmly answering three phones at once.

She waved for me to come over. When she finished her last call she said pleasantly, "You must be Al's boy." She glanced at the clock and smiled. "Right on time. I'm Marge, the Senator's secretary."

I nodded, still catching my breath.

Marge rose and led me down a long corridor with thick green carpet. My nerves jangled. It occurred to me that the Senator might just want to bawl me out for throwing up on Alice. We stopped in front of a heavy mahogany door with a gold ear of corn carved in the middle. "Don't be nervous," Marge told me.

I swallowed. Marge rapped on the door.

"Open sesame," a gravelly voice called.

We entered a huge oval room. A short, stocky man with a ruddy face stood up from behind a gigantic honey brown desk. He strode over to us and extended his huge paw of a hand.

To my surprise, his hand was strong and callused. "Thanks for seeing me, Senator." I hoped he wouldn't notice that my hand was trembling.

The Senator had bushy black eyebrows and thick white hair combed into a high pompadour. He motioned to an overstuffed gold chair that faced his desk. "Take a load off."

My feet sunk into a plush green carpet with a big round crest in the middle. Inside the crest was an ear of corn. The kernels weren't yellow but green as a dollar bill.

He tilted back in his chair and studied me silently. His black and white checkered sport coat gaped open, revealing a white shirt and a bolo tie laced through a golden ear of corn. Its kernels, too, were green. Framed pictures of the Senator with Jack Benny, Fred Allen, Alice Fay, the Lone Ranger, and other celebrities covered the curved wall behind him. There was also a picture of the smiling Senator, an unsmiling Alice and a black Scottie dog.

"Your father tells me you need a favor."

My throat was so parched I just nodded.

"Well, let's hear it."

I clenched the arms of my chair. "First off, I guess you heard about my accident with your granddaughter, Alice. I'm really sorry—"

The Senator waved his hand. "A little humbling will do her good."

I was perplexed, but felt a big weight lift from my shoulders.

"Now, about this favor."

'Well, sir, we're starting a class newspaper and I have this idea for a story that may sound a little off base but—"

Garney chuckled. "Get to the point."

I swallowed. "I need you to clear the way for me to interview a German POW here. His name is Eric."

The Senator's expression didn't change.

I told him about the two times I'd seen Eric. How I had a hunch we were very much alike. How other prisoners tormented him.

The Senator looked unimpressed. "Folks today don't have much sympathy for Nazis."

I edged forward in my seat. "That's just it. Only one in ten Germans are Nazis. I looked it up in the library."

The Senator picked up a letter opener and scraped under a fingernail. "Maybe this Eric is the one in ten."

"Could be, but I doubt it. I've got a hunch Eric doesn't like the Nazis any more than we do. And he's probably not alone. If I'm right, people should know that."

Garney set down the paper opener and formed a steeple with his fingers. Given his expression, I had a clue what he might be thinking.

I leaned forward with my hands on the chair arms. "Night before last I heard Prime Minister Churchill talk to all you Senators. He made a big point that hard as it might seem now, we have to make friends with the good Germans after the War. Otherwise it'll just be a matter of time before we have another one."

"He was very impressive." The Senator drummed his fingers on the desk for several seconds then looked me in the eye. "Well, young man, I'm not sure if you're inspired or just plain cuckoo. But I agree with Mr. Churchill. And I respect your spunk." He turned his attention to a letter on his desk. "I'll see what I can do."

I swelled with joy. But in seconds it was cut short by the reality of what I'd just gotten myself into. *Did I really have the guts to do this?* I tried to get up but felt glued to the chair. The Senator looked up with a hint of annoyance. "Something else you wanted to talk about?"

I forced myself up and left.

CHAPTER 10

FRIDAY, FEBRUARY 9, 1945

We held a newspaper status meeting during lunch. Cleo passed out her typewritten "Vacuum Cleaner" column. It started with "Secrets to Snaring That Guy or Gal" and went downhill from there. Miss Morris and Alice nixed every item. Cleo grabbed her papers in a huff and started to storm out. Miss Morris sat her down. She complimented Cleo on her writing and suggested Cleo write another column that wasn't quite so "controversial."

Cleo fumed for several minutes, then brightened up. "I know. I'll write a column about who would make the perfect eighth grader. You know, perfect face," her hands traced her body. "Perfect eyes, nose and so forth."

"Great idea!" Miss Morris enthused.

I agreed.

Alice looked less than enthusiastic. "I guess it's all right, so long as you emphasize important things like the brain."

Cleo sniffed and sashayed away.

Alice turned in two stories, one on War Stamp sales and the other on the Scrap Paper Drive. By coincidence, Alice had bought more stamps and gathered more scrap paper than anyone else. I had to admit, her stories were well written. She only mentioned herself three times in each.

"So, where's your 'mystery man' story?" interrogated Alice.

"I hope to know today if I can see him."

"It has to be in by Monday," she needled.

I nodded nervously.

Alice smiled and pulled two typed sheets out of her notebook. "But don't worry. If yours doesn't work out, I wrote an extra story on our Spring play."

The final bell rang. I zipped out of class and took the short cut home. Fortunately, Bo and Lester were nowhere in sight. Maybe Chester scared them into laying off me.

A block from home I slowed down to greet Chaplin. He met me at the same time and place every day. Not today. No yowl, no tail wag, no slurp. At first I felt put out. Then I panicked. What if a car had hit him? I took off running. At the corner, I stopped cold.

Chaplin was sauntering toward our house with a jaunty lilt. He looked like he had eight legs—his four long ones and four stubby black and white ones in between.

I scratched my head. "Chaplin?"

Chaplin stopped, stretched a leg up to his ear and scratched. A beautiful little black and white female Cocker Spaniel pitter-pattered out from behind him. She blinked her big, round, shiny black eyes at Chaplin and started scratching, too.

I crossed the street and knelt beside Chaplin. "So, who's your girlfriend?"

He gave me a silly grin. The Spaniel jumped up and set her front paws on my knee. She wagged her tail and licked my mittens. I lifted a red heart-shaped tag hooked to her collar and read it aloud: *"Cinderella 232 Pearl Street."* That was Darrel's address; I'd delivered something there for Mom just the other day.

The sky lowered into a low blackish-grey ceiling. A numbing wind whipped at us. "We better all get inside before we freeze to death." I pointed down the street and told Cinderella, "Go home."

She stayed glued to the sidewalk wagging her tail. Chaplin didn't move. He looked at Cinderella then me.

"Go," I said firmly, shooing Cinderella with my hand. With a diminutive little yip, she scurried home.

Chaplin and I raced into the kitchen and headed for the heat register. "Dad home?"

Mom narrowed her eyes. "What's going on between you two, anyway? Something's up, I can feel it."

I tried to sound offended. "Can't a father and son talk occasionally?"

"Not tonight. Dad has a personal appearance tonight in Sioux Falls. He won't be home until late."

The creak of my bedroom door awoke me. The radium dials on my Baby Ben clock glowed twelve forty-three.

Dad bent over me and whispered, "I talked to the Senator before we left for Sioux Falls."

I held my breath. "And?"

"Everything's set. Be at the POW camp gate at eleven o'clock tomorrow morning. A Sergeant Atkins will meet you."

I gasped.

"We better tell your mother," Dad said.

"Can't we wait 'til after I see Eric? If it's a bust, we might have opened a hornet's nest for nothing."

Dad thought it over. "Okay. Meet me at the station after you're done. I'll give you a ride home. We'll talk then."

"Thanks, Dad. Thanks...for everything."

Dad gave me a quick hug. "Now get some rest, DB. I've got a feeling you're gonna need it."

My mind reeled. What if Eric was nasty? What if he hated me? What would Mom do when she found out?

CHAPTER 11

SATURDAY, FEBRUARY 10, 1945

I tossed and turned all night. Chaplin got so annoyed he slept on the floor. I got up around eight and put on what I wore every weekend: dungarees and a heavy shirt. Hopefully Mom wouldn't get suspicious when I left for the camp.

Dad sat in the living room listening to the radio.

"German troops in Aachen refused repeated Allied demands to surrender. As a result, the US 991st Field Artillery Battalion commenced a devastating bombardment today. The historic city is home of the famed Aachen Cathedral, commissioned by the Emperor Charlemagne in 790 AD."

"Come to breakfast, guys," Mom called.

I was so nervous, Mom nearly had to force me to eat my eggs. Dad ate even less. He drank two cups of coffee and squelched several belches.

Dad had been belching a lot the past couple of days. Paul Whiteman had invited him to be on his radio show and promote his new record. But Mr. Cody said there were too many problems at the station for Dad to leave. Dad talked to the Senator and got an okay to go, which made Cody mad as hell. He'd been making life miserable for Dad ever since.

When Dad got ready to leave for his noon program, I casually said I'd go along.

Mom looked at me skeptically. "You hardly ever want to go to the station."

"Anything wrong with wanting to spend time with Dad?"

"Of course not, but something funny's going on between you two. I can feel it."

"Well, you know what happens next week, don't you?" Dad said.

Mom looked puzzled, then exclaimed, "You mean Valentine's Day?"

Dad gave her a sphinxlike smile.

A chilling wind swirled around me as Dad let me out at the camp gate. I checked my watch. Eleven o'clock on the nose.

An MP Sergeant who was at least six feet tall stood next to the guardhouse. He looked cold and annoyed. His white-gloved hands were hooked into a thick white web belt with a .45 holstered to it. He was the same MP who pulled us over when we came into town, and the one who had helped Eric when he got tripped.

I approached him timidly. "Excuse me, are you Sergeant Atkins?"

"Roger," he grumbled in a Southern drawl. "You must be the Cook boy." He opened the gate and the earth shuddered beneath me. About 100 yards away, a steam crane was hammering piling the size of a telephone pole into the bank.

"Wanna prisoner named Eric, eh?" Atkins shouted over the din.

I nodded.

Atkins frowned. "Lots of Krauts here named Eric. What's he look like?"

The pounding had stopped, so I could be heard. "Light brown curly hair, not very tall. Doesn't seem much older than me."

Akins pursed his lips. "What else you got?"

"I was at the station the other day and saw him struggling with a wheelbarrow full of rocks. Another prisoner tripped him with a pickaxe. Eric hit his head and started bleeding. You drove up and helped him."

Atkins nodded. "Oh, Stiendler. Eric Stiendler." Atkins shook his head. "Too bad."

My heart stopped. "Something happen to him?"

"Naw, just doubt he'll see you. He's a loner. Hardly speaks to anyone, GI or Kraut."

"Could I at least ask? Long as I'm here, anyway?"

Atkins shrugged. "Brass said to help you, so okay. But I think you're pissin' up a rope."

He took off at a brisk pace. "Follow me."

We came to a squat Quonset hut. It looked like a giant metal barrel that had been cut in half, tipped on its side and painted a drab green. Its two front windows resembled dull yellow eyes. Atkins opened the front door and motioned me inside. "Grab a seat. I'll try to round up Eric."

The sweet scent of fresh cut plywood filled the room. Four curved metal beams like dinosaur ribs held up the corrugated metal ceiling. A string of bare light bulbs ran the length of the room. A balding, squat soldier with a five o'clock shadow and thick round glasses sat at a small table thumbing through a book.

I walked toward him hesitantly. "Sergeant Atkins told me to take a seat. He went to get someone."

"Yeah. That's why I'm here," the soldier said pleasantly. "I'm Corporal Schumacher."

He put down his book, rose and crossed to a Franklin stove. "Coffee?"

he held up a blue and white enamel percolator.

Mom said I was too young to drink coffee. "No thanks."

Schumacher poured a cup. It smelled so warm and tangy that I wished I'd said yes.

I hung my pea coat on the back of one of the table chairs and sat. Glancing at Schumacher's book, I saw that it was in German. I took out a pencil and a small pad of paper from my pea coat pocket. Schumacher sat back down and resumed reading.

I started shivering. It had to be from nerves since the room was almost boiling. The door opened. Atkins came in followed by a sullen-looking Eric.

Atkins motioned for Eric to sit across from me. "Let's get this show on the road." Atkins pointed to the balding soldier. "Corporal Schumacher here is our translator."

I felt like an idiot. It hadn't crossed my mind that Eric wouldn't speak English.

Atkins touched the young German's shoulder. "This here's Private Eric Stiendler, Medical Aid German Infantry."

I held out my hand. "My...name...is...Donald...Cook."

Eric's violet eyes were as forlorn as the first time I saw him. He dropped his gaze and did not extend his hand. Schumacher rattled off my name in German. From his lack of response, Eric might as well have been deaf.

I gathered up all my courage and spoke. "I'm not sure if you remember, but I saw you in the convoy when you came to town. My Dad pulled our car over to let you pass. It seemed you noticed me, too."

Schumacher translated.

No response. I told him I also saw the other POW trip him. Schumacher translated.

Eric remained silent.

"I understand most Germans are not Nazis. In fact, I believe many Germans have been killed because they didn't go along with Hitler."

Eric's eyes flickered.

I swallowed to moisten my throat. "When I saw you, I got a feeling we were alike. Maybe you hated the War as much as I did. If so, I'd like to write about you for our school newspaper."

Schumacher translated. Eric remained silent.

Atkins scraped his chair back. "Son, I'm afraid you're fishin' a dry pond."

"Please," I pleaded.

Atkins locked his arms across his chest. "Only a minute or so more." Schumacher yawned and sipped his coffee.

"Look," my voice rose as I leaned in to Eric. "If I'm all wet about you, just say so. If not, knowing what a German is really like might help change people's minds about things." I looked desperately for some reaction from Eric.

Nothing.

The room became eerily quiet. Eric stared into space as though he hadn't heard a thing.

Atkins stood. "Well, that's it."

Schumacher rose, too.

I lumbered to my feet dejectedly. "Sorry to trouble you," I apologized and turned to get my coat from the back of my chair.

"Vait," a soft voice said.

I wheeled around.

Eric gestured for me to sit. "Please," he added politely.

I fell into my chair, stunned.

"I'll be damned, you speak English!" Atkins said, flabbergasted.

"*Ja*. But not *gut*," Eric replied. "In school, I study two years." His face creased into a slight suggestion of a smile. "*Und* also I learn from your soldiers."

Atkins raised his eyebrows.

I turned to Eric eagerly. "Could I ask you some questions?"

He hesitated for a moment. "*Ja*."

I took a moment to catch my breath. "First of all, could you tell me about you and your family?"

Eric closed his eyes as though recalling a painful memory. "Me, I have 19 years old." He opened his eyes slowly. "*Mein vater* is Valter Stiendler. *Mein mutter*, Sigrid."

"Any brothers or sisters?" I wrote as fast as I could.

"Inga, younger sister."

"And your home?"

"Aachen."

I tensed remembering the news about the bombing there. "Your father. What does he do?"

"He vas Professor History. Aachen *Universität*."

"Was?"

Sorrow shone in Eric's eyes. "Gestapo take him."

I noticed Atkins and Schumacher were as caught up in Eric's story as I was. "Why?"

Eric lowered his eyes. "He say thing they not like."

I felt a tremor of fear. "Is he all right?"

Eric shook his head. "Executed."

His answer felt like a kick to my stomach. "What about your mom, sister? Are they still in Aachen?"

Eric nodded. I asked how he happened to be in the Army.

"At *Universität*, I join *Bekennende Kirche*. Jung people against war. SS arrest us. They vant to send me to concentration camp, but need soldiers. I tell them I not fight. They send me to Normandy. Stretcher-bearer." His eyes glazed with sorrow. I realized that I'd stopped taking notes.

A siren jarred us.

"Chow time," Atkins slapped the table and stood. "Then Eric's gotta go back to work."

A wave of revulsion swept through me. My problems were so petty compared to Eric's. I managed to stand, but held onto the table for support. "Could I see you again?"

"For me, *ja*. But..." Eric turned to Atkins.

The Sergeant shrugged. "Way above my pay grade, boys. That's something the Senator would have to set up."

Eric shuffled out the door with Schumacher.

Atkins drove me to Garney Castle. "You know, kid," his voice lost its gruffness, "I figured you came here just so you could brag about being up close to a live Nazi. Then, when I found out you wanted to see Stiendler, I really got my dander up. With all the crap Eric gets from that SS bastard Krueger, I figured he needed you like a boar needs teats."

He slammed to a stop in front of Garney Castle. "But I gotta hand it to ya." Atkins rapped his white helmet. "I think you cracked his shell."

The instant my feet hit the ground, the Jeep squealed around in a circle and shot back to camp. I skipped up the front steps and started through the door when a horn tooted behind me. Dad. He motioned for me to hop into the Buick.

"Well, how did it go?" he asked.

I scooted around to face him. "Good. Real good. But I'd rather not say anything to you or Mom about it 'til I write the story. I need to really think it out."

Dad frowned. "She knows you're up to something."

"Please. Just give me 'til tomorrow."

His exhale fogged the windshield. "It's against my better judgment, but okay."

We stopped at Jacoby's Drug Store. Dad bought Mom a Whitman's Sampler for Valentine's Day, the same thing he got her every year. I got her a small red heart filled with Russell Stover chocolates. For some dumb reason, I had an urge to get one for Alice, too.

The instant we got home, I locked my bedroom door and holed up in my room. Mom demanded to know what all the mystery was about. Dad told her I was writing a story for the school paper and it was due Monday. Mom got excited and wanted to know all about it.

Dad told her I wanted to surprise them, and that I'd show them the story tomorrow.

I sat at the desk in my room chewing on a pencil, wondering where to begin.

CHAPTER 12

SUNDAY, FEBRUARY 11, 1945

I wolfed down my breakfast and hurried back to my room. Crumpled balls of tablet paper littered the floor. I sat at my desk carefully printing the final version of my story. My fingers were so cramped it hurt to open them. My neck burned from bending over. I checked the clock: eleven fifty-five.

Dad came into the room. "Ready?"

"Just a few more minutes. Promise."

"Mom's waiting in the living room. Cody just called. I have to make a quick run to the station. Tim and Tessie Mae just had a nasty fight over the Colorado Cow Gal."

"Can't you wait?" I hated to face Mom alone.

"Sorry. I'll make it fast as possible."

I finished printing the last page. The story seemed like one big blur. I had no idea if it even made sense. I'd soon find out.

Mom sat on the living room couch, her nimble fingers a blur as she crocheted a white lace tablecloth. "Well, Shakespeare," she smiled as I entered. "Is your masterpiece finally ready?"

My hand shook as I placed a six-sheet manuscript on the arm of the couch. She set down her crochet hook, lit a Chesterfield and picked up the pages eagerly. No sooner had she started reading than the house shook from a deafening clap of thunder. Seconds later, rain pummeled the roof. I hoped it wasn't an omen.

The more Mom read, the more her smile faded. The longer her cigarette ash grew. I plopped in the chair across from her. Doubts buzzed through my brain. *She's sure to hate it. Why am I causing all this trouble?*

Her breath caught in her throat from time to time. When she finished, she stared at me with hollow eyes.

Dad came in the back door stomping his feet. "It's a monsoon out there." I ran to him, anxious to escape from Mom at least for a bit. "Did you get them calmed down?"

Dad snorted. "Nobody was killed if that's what you mean. But if I was the Colorado Cow Gal, I'd never want to be caught in a dark alley with Tessie Mae."

Dad hung his dripping raincoat on a peg and kicked off his galoshes. He poured a cup of coffee, grabbed a dish towel and started drying his head.

"That's a dish towel, Al."

Dad shrugged. "Works just fine." He sat on the arm of the couch. "Well, how'd you like DB's story?"

"You knew about this?" She asked accusingly.

Dad nodded. "About meeting the German? Sure. Haven't read the story yet."

"You let Donnyboy meet with an enemy soldier?" Mom's voice crackled with hurt and anger. "Someone who could have killed our son?"

Dad set his cup on the coffee table. "Now hold on. DB was never in any danger. The Senator assured me there'd always be MPs with him."

"People get killed all the time, in spite of guards." Mom rubbed the back of her wrist across an eye.

"Not here," Dad barked. "Besides, from what I heard this Eric is a good kid. He refused to fight, so they made him cannon fodder on the front line."

"That's right," I jumped in. "And those SS guys who torment Eric? They're like Bo and Lester picking on me."

Mom cradled her forehead. "How could you do this behind my back?"

I reached for my pages. "Sorry you didn't like it."

She jerked them out of my grasp. "I didn't say that. Truth is, it's amazing. Like something Edward R. Murrow would write."

My jaw dropped.

She handed the pages to Dad. "Here."

No one spoke as Dad read. After he was finished, he looked at me proudly. "Good job, son. This is really something."

A joy swept over me that I'd never felt before.

Mom's face grew ashen. "But it worries me. Making friends with a German soldier—after all the horrendous things they've done—there's no telling what people will think. They can brand us as Nazi lovers. I'm sorry, Donnyboy," her eyes became glassy, "but you can't turn it in."

Years of pent-up fury exploded inside me.

"Damn it! You're always worrying about what other people think," I shouted. "This has nothing to do with you. It's my story and I'm going to turn it in. If Miss Morris or Alice say no, so be it. But I've got to take a chance." My whole body quivered in exhaustion.

Mom reacted like I'd slapped her in the face. She turned pleadingly to Dad. "Al, tell Donnyboy he can't turn it in. Tell him."

Dad took a long drag on his cigarette. He held it for several seconds before he exhaled. "No, Jane. He deserves a chance."

Tears streaked with black mascara streamed down Mom's cheeks. I reached over and hugged her. "I don't want to hurt you, Mom. But this is really important to me. Maybe the most important thing ever."

Mom wailed and buried her face in my chest.

CHAPTER 13

MONDAY, FEBRUARY 12, 1945

At lunch Miss Morris gathered Alice, Billy, Darrel, Cleo, and me together to discuss our stories. As circulation manager, Pete invited himself.

Alice had already read her pieces, so Billy started with his story about an upcoming intramural track meet. It was short and funny, and everyone liked it.

Miss Morris asked Cleo to read her new column. Cleo held up a paper full of eraser marks and hastily crossed-out lines. "Okay. But nobody can breathe a word about this until the paper comes out."

We vowed silence.

Cleo took a thick wad of green gum out of her mouth, stuck it to the top of her paper, and began reading.

"The Perfect Eighth Grader, by Cleo Sampson." With a quick wink, she continued. *"Perfect Boy Athlete: Billy Rogers."*

Billy grinned and sat up straight.

"Perfect Girl's Figure: Cleo Sampson." Cleo puffed out her ample chest. She did a good job of mentioning at least half the class, including Pete for "Perfect Sense of Humor" and Darrel for "Perfect Boy's Brain." I didn't expect to be named anything, and I wasn't. I noticed Alice wasn't mentioned either. She stood there gnawing a fingernail and looking like she might burst into tears at any moment.

I looked at Cleo. "I didn't hear 'Perfect Girl's Brain?'"

Cleo looked at me in annoyance. Miss Morris spoke up. "I didn't hear it either."

Cleo put a hand on her hip and gave her gum an angry crack. She pretended to go over her list. "Huh. Guess I forgot," she said in a monotone. *"Perfect Girl's Brain: Alice Cody."*

Alice's superior smile sprang back to life. Miss Morris turned to me eagerly. "Your turn, Donald."

My hands trembled, and my throat turned to chalk. *"Two of a Kind,"* I croaked. After clearing my throat and taking a deep breath, I continued.

"Eric Stiendler is nineteen. If you glanced at him on the street, you'd take him for a happy-go-lucky Farmington High School junior or senior."

Sweat seeped out on my upper lip. The tick of the classroom clock hammered inside my head.

"But you won't see Eric on the street. And he's not happy-go-lucky. He's a German Prisoner of War here in Farmington, and he's friendless. Fellow prisoners torment him because he refused to fight for Hitler. Most Americans hate him simply because he's German."

I peeked up. All eyes were on me. I buried my face in the pages.

"Eric's father was a Professor at the university in Aachen, Germany. Professor Stiendler despised Hitler and the Nazis, and spoke out against them. One day, the Gestapo banged into the Professor's classroom and arrested him. They sent him to a camp with thousands of other dissenters, where he was executed. About a year ago, the Gestapo arrested Eric for belonging to an anti-Hitler youth group at the university. Because they were running low on soldiers, the Nazis forced him into the Army. He refused to fight. They sent him to the front lines as a stretcher-bearer—a job that almost no one survived."

I had to take a breath. The kids' faces were as expressionless as oil paintings. My stomach curdled.

"Eric's mother and younger sister remained in Aachen. Recently, their town has received some of the heaviest Allied bombing in the War. Thousands of Germans civilians have been killed. Eric has tried desperately to get news about his family, but without success."

My hands started trembling.

"I titled this story 'Two of a Kind' because I believe Eric and I are kind of alike. Until I came here a short time ago, my only friend had been my dog, Chaplin. Kids have picked on me because I didn't dress or think like them.

But that's where the similarity between Eric and me stops. Eric's had the guts to stand up for what he believes in, whatever the cost. I've just backed off and felt sorry for myself."

My chest tightened. It hurt to breathe.

"But thanks to what I've learned from Eric and, strangely enough, my brave dog, Chaplin, I realize that it's better to take a chance and fail than to live in fear and be constantly miserable. So this story is my first step out on a limb. After the War, I hope every single Nazi gets exactly what he deserves. But I also hope we can sympathize with Eric and other decent Germans who've suffered personal losses as great as our own. And that we can shake hands and work together for lasting peace."

I lifted my head. I was met by wide eyes and held breaths. A sliver of a tear glistened in one of Alice's eyes. She ran from the room.

My body went limp. "Was it that bad?"

Miss Morris' eyes glistened. "No, that good."

Right after the lunch bell rang, Cleo hurriedly corralled Miss Morris, Alice, Billy, Pete, and me together. She announced there was another "Perfect" she'd forgotten to tell us about.

I kind of half listened, knowing it would just be another kid.

Cleo held up her paper and cleared her throat. *"Perfect Boy's Legs."* She turned to me, *"Donald 'Cookie' Cook."*

At first I thought Cleo was mocking me. But her delight seemed genuine. Miss Morris congratulated me. Billy clapped me on the back. Pete whooped. Alice actually smiled.

For the first time in my life, I felt giddy.

My joy quickly evaporated after lunch. Miss Morris seemed stern and avoided even glancing at me. I had a sneaky suspicion it had to do with my story.

The final bell screamed. Over the din of slamming desktops and kids racing for the cloakroom, Miss Morris said, "Donald and Alice? Come here, please."

My spirits sank. Alice looked annoyed. Miss Morris waited until the room cleared, then looked at me solemnly. "Mr. Chester wanted to see the stories before they were mimeographed. I sent them to him." She dropped her eyes. "He said we couldn't run your story."

Alice almost turned blue. "That's censorship!"

Miss Morris shook her head sadly. "He's the boss. He's afraid some parents—or the School Board—might consider it pro-Nazi and put him on the spot."

Blood raced to my head. "Eric hates the Nazis as much as we do!"

Miss Morris sighed. "I told him that. He just won't take the risk."

I mashed the palm of my hand against my forehead trying to erase the hurt and anger inside. "All right. Can I have my story back?"

Miss Morris reached for it but stopped. "Let me hang onto this for a day or so, okay?"

I sulked. "Why?"

She touched her temple. "Got an idea."

"Well, I guess there's nothing to lose."

Alice slammed her desk shut and strode away. "Chester's a fool. It's the best story in the paper—by far."

I was so shocked I clutched Miss Morris's desk to keep from keeling over.

CHAPTER 14

WEDNESDAY, FEBRUARY 14, 1945

I told the folks Chester killed my story. Mom acted shocked, but I could tell she felt relieved. Dad got mad and wanted to call the Senator. Mom stopped him. She said the principal would make things tougher for me if we went over his head. I agreed but said nothing about Miss Morris having an idea.

After breakfast, we gathered in the dining room to open Valentine's Day presents. Mom gushed when Dad gave her the Whitman's Sampler—just like she did every year. She hugged me for her Russell Stover heart. Mom gave Dad a red sport shirt with a roulette wheel on the back. I got some underwear with red hearts on them and a huge Hershey bar with almonds—more precious than gold during the War.

Chaplin made out, too. Mom gave him a big bag of Gaines Meal tied in a red ribbon. Dad gave him a ham hock from Mr. Farberow, the butcher. I got him a name tag in the shape of a bone with our new address engraved on it.

The celebration made me late, so Dad drove me to school. Mom insisted I give a Valentine to each kid in class. My fingers stung from the paper cuts I got punching out the Valentines Mom picked up at Woolworth's.

Bo and Lester were in the cloakroom when I entered. I slipped my coat on the nearest hook and hurried out. Except for an occasional dirty look, they had ignored me since their talk with Chester. I still didn't trust them.

After everyone took their seats, Miss Morris asked us to line up and drop our cards into a heart-shaped box Alice had made. It was covered with pink and white crepe paper and cut-out red hearts and cupids. It looked as good as anything you'd buy in a store.

Pete cut in front of me and thumbed through the names on my envelopes. I turned away and covered them with my hand. Pete acted insulted. "We don't have Valentine's Day in Persia, anyway." He strode away without depositing anything in the box.

I felt apprehensive all day about the Valentines being handed out. I rarely ever got one.

At two o'clock, Miss Morris covered the art table with a white tablecloth that had red hearts all over it. Alice and Peggy put stacks of matching cups, plates and napkins at one end. Cleo and Darrel added pitchers of red punch, plates full of cupcakes and sugar cookies, and baskets of tiny pastel mint hearts printed with phrases like "Love You" and "Heart's Desire."

We formed a line on each side of the table and picked up our treats. I noticed that Bo and Lester weren't there. I almost envied them. They probably didn't expect any Valentines either.

Miss Morris placed the heart-shaped box on her desk and asked who'd like to be "Cupid's Messengers?" Cleo and Peggy raced up to the front of the classroom. Miss Morris lifted the lid and instructed them to close their eyes and draw out two or three cards at a time. Before delivering the Valentines, they were to announce the recipient's name clearly.

I could sense the excitement in the room, which made me feel even more despondent.

Peggy and Cleo were fast as blue lightning. Soon everyone around had at least one Valentine—everyone except me. More names were called. None were mine. I tried to become invisible by sliding down in my desk.

Billy got so many cards he stopped opening them. Alice got lots, too. Darrel leaned over and whispered she'd probably sent most of them to herself.

Peggy called Pete's name. He tried to act blasé but I could see his face light up. He tore open the envelope and looked to see who had sent it. He put the palms of his hands together and bowed at me.

Cleo called my name. Startled, I blurted, "Here!" The class erupted in laughter. My face flushed as Cleo sashayed over. She held the card by one edge high above my open hands and cried out, "Bombs away!" She made a whistling sound as it fell.

Trying not to appear eager, I slowly slid my finger under the flap and pulled it open. The card showed a boy in short pants swinging a golf club. It said: *"Take a swing at being my Valentine."* I turned the page to see who had sent it. Careful not to show my disappointment, I mouthed, "Thank you" to Miss Morris.

Peggy closed her eyes and swept her hand across the bottom of the box searching for a stray card. "Guess that's it," she announced. Cleo walked over with a quizzical expression. "Let's make sure." She picked up the box, peered inside and pulled out a thick pink envelope. "Donny Cook," she announced with an eyebrow jiggle.

I gulped. Nobody called me "Donny." Was this somebody's idea of a sick joke? The envelope landed on my desk with a *thunk*. The front had a red Cupid stamp, and "Donny Cook" in a fancy script. I sniffed. The envelope smelled of Mom's favorite flower, gardenia.

I edged my finger under the heavy triangular flap until it popped open. I slipped out the card. The front page had a large cut-out heart. Through the heart I could see a sucker. Not just any sucker—a sucker molded like a beautiful red rose. I felt elated but looked over my shoulder, worried one of my neighbors might see it and make fun of me. But they were all too busy counting their Valentines.

I lowered the card onto my lap and opened the cut-out page. Printed under the rosebud lollipop was: *"I'm a sucker for you. Be my Valentine."* Below that: *"Love, Guess Who?"*

It was too expensive to be a joke, and it had to have come from a girl. But who? I scanned the room. Most of the kids were still busy looking over their cards, but Cleo appeared to be glancing at me out of the corner of her eye.

It had to be her. She was always squeezing through the door at the last minute with me. And hadn't she written that I had perfect boys' legs? I definitely felt flattered. But I also had a gnawing disappointment that it didn't come from someone else. I shoved that thought out of my mind as a pipe dream.

After everyone left, I slipped my Valentines inside my Geography book. The classroom door opened and a young man with unruly black hair, a sharp nose and a rumpled grey suit entered. He had a black scarf wrapped around his neck and carried a heart shaped box with a red ribbon around it. He tiptoed toward Miss Morris.

"Bob!" She looked up in surprise.

"Happy Valentine's Day," Bob said with a goofy smile. He handed her the box.

"Why, thank you, darling!" She stood up to give him a kiss. She noticed me and blushed. "Oh, Donald! I didn't realize you were still here. This is my, uh, friend, Bob Lyle."

I walked over and shook his hand.

"Donald wrote the POW story I gave you last night."

Bob nodded. "Nice piece."

I lowered my eyes. "I'm sure it sounded pretty amateurish."

"Not at all. In fact, I'd like to talk to you about maybe running it."

I almost fell over. "Really? When?"

He screwed his mouth to one side. "It's pretty timely, so sometime soon. Drop by the *Dakotan* when you can."

"You bet." I floated out the door.

"Hi, Mom. Chaplin here?"

"No. Wasn't he waiting for you outside?"

"No."

"Well, he's probably out gallivanting with Cinderella."

Something made me uneasy. "Hope so."

Mom finished rinsing a dish and dried her hands on her apron. "How was your Valentine's Day?"

"Good," I replied, more worried about Chaplin. I went out to the back landing and called for him. He didn't come, which really bothered me. Chaplin never missed a meal.

Dad had a personal appearance, so we ate early. I wolfed down my dinner and rinsed my dishes in the sink. "I'm going out to find him," I announced, and slipped into my pea coat.

Mom took a flashlight out of a drawer and put it in my hand. "It's dark out there." She tugged a stocking cap over my ears. "And freezing."

"Ouch." The gash on my temple was still tender. I rolled the cap above my wound and sped out the door.

Shouting and shining my flashlight into every bush and dark cranny, I combed my street. "Chaplin. Here, Chaplin. Come boy. Food. Come get your dinner. Time to come in."

I heard the clink of a dog tag heading my way. Relieved, I swung my flashlight toward the sound.

It was a Red Setter that lived down the street. My fear turned to anger. "Quit playing games, Chaplin!" I shouted. "Get over here right now!"

Nothing.

I crumpled to the curb. "Where *are* you, Chaplin?" Then it hit me. He could be with Cinderella. I galloped to Darrel's house.

Panting, I stomped up the front landing and rapped on the door. I heard footsteps. A hand pulled back the lace curtain over the door window. An eye peered out at me. I heard a woman's voice call from inside, "Darrel, it's the Cook boy."

The front door swung open. Darrel looked out. "Hey, you look awful. What's wrong?"

"Chaplin, my dog's missing," I wheezed. "He likes Cinderella. I wondered, is he here?"

Before Darrel could answer, Cinderella pranced up, wagging her tail. "Haven't seen him," Darrel shrugged.

Dread swamped me. "Oh. Tell your mother I'm sorry to have bothered you." I turned and slumped down the stairs.

Darrel called out. "I'll keep an eye out for him, Cookie."

My bed seemed vast and desolate without Chaplin. I stared at the ceiling, numb from worry. When Dad got home, he and Mom came in to say goodnight. "I'll put food out on the back porch," Dad said. Mom stroked my hair. "I'm sure he'll show up in the morning."

I couldn't sleep. To stop myself from fretting about Chaplin, I tried to think about my elaborate Valentine and Bob Lyle wanting to see me.

It didn't work.

CHAPTER 15

THURSDAY, FEBRUARY 15, 1945

At the first glint of dawn, I jumped out of bed and threw on dunga-rees and a flannel shirt. To my surprise, I only had to roll up the cuffs twice. It usually took three rolls to keep them from dragging on the ground.

I grabbed my loafers and tiptoed out of my room. The floor creaked, but I made it to the back porch without waking Mom and Dad. I slipped into my pea coat, crossed my fingers and opened the back door. My heart sank. Chaplin's Strongheart dog food was still in the bowl—crusted over with frost.

I spent the next 45 minutes searching Pearl, Elm and Mulberry Streets. No sign of Chaplin. When I got back, Dad had left for the station. Mom had Shredded Wheat and cream set out for me. Steam drifted from my cup of hot chocolate. She sat at the breakfast table in her pink chenille robe smoking a cigarette. "No luck?"

"No."

"He'll probably show up while you're at school," she said cheerfully.

"No he won't!" I wailed. "Quit pretending he's all right. Something's happened to him. I know it."

"Just calm down, young man," she scolded. "I know you're upset. We all are. But thinking the worst will just make you more miserable."

I picked at my cereal and ignored my hot chocolate. Mom checked the kitchen clock. "It's late. You don't have to finish your breakfast." She held up my lunch bag and smiled. "I packed extra cookies in case Pete raids you."

I got up and gave her a quick hug. "Thanks. Sorry for yelling."

"I understand. Now hurry up and change your pants and scrub your teeth."

"These pants are fine."

"They're dungarees." She looked at me with disbelief. "You can't wear dungarees to school."

"All the other kids do."

Mom started wringing her hands. "What's gotten into you lately? You argue with me about everything."

"I'm tired of being a freak!" I threw my napkin on the floor and stood. "You don't give a tinker's damn what I think. All you care about is what everyone else thinks!"

Mom's lips trembled. The lunch bag fell from her hand and hit the floor. She ran into her bedroom, slamming the door behind her.

"Hey, Cookie." Pete was all smiles at the corner.

"Don't call me 'Cookie,'" I grumbled, stomping past him.

Pete hurried to catch up. "My! Look who got up on the wrong side of the bed this morning."

I slowed down. "Sorry. I'm in a rotten mood. Chaplin's been missing since yesterday afternoon."

Pete chuckled. "That all? Don't worry. Our dog runs off all the time. Dogs do that."

"Not Chaplin."

Pete squeezed my bulging lunch bag. "What you got in there?"

I handed it to him. "Help yourself."

The morning passed in a daze. I couldn't think of anything but Chaplin. Alice came up to me at recess. "I've been thinking about Mr. Chester rejecting your story," she said, her tiny lower lip jutting out. "Maybe I could talk to my grandfather about it?"

"My Dad had the same idea," I told her. "But my Mom felt it would rile up Chester. Besides, the only thing on my mind right now is my missing dog, Chaplin."

"Oh, that's awful. If something happened to my Coco I'd just die." She patted the black Scottie in the middle of her swollen sweater.

I wanted to be alone at lunch, so I broke the rules, left the schoolyard and walked over to Lynn Creek. The tree branches on the bank were coated with clear ice sleeves. Silver ice mirrors floated in the stagnant stream. I threw a rock at one. It shattered into slivers of shimmering tears.

Moments spent with Chaplin played in my mind like a slideshow. I remembered cradling his head under my arm as we lay in the grass, staring up at scudding clouds; cowering under him as he snarled over me playing "Devil Dog"; holding him up by his front paws and dancing to my records. The thought of not having him in my life was too much to bear.

It seemed like the afternoon would never end. The instant the final bell sounded, I shot out of the building and ran for home.

Clutching the rail with both hands, I scrambled up the front porch stairs two steps at a time. "Please, *please*," I prayed. "Let Chaplin be home." I lurched onto the top landing and looked at his bowl. The food was still there. I stumbled into the house. Mom stood waiting for me. Her expression said she hadn't seen Chaplin.

I started to cry. "Something awful's happened to him. I know it," I sobbed.

Mom massaged my neck. "It's only been one day."

"He's never been gone this long."

Mom cupped my face in her hands, stared at me tenderly and kissed me softly on the cheek. Tears dropped from her eyes.

I wiped my eyes with my sleeve. "I'm going to look some more." For the next hour and a half, I searched from Garney Castle to the train station. I called and called until I was hoarse.

No sign of Chaplin.

The sun was setting as I shuffled up our driveway. Long wispy clouds on the horizon glowed an iridescent orange and pink. The cold bit at my fingers. A stream of fog shot from my mouth every time I exhaled. I heard the jangle of tags on a dog collar. Soft feet padded down our back stairs.

"Chaplin!" I cried, running to the rear of the house.

Cinderella bounded off the last step and ran toward the garage, Chaplin's food bowl clamped in her teeth.

"Stop!" I shouted. "That's Chaplin's!" I ran after her. Her legs were little, but they moved fast. She flew past the garage into the vacant field and scurried through the high dead weeds—all the while keeping a tight hold of Chaplin's dish.

Just as I was about to run out of breath, Cinderella stopped abruptly and gently set Chaplin's bowl on the ground. I slammed to a halt beside her. Chaplin's dish rested next to a reddish-brown heap lying motionless on the ground.

"Chaplin!" I dropped to my knees and hugged my beloved friend. His head felt limp and lifeless. His eyes were open and glazed. His tongue drooped out of one side of his mouth. He wheezed short, painful breaths.

I collapsed beside him and pulled his face to mine. "Where've you been? What's happened to you?" His only sign of life was labored breathing. Cradling my arms under his belly, I found the strength to lift him.

Cinderella pattered beside me as I lumbered home. "Good dog, Cinder," I sniffed gratefully. She started to follow me up the back steps but I ordered her home. She moved off, her head drooping.

I kicked at the back door. "Mom! Dad! Open up, quick! I found him! I found Chaplin!" I heard rushing footsteps and the door burst open.

"Oh, thank goodness!" Mom cried. Dad noticed Chaplin's slack body. "Jesus. What's wrong with him?"

"Don't know. But it's bad. We've got to get a doctor. Right away."

"Al, give Donnyboy a hand," Mom said. "I'll call a vet."

Dad took Chaplin from me.

"Put him on my bed," I said, shaking my arms to get feeling back into them.

"Donnyboy, get some blankets out of the closet," Mom ordered as she paged through the phone book.

"What do you think it is?" I asked Dad as we wrapped Chaplin in blankets on my bed.

"Beats me, DB. I don't see any cuts or bites."

"Think it's some kind of disease?"

Dad looked perplexed and shook his head. "He's had all his shots."

Mom scampered into the room. "I got hold of a vet, Dr. Schultz. He's on his way."

I said a silent prayer.

Mom lifted Chaplin's head and tried to spoon water into his mouth. Most of it dribbled onto the blankets. Chaplin panted for air. I stroked his head and prayed more fervently.

Mom led Dr. Schultz, a stocky white-haired man with a ruddy face and rough hands, into my bedroom. He nodded pleasantly and knelt beside

Chaplin. He pulled back Chaplin's lips and checked his gums. They were a sickly yellow instead of pink. The vet pressed what looked like a wide popsicle stick on Chaplin's tongue, which drooped to one side.

Dr. Schultz shined a flashlight into Chaplin's murky, unblinking eyes. Finally, he took out his stethoscope and listened to Chaplin's heart. The vet signed, leaned back on his haunches and looked at us.

"What is it?" I cried.

"Appears to be poison."

Mom gasped. "Where would he get into poison?"

Dr. Schultz shrugged. "It's all around. Garages. Basements. Trash cans."

I moaned, remembering how Chaplin scrounged through trash cans for food. Pushing the thought out of my mind, I tugged on the vet's sleeve. "But you can fix him, doctor. You can, can't you?"

The vet looked solemn. "I'll take him back to my place and do what I can."

"I'll go with you!" I exclaimed.

He shook his head. "Best you get some sleep." Dr. Schultz packed his instruments into his black bag. "I'll let your folks know what's what."

"But he's my best friend!" I sobbed.

"Sorry, son," Dr. Schultz said softly, and put his hand on my shoulder. Every feeling in my body switched off.

The doors of the vet's van shut with a *clunk*.

"Call as soon as you know something," Dad said. "Day, night—doesn't matter."

The vet nodded and climbed into the driver's seat. The engine groaned a couple of times and then rumbled to life. I stared at its red tail lights until the night swallowed them.

Dad and Mom took my hands and squeezed. My stomach convulsed. I leaned over to retch. Nothing came up.

CHAPTER 16

FRIDAY, FEBRUARY 16, 1945

The phone rang at a little after six o'clock in the morning. I sprang out of bed and ran to answer it, but Dad beat me. He looked like he'd been up all night. When he hung up, there were tears in his eyes. I'd never seen him cry before. "I'm sorry, DB. Chaplin was too far gone."

I sleepwalked to my bedroom and locked the door.

Dad rattled the doorknob. "Donnyboy."

"Please. I want to be alone."

He let go of the doorknob. "I understand."

Mom rapped on my door a few seconds later. "Are you all right, Donnyboy?" She was sobbing.

"Yeah," I said numbly.

"Want to stay home from school today?'

"Please."

"I'll call." She paused. "Just so you know, our hearts are broken, too. Dad's got a terrible stomach ache"

"Sorry."

The noonday sun lit up the frost caked on my bedroom window. It sparkled blue and white as a diamond. I remembered how Chaplin liked to lick it.

I wondered why I didn't throw up last night. All the usual signs were there. But somehow, I just didn't care. Then. Or now.

Mom came to the door. "Donnyboy," she said softly. "May I come in?"

"Not now."

"You need to eat something."

"No, thank you."

"Guess what?" She tried sounding happy. "Dad says he'll get you another dog. Whatever kind you like."

A river of hurt poured out of me. "I don't want another dog! I want *Chaplin*." I burst out bawling.

Mom moaned. "Please, open the door."

I shuffled over and turned the key.

Mom threw her arms around me. We squeezed the breath out of one another and cried until we didn't have a tear left between us.

Dad told Dr. Schultz to cremate Chaplin. That way I'd at least have his ashes to keep.

I finally managed to get down a poached egg on toast. I spent the rest of the day listening to records and reading. Mom baked a chocolate cake with seven-minute icing—my favorite—and brought me a piece. I took a bite. The chocolate tasted too bitter, the frosting too sugary. I told Mom I'd finish it later.

Traces of Chaplin were all around me. The scratches he made on the side of my bed when he scrambled up to sleep with me. His scent on my pillow. And there, on my nightstand, a small clump of red fur from a burr I pulled off his tummy.

Dad came in before going to Chicago for the Paul Whiteman show. "You going to be all right? I could stay, you know."

I knew he'd give up a big chance if he did. "No, you should go. Sorry about your stomach."

"I'll be fine. Tune in Monday night for the show. I'll be back Tuesday."

"Good luck."

"I'll bring you back something. What would you like?"

I didn't answer. The only thing I wanted was Chaplin.

CHAPTER 17

MONDAY, FEBRUARY 19, 1945

Over the weekend, I made a twig cross and staked it in the vacant lot where I found Chaplin. Dr. Schultz delivered his ashes Saturday night in a plain brown box. I printed "Chaplin Cook" on it in my best penmanship, and put it on the shelf of my bedside table.

I felt numb as I left for school. Pete waited at the corner, puffing into his gloveless hands to warm them. I wondered how he kept from freezing in his flimsy black balloon pants and rust-colored jacket—to say nothing of his bare feet in sandals.

"Sorry about your dog," he said. "Chester told Morris after your Mom called last Friday. She told the class."

"Did she mention Chaplin was poisoned?"

Pete's thick brows slid together. "No. How?"

"I think somebody did it on purpose."

"Who?"

"Think I know. But I can't say 'cause I've got no proof." We walked on in silence.

Pete let out a whoop. "Hey, did you hear about Bo?"

My body tensed. "What about him?"

"Quit school."

I stopped cold. "When? Why?"

"Chester announced it Friday. Didn't say why." Pete's eyebrows danced. "But Bluehair eats at the café every Friday night. She gave Pop the whole story."

"Which was?" I pressed.

"Well, when Bo skipped class last Wednesday afternoon, Chester blew a fuse. He drove out to the Foley's for a showdown."

"And?"

"Bo wasn't there. Ole man Foley said Bo was sixteen and didn't have to go to school. Far as he was concerned, Bo should get a job and pull his weight around the house—if you could call it that. Ever seen their dump?"

I shook my head.

Pete held his nose. "They got a shanty in the hollow next to the stock-yards. Filthier than a pigsty. Anyway, Chester said good riddance and left."

My mind started racing.

Almost everyone in class told me they were sorry about Chaplin. I thanked them but didn't feel like talking about it. To my relief, Pete had to wash dishes at the diner after school, so I got to walk home by myself.

David sat on our front porch steps, his arm in a sling. "What happened?" I asked.

He laughed a little too hard. "Wrenched it throwin' my fast ball."

"Sure you did."

David ignored my sarcasm. "Came by to see your pop. Nobody's home."

"Mom's probably playing Bridge. Dad's in Chicago. He's going to be on the Paul Whiteman show tonight."

"That's great." He looked at me questioningly. "How come you seem so down in the dumps?"

"Chaplin's dead. Poisoned."

David's face crinkled. "That's raw. How'd it happen?"

I slumped down on the steps beside him. "Can't say for sure. But I think I know who did it."

"Who?"

I raised my shoulders and let them drop. "Bo. But I've got no proof." I told David how Bo promised to get even with Chaplin after Chaplin came to my rescue.

David's eyes grew wide. "Hey! Last week—yeah, Valentine's Day—I came by to see if your pop was home."

"So?"

"I rounded the front of your house and heard arguing. A trash can slammed shut. When I reached the backyard, Chaplin was eating something and I think I saw Bo dart behind your garage."

I bolted up. "Wednesday's when Chaplin disappeared." I paused. "You said you heard voices. Who else was with him?"

David snorted and stood. "Knowing Bo, he was probably arguing with himself." He shook a pack of Camels, pulled one out with his lips, bent a paper match over and struck it aflame. "I've gotta get going. Real sorry about your dog."

I clenched his arm. "When Dad gets back, I'll make sure he sees you."

"Much obliged." David strutted off.

Today was trash day. I rushed to the garage hoping the trash man hadn't come by yet.

He hadn't.

I tore off the lid. The stench of rancid garbage assaulted me. I breathed through my mouth and rummaged through a week's worth of tossed food and papers, not knowing what I was looking for but hoping I'd know it when I saw it.

Halfway down I found a soiled yellow box.

E-RAT-ICATE
KILLS 'EM DEAD.
CAUTION! POISON

With bone-deep sorrow, I slipped the box into my pea coat. My legs quivered. My chest felt as if a steel cable was squeezing the life out of me.

I didn't tell Mom about my conversation with David or what I'd found. I didn't want her to know.

After dinner we gathered around the radio to listen to the Whiteman show. I sat on the floor, Mom on the couch. We listened impatiently for ten or fifteen minutes before Mr. Whiteman introduced Dad. They kidded about some of the funny experiences they had when they were on the road. Then Dad played "Crossbow" with the entire Paul Whiteman orchestra. I'd never heard Dad play with such artistry. When the applause finally died down, Mr. Whiteman declared, "Al, anytime you want your old job back, let me know." Dad laughed heartily and told the maestro he would.

Mom tried to laugh it off, but couldn't hide the sorrow in her eyes.

CHAPTER 18

TUESDAY, FEBRUARY 20, 1945

Dad's train was scheduled to get into Sioux City around two o'clock this afternoon. Mom wanted to leave early so she could do some shopping. The timing couldn't have been better.

As Pete and I made our way to school, I grimaced and grabbed my stomach. "I think I'm going to be sick."

Pete edged away. "You gonna barf?"

"Not sure."

Pete backed off a little more.

I fake moaned. "I should go home. Tell Miss Morris, will you? I'm sure I'll be better tomorrow."

"Sure." Pete's eyes fell on my lunch bag. "Probably shouldn't eat, right?"

"Take it."

As we went our separate ways, I heard the crinkle of wax paper and the crunch of a Hydrox cookie.

I checked the garage. The Buick was gone. I opened the back door and called, "Mom?" The only answer was the hum of the Frigidaire and the usual household creaks. I took off my shoes and tiptoed to the folks' bedroom. The door was ajar. No one inside. I slid through the doorway.

I searched every square inch of their closet. It wasn't there. My hands began to sweat. I looked in their bathroom. The only place it could fit would be under the tub. Not there, either. I pulled back the drapes in the bedroom. Nothing. I was about to give up when I pictured Bo bellowing, "Ah'll git ya, gawdamit! You an yer gawdam dawg!"

I scanned the room one more time and realized I'd missed the most likely place. Kneeling on my hands and knees, I lifted their white chenille bedspread. Dad's rifle and shotgun lay an arm's length away.

I pushed a black sock out of the way and pulled out the rifle case. Dad had taught me how to load and shoot the .22 the first time he took me hunting. I checked the chamber. Empty. The same went for the bullet tube below the barrel. No bullets inside the rifle case either. A box of Peter's High Velocity shells could easily fit in the palm of your hand. Dad could have hidden them anywhere.

Sweat dripped from my forehead. My doubts grew. I forced them out of my mind and crossed to my folks' dresser. Nothing in the top three drawers. I opened the bottom drawer and snaked my hand through the soft piles. My hand touched three small, heavy boxes. I grabbed one and slammed the drawer shut.

Dad's raincoat hung on a hook by the back door. It nearly dragged on the ground when I put it on. But it would hide the rifle, and I could carry the shells in one of the pockets.

From what Pete said, the Foleys lived in a shack just past Lynn Creek next to the stockyards. Like a robot, I headed there.

It took ten minutes to reach the creek. It ran at the bottom of a steep hollow. I unbuttoned Dad's coat and pointed the rifle barrel in the air. After making sure the safety was on, I edged down the steep bank.

After about four yards, my feet slipped and I fell on my butt. I slammed my hand against the rocky ground and came to a halt just shy of the creek. I struggled to my knees and rinsed my scraped hand in the frigid creek water. It stung something fierce, but I didn't make a peep.

I reached the top of the bank and knelt behind some high weeds to catch my breath. In the distance to my right were a cluster of red barns and white pens. A terrible smell hit me—a sickening mix of manure and blood and fear.

I glanced to my left. Through the weeds I saw what appeared to be an abandoned shack. I rose up for a better look.

The walls were made of different-shaped pieces of wood fit together like a nonsensical puzzle. Some were painted, some not. A section from an old circus poster was pasted on one. The shack drooped in the back. Grey smoke trickled from a narrow flu in the tarpaper roof.

Three filthy red-haired kids ran out of the shack door, slapping and taunting each other. I recognized them from the clinker ambush. My heart thumped. I bent down and stalked through the brush.

Rusted carcasses of farm equipment surrounded the shack. Two fat sows snorted and rooted in a mud wallow out front. A dozen scrawny chickens strutted around the yard. The majority sported patches of raw skin from having their feathers pecked away.

I stopped at the edge of the weeds where I still had cover. Shrugging out of Dad's raincoat, I set the rifle butt on the ground and unscrewed the bullet tube. I reached into the coat pocket, opened the bullet box and took out a single shell. It was all I needed.

I loaded it into the chamber and thumbed the safety off. A door slammed. My head swung to the sound. Behind the shack, a Foley boy about eight years old stepped out of a rickety privy. A putrid smell fouled the air. The boy wiped his hands on the front of his dirty overalls and crossed to a water pump beside the shack.

My arms trembled. Only the memory of Chaplin lying in the field kept me going. I stood, hitched the rifle to my hip and walked into the yard. When the kids saw me, their eyes bulged.

"Where's Bo?" I asked a little girl.

She stared at me with a vacant look.

"You've got a brother named Bo, haven't you?"

"Bo?" she seemed befuddled.

"Bo's inside," said the boy who came out of the privy.

I nodded and moved toward the front door, which was really just a collection of boards nailed together haphazardly. There were large gaps between the boards. I knocked. Nobody answered. I knocked again. Nothing.

I peered through a gap and could make out someone sitting inside. "I'm coming in," I announced. Lifting the rifle to my chest, I kicked the door open.

There was only one room, which was jammed with junky furniture. My eyes shot from side to side. Beat-up Army cots crowded against one wall. Clothes and canned goods were stuffed into orange crates along the other. Two railroad lanterns hung from rusty nails, their kerosene smell filling the stuffy room.

Bo sat at the table facing me, spooning thick white stuff out of a crock onto a hunk of dark bread. When he saw me, he screamed, "Ma!"

A skinny woman with grey-streaked red hair turned to face me. She stood at a sink rubbing soapy clothes against a washboard. "What ya want?" she asked in a tired voice.

"I came for Bo." I tried to sound polite and angry at the same time.

"What yew want Bo fer?"

"Yeah! What fer?" Bo asked, his voice quivering with fear.

"For killing my dog." I swung the rifle at him.

He screamed, "I dint do it!"

"You kill his dawg, Bo?" the woman asked.

"Shit no, Ma!"

"Yew lyin' agin, Bo?"

"No, Ma. He's mistook. Honest."

Her sad eyes moved to me. "Bo say he didn't do it, boy."

"He's lying, ma'am. I've got proof." I held up the yellow box. "Rat Poison. Bo was in my backyard the day my dog got poisoned. My friend saw Bo put this in our trash."

I raised the rifle to my shoulder. Touched my finger to the trigger.

Bo whimpered and ran for his Ma. "It weren't me, Ma." In his panic he knocked over the crock of white stuff he'd been spooning. It rolled to a stop at my feet.

My stomach quaked. Lard. Bo was eating lard. I felt dizzy. Sweat bleared my eyes.

"It were jest a dawg, boy," his Ma mumbled. "Don't shoot Bo 'cause of no dawg."

The rifle wobbled in my hands. I tried to line Bo up in the sight. He tried to shrink behind his Ma. A yellow puddle spread out at the bottom of his bare feet.

Mrs. Foley stared at me pathetically. "Why yew doin' this?"

I searched for a reason other than revenge, but failed. The hate that had been raging inside me abated, and was replaced by shame. I dropped the rifle to my side. By accident I pulled the trigger.

KAPOW!

Dust and splinters burst from the floor inches from Bo's toes. He screamed.

I snapped on the safety. "Oh my God! It was an accident."

"What the goddam hell's goin' on?" a raspy voice shouted from the doorway.

I spun around and saw an unshaven, gnarled, red-haired man. He had stubbly salt-and-pepper whiskers, and his face was splotched with broken veins. The bib overalls he wore over his soiled long underwear were missing a strap. Two of his front teeth were gone, and the rest were stained a deep yellow. Behind him, four Foley kids peered at me with fear and curiosity.

"He tried ta kill me, Pa!" Bo blubbered.

"What the hell fer?" Mr. Foley demanded.

"For poisoning my dog," I replied weakly. "But I didn't try to shoot him. It went off by mistake."

Mr. Foley sneered and strode over to Bo. "You kill that boy's dawg?" he challenged, standing nose to nose with his son.

"No, dammit," Bo whimpered. Mr. Foley whacked Bo across the mouth. Bo brought his hand up to his lips. Blood streamed through his fingers.

Mr. Foley turned and drilled his eyes into me. "That satisfy ya, boy?" He spat on the floor.

I lowered my eyes in humiliation, walked out the door and took off running. When I reached the edge of the weeds I stopped. I wrapped the rifle in Dad's raincoat and pushed through the brush. Somehow I made it home.

I cleaned the gun and put it back exactly the way I found it. The kitchen clock said two o'clock. The folks would be home soon. I made a cup of hot chocolate hoping it would soothe me.

For the next hour, I imagined all sorts of dire consequences. I expected a screaming police car to pull up and arrest me any second. Or Mr. Foley to storm into our house to confront me in front of the folks. But nothing like that happened.

When I heard Mom and Dad climbing the back stairs, I jumped into bed and began groaning and holding my stomach. Unfortunately, I'd forgotten that Mom had a deadly fear of appendicitis. Her brother Steve nearly died when his appendix burst. She immediately pulled my PJ bottoms down and started pressing the right side of my stomach. "Does it hurt here?"

"No."

She pushed a little harder to the left.

I shook my head.

She put her full weight on it. "Here?"

I woofed in pain.

Mom nodded solemnly. "I'm calling the doctor."

I grabbed her arm. "Mom, it's not my appendix, it's your *fingernails*. They gouged me."

She curled her fingers and scrutinized them. They were red as ripe cherries and sharp. "You sure?"

"Positive. Besides, my stomach pain's gone now."

Mom gnawed her lower lip. "Well, it may come back. I'll get some milk of magnesia."

I tried to talk her out of it, but she forced two heaping spoonfuls of the chalky dreck down my throat. To make things worse, Dad had brought me three Hershey bars with almonds from Chicago. My mouth juiced at the sight of them.

Mom snatched the precious candy. "Not yet. Not 'til we know for sure you don't have appendicitis."

For dinner Mom made me a cup of chamomile tea. She said it would soothe my insides, and made me sit at the table so she could be sure I drank it all. Without thinking, I reached under the table for a lick from Chaplin. My fingers twitched in empty space. A hollowness filled my stomach. I was on my own.

CHAPTER 19

FRIDAY, FEBRUARY 23, 1945

The three days following the incident at Bo's house were an emotional hell. I expected to be arrested at any moment, or for Mr. Foley to bust through the door. When that didn't happen, I worried even more. Maybe the Foleys had some evil plan to kidnap or kill me.

But on the fourth day, I forced the whole mess out of my mind. I had something much bigger then me to tackle.

The air in the huge open room reeked of cigarettes. A low haze billowed beneath the ceiling and stung my nose. "Is Mr. Lyle here?" I asked a gaunt woman at the front desk. I had to raise my voice to be heard above a couple dozen men and women pounding typewriters or chattering on telephones.

Without looking up she hollered, "Hey, Lyle."

Miss Morris's boyfriend raised his head like a turtle. His shirtsleeves were rolled up and a cigarette was pinned against his head by the black frames of his horn-rimmed glasses. My uneasiness ratcheted up when I saw the annoyance on his face.

"Hold on," he hollered back. After sticking a pencil sideways in his mouth, he continued typing.

"Take a seat." the gaunt lady nodded at a wooden chair against the wall. Copies of the *Farmington Dakotan* were strewn on a table next to it.

Bob strode up to me. "Wanna see me?"

I jumped up. "Yes, sir. I'm Donald Cook. Miss Morris's class. I wrote the story about the German prisoner. You said you'd like to talk about it."

"Oh, right. Nice piece."

I took a breath. "Any chance you might print it?"

"It crossed my mind."

A wave of exhilaration and fear swept over me.

Bob nodded over his shoulder to a bald-headed man wearing round glasses. "Have to check with my editor. But it might be a good editorial for Sunday."

"This Sunday?"

"Right. I'm on deadline now. I'll check with him after I'm done."

"Do you still have the story? It's my only copy."

He paused in thought. "Yeah. In my desk." He started to turn away. "Oh. Are your folks okay with this?"

A tremor went through me. "Uh, sure. They really liked it."

CHAPTER 20

SUNDAY, FEBRUARY 25, 1945

"Donnyboy, how could you?" Mom screamed in my dream. Only it wasn't a dream. Mom stood over me in her chenille robe shaking a newspaper in my face.

I rubbed the sleep out of my eyes and mumbled, "What's wrong?"

"Your story. It's in here."

I reached for the newspaper.

Mom pulled it back. "How did it get in here?"

I related the whole story.

"What made you do it?" Mom's voice crackled with grief.

I lowered my eyes. "I know it sounds crazy, but I had a dream. Chaplin said I had to get my story printed."

Mom slumped to the bed, her lower lip quivering.

"What's all the ruckus about?" Dad ambled in wearing his blue robe.

Mom held out the folded newspaper. "This."

Dad started reading. A sliver of a smile snuck onto his lips. "Pretty slick, DB," he nodded.

"*Slick?*" Mom spat. "You think it's slick your son snuck around behind our backs and unleashed something that'll probably set half the town against us?"

"Hold on!" I snapped. "You said you liked the story. And you sure acted disappointed when Chester killed it. Why are you so upset now?"

Mom wrung her hands.

Dad said, "Let's just see what happens."

The phone started ringing before breakfast. Dad answered. After a long silence, he slammed the receiver down.

"Who was it?" Mom asked.

"Nobody," Dad growled.

Less than a minute later, the phone rang again. Dad answered. The same thing happened.

"It's about the story, isn't it?" Mom turned pale.

Dad didn't answer.

"What are they saying?" I tugged the sleeve of his robe.

"Nothing you need to hear," Dad muttered, squelching a belch.

I looked at Mom expecting her to scream at me. Instead she stood motionless, as though in a trance.

Dad took the phone off the hook during breakfast. Six more calls came in during the rest of the day. Two said I had no business making friends with Germans. Three said they agreed with me.

The last one said I ought to be shot.

CHAPTER 21

MONDAY, FEBRUARY 26, 1945

Mom insisted on driving me to school. "After that phone call, we can't take any chances," She reasoned. While I waited for her to get dressed, I went out front for the morning paper. I bent down to the sidewalk and my heart almost stopped.

The newspaper lay next to a freshly painted black swastika. If Mom saw it, she'd probably lock me up in my room for a year. I had to get rid of it, but how? A desperate idea came to me.

I ran to the garage and scoured the shelves. Behind the Simoniz I found a narrow green can of turpentine. I snatched it along with the stiff-bristled brush Dad used to clean his white walls, and raced to the front yard.

After minutes of furious rubbing, a whole can of turpentine and most of the bristles on Dad's brush, the swastika dissolved into a greyish blotch. Just as I got the stuff back in the garage, Mom tromped down the back stairs.

I reached the classroom door just as the final bell rattled to silence. Miss Morris stood talking with Mr. Chester. He seemed steaming mad. When he spied me, he waved me over.

"Okay, big shot. Explain this!" He thrust a clipping of my story in front of my face.

"Explain what?" I said innocently.

"Don't play dumb with me. You know what this is!" Chester barked.

"Yes, sir. But I don't understand what I'm supposed to explain."

"Going over my head is what. You knew I killed that story."

"Yes, but that was for the school paper. Nobody said it couldn't run somewhere else."

Miss Morris nodded in agreement.

"Stay out of this, Morris!" Chester's face splotched red.

In spite of my heart hammering, I did my best to sound calm. "Look, sir. A reporter at the *Dakotan* saw what I wrote and thought it was worth printing."

"Bet I can guess who *that* was," Chester glowered at Miss Morris.

"Anyway, I didn't try to go over your head. As I understand it, you don't have any say over what happens outside of school. At least, that's what you told my mom when Bo and Lester ambushed me on my way home."

Chester shivered like a dog with distemper. "Nobody, *nobody*," he waggled his finger at me, "goes behind my back and gets away with it. You'll regret this!" He spun on his heels and stomped off.

Miss Morris sighed and escorted me into the classroom.

After the Pledge of Allegiance, Pete jumped up. "Hey! How many of you saw Cookie's story in the paper yesterday?"

"Nazi propaganda!" Lester shouted.

Alice dismissed him with a wave. "It was wonderful."

I almost fell over in shock. Billy circled his thumb and finger and whistled his approval. Cleo flashed me a toothy grin. "I haven't read it yet, but I'll bet it's good."

"What's wrong with you guys?" Lester's tiny eyes blazed. "That punk's been nothing but trouble since he came. Pukin' on folks. Wearin' short pants like Krauts do."

Miss Morris slapped her desk with a ruler. "Quiet down, Lester."

Lester slammed his desk with his hand. "Why should I?"

Miss Morris lowered her voice. "Look. I realize some of you may not agree with Donald about making friends with a German prisoner." She turned to me. "But he has the right to write what he believes in. What's the first amendment to our Constitution?"

"Freedom of speech," Alice blared without raising her hand.

As soon as Pete and I walked outside for recess, I heard someone run up behind me at full tilt. Before I could turn around, two hands slammed into my back and sent me reeling.

It was touch and go for quite a ways, but I eventually got my balance. I spun around to see who pushed me. Lester. As he strode toward me, his face contorted and his fists balled.

"Filthy Kraut."

Out of the corner of my eye I saw Pete back away.

Lester was four inches taller and a good 25 pounds heavier than me. He stuck out a finger and poked me hard in the chest. "Nazi scum." He poked me again, harder.

I turned to walk away.

"Look out!" a voice cried.

I looked back just as Lester let go with his right fist. It landed in my stomach and knocked the wind out of me.

Lester gripped me in a bear hug and slung me to the frozen pavement.

After scrambling on top of me, he quickly pinned my shoulders. One fist slammed the side of my head, and the other followed with an uppercut that jammed my lower teeth into my top lip. My head throbbed with searing white pain. Warm, salty blood spurted into my mouth.

I bucked and twisted but couldn't get free. Lester's eyes were burning slits. He reared back with both fists to pound my face.

Suddenly he let out a scream. His face vanished, and his body rocketed off me.

Turning on my side, I saw Billy straddle Lester. "How 'bout fightin' someone your own size?" Billy growled. Grasping the bully by the hair, Billy bounced Lester's head on the asphalt.

Lester screamed in pain. "He's a Nazi lover!"

"And you're a jerk," Billy spat.

Several kids had gathered to watch the fight. They cheered.

Billy lifted Lester's head higher.

Lester started sobbing. "Please, you're gonna crack my skull!"

Billy dropped his face inches from Lester's. "Listen, Dumbo. This is just a sample of what you'll get if you ever hassle Cookie again. Got it?"

"Yeah, sure. Jest let me go!"

Billy gave Lester's hair a final yank and rose to his feet.

Lester scooted backwards like a crab. I got to my feet and crossed to Billy. "Sorry you got involved, but thanks."

Billy waved me off. "You did me a favor. I've been lookin' for an excuse to put that crumb in his place forever."

Pete appeared out of nowhere and struck a Joe Lewis pose. "Dang. You got to him just before I could."

A throng of adoring kids crowded around Billy, edging me to the side. Looking at my reflection in a puddle of water, the only visible damage I could see was a cut on my chin. The pain inside me was a different story.

I turned around and noticed Lester sitting alone on the playground, cursing, moaning and rubbing the back of his head. His shirtsleeves had been torn and fell to his elbows.

Splotches of paint dappled his arms. Black paint.

I tried my best to hide my jaw, but Mom saw the cut right away. After lamenting that the story would probably get me killed, she scrubbed my face with Lifebuoy and doused my chin with iodine.

I snacked on some canned apricots, went to my room and stared out the window. While I regretted the trouble I'd caused Mom and Dad, I knew that I'd done the right thing about having the story published.

Lightning winked across the heavy pewter sky like blue flashbulbs. A torrent of rain crashed onto the rooftop. The air felt charged, like tiny soda pop bubbles floating up my nose. I stood there, mesmerized by the symphony of thunder and rain and the flash of lightning.

Dad's voice jolted me out of my reverie. "Donnyboy."

I spun around. Dad stood inside the doorway in his drenched raincoat. Mom appeared next to him looking distraught. He reached into his coat pocket and pulled out a box of .22 shells. "Know anything about these?"

My legs turned to rubber. I leaned against the window for support.

"What's this all about?" Dad groaned.

It took a lot of fits and starts, but I finally gave them the whole story—from David telling me what he saw, to finding the rat poison, to confronting Bo. "But I didn't hurt a soul! Honest," I insisted. "And the Foleys must not be too mad. They haven't called the police or anything."

Mom's face turned white. "This could ruin your whole life."

"You're sure no one got hurt?" Dad prodded.

"Positive. I just loaded one bullet. The rifle went off by mistake, but it hit the floor in front of Bo."

Mom sighed. "But you could still be arrested."

"Believe me, I've thought about that," I admitted.

Dad started pacing. "If the Foleys were going to report DB, they'd have done so by now."

"We can't take any chances!" Mom cried. "Donnyboy, you've got to apologize! Now!"

"But it's storming," I reasoned. "Besides, there's no telling what they'll do if I show up again."

"You'll have to take that chance. Dad will go with you. I baked oatmeal cookies this morning. Take them to the Foleys."

I started to protest but Dad cut me off. "I'll take you. But you're doing all the talking, understood?"

I gulped. "Yes."

Dad parked on the edge of the stockyards. Rain and hail pelted us as we sloughed through a thicket leading to the Foley's shack. With every step we took, our galoshes sank ankle-deep in the mud. We halted at a rise on the perimeter of the Foley's property.

Mr. Foley stood in the pig wallow pouring fruit peels, eggshells and slimy garbage into a trough. In his ragged grey stocking cap and torn grey poncho, he seemed indifferent to the rain. I started to call to him, but the words stuck in my throat. Dad nudged me in the back.

"Mr. Foley." I called out.

He swung around. "Whatcha want?"

"Came to apologize." I hollered over the storm.

The two sows rushed for the trough and almost knocked Mr. Foley over. He cursed and kicked them. "Don't want no apology. Jes git." The slow-witted girl I saw when I came after Bo slipped out of the shack and stood next to her father.

I held up a red tin. "Mom made cookies for you. Oatmeal and raisin. Can I bring them over?"

Mr. Foley started for the shack. "Keep yer damned cookies."

"Cookies? Cookies?" The girl repeated excitedly.

Mr. Foley drew back his hand. "Shut up, Sara." The girl backed away from him, her face withered with disappointment.

My teeth chattered violently. My mackinaw and Pendleton shirt were soaked through from the icy rain. I looked at Dad helplessly.

"Look, Mr. Foley," Dad called out. "You've every right to be angry with my son. He knows what he did was wrong. He came here to make amends."

"None expected, none needed," Mr. Foley called back.

"Could I please see Bo?" I hollered. "I'd like to apologize face to face."

"Bo ain't here."

"Will he be back soon?"

"Nope."

"I could come back tomorrow."

Mr. Foley spit. "Won't be back tomorrow."

"When then?" I persisted.

Mrs. Foley opened the shack door. She looked even sadder than the last time I'd seen her. "Bo run off the day you come by," she said in a fragile voice.

I cringed. "Because of me?"

"Hell, no!" Mr. Foley snorted. "'Cause I made him git. Never did a lick a work. Nothin' but a troublemaker."

"Where did he go?"

"Who cares?" Mr. Foley flapped his hand at me. "Now off with ya." He pushed past Mrs. Foley and entered the shack.

The little girl stared longingly at the tin in my hand. I looked to Dad for what to do. He motioned for me to leave the tin on a tree stump.

"Let's go, DB."

When we reached the beginning of the thicket, I glanced over my shoulder.

The tin was gone.

CHAPTER 22

TUESDAY, FEBRUARY 27, 1945

It didn't take long for Chester to get even. Less than 24 hours after chewing me out about my story, he took his revenge during gym class. No sooner had I joined the rest of the boys in a semicircle around the principal-coach than Chester reached out and grabbed two thick ropes that hung from the gym ceiling. "Okay, Rogers and Cook!" he yelled hoarsely. "Shimmy on up to the top. And I wanna hear a loud slap on the ceiling when you get there." He bit down on his whistle and blew shrilly.

Billy leaped onto one of the ropes. I froze. Chester knew heights scared me because I had only gotten up a few feet the last time we had rope climbing. He frowned and stepped toward me. "No excuses, Cook."

I forced myself off the floor and shuffled to the rope. It reminded me of a noose. By the time I'd grabbed a hold of it, Billy had already climbed a third of the way to the top of his.

I clutched the thick rope in both hands and pinched it between my legs. The sisal was black from years of sweat and dirt. It was knotted every foot and a half for hand and footholds. I reached for the first knot and pulled myself up.

With each knot I passed, my anxiety grew. Stinging sweat drowned my eyes. My hands got so slippery I could barely hold on. Ten feet off the ground, I stopped and clung to the rope sheer terror. I couldn't go any higher.

A loud *SLAP* resounded throughout the gym. Billy looked down from the ceiling. He bellowed a Tarzan call, gave his chest a thump and spiraled down like a spinning top. In no time he swirled right past me.

Humiliated, I slid to the floor. I stared at my feet in shame.

Chester strode over. "What's wrong, Cook? Rope too icky for you?" His sarcasm cut me to the quick.

I didn't look up.

He crouched beside me. "Well, Mister Hot Shot Writer! Is there anything *physical* you can do? This *is* a gym class, you know."

Lester led several boys in scoffing.

My eyes blazed with fury. "Yes. I can run."

Chester raised his hands high. "Well, Hallelujah! Let's have a race!"

The principal-coach lined us up across one end of the gym. "Now, when I blow my whistle, everyone take off like your butts are burning. Slap the far wall and run back here. That's one lap. Do five." He fumbled for his whistle, stuck it in his mouth, and blew.

The gym floor thundered from the beat of our feet. Billy shot out ahead of the pack. I got bogged down in the crowd and ended up about 15 feet behind everyone else.

Hands slammed against the wall. Shoes squealed at the sharp turns.

One lap. Two. Three.

After four laps, Pete, Darrel and about half of the other boys started losing steam. Lester clutched his side, moaned and dropped out.

My lungs begged for air and my legs burned, but I wouldn't let myself give up. Lester dropping out gave me even more incentive.

Billy and I hit the wall at almost the same instant. We whirled around for the final lap. Billy looked shocked to see me so close.

Halfway to the other wall, Billy slipped on a pool of sweat. He started to fall. I thrust out my hand and caught his elbow. We swayed back and forth like two drunks. By some miracle, we regained our balance.

Billy wrenched his arm free. We surged forward, neck and neck.

The wall rushed toward us. I stretched out my arms.

WHACK!

My palms slammed into the wall. An electric shock shot through my arms and up my spine. My arms jackknifed back. My forehead banged against the wall. I saw a blinding white flash and crumbled to the gym floor.

When I came to, Billy, Pete and Chester were standing over me. "The winner and new champion!" Pete announced, hiking my limp arm in the air. Chester looked churlish but worried. "You all right, Cook?"

My head throbbed, but it was nothing compared to the joy I felt at winning the race. "Think so."

I carefully rose to my hands and knees. After pausing a moment, I stood up. I circled my head one way and then the other. I shook my hands and legs. "I'm okay," I said gruffly, and headed for the showers.

Lester slipped out of the locker room without taking a shower. Pete made a big deal out of telling the other guys we were best friends. Billy avoided looking at me. I figured he was sore about losing.

Just as I was starting to leave, Billy called out to me.

"Hold up." He walked over slowly and zeroed his eyes in on mine. "Helluva race, Cookie." A warm smile spread across his face. He draped his arm over my shoulder and shepherded me out the door.

CHAPTER 23

The class paper came out today. As expected, Cleo's "Perfect Eighth Grader" story was a hit with everyone she named. Everyone she didn't mention hated it. Several kids ribbed me about my "Perfect Legs."

Alice's story about the Spring play caught my eye. Miss Morris had written it. She called the play *Becky Thatcher*, and it was based on Mark Twain's *Tom Sawyer*. I had always kind of hankered to be in a play, but never had the nerve to try out.

On the way in from afternoon recess, Alice motioned that she needed to see me. "Go ahead, fellas," I said to Pete and Billy. I reached down and pulled off a loafer. "Got a rock in my shoe."

My friends disappeared through the door. Alice slid up next to me.

"Hi, Donny—I mean, Donald."

"Oh, Donny's just fine."

She crinkled her nose. "Well. It does suit you better."

Her sweetness made me uneasy. "You wanted to see me?"

Alice's eyes darted from left to right. "Yes," she said, reaching into her jacket pocket. Cleo stepped between us, seemingly out of nowhere. She slipped her arm under mine and tugged me toward the door. "C'mon, Cookie, can't be late."

I dragged my heels but Cleo herded me away. Alice hissed and jerked her hand out of her pocket. It held what looked like a small envelope.

All afternoon, it seemed like Alice was going out of her way to ignore me. Apparently she'd decided against giving me whatever it was she had in her jacket pocket. In the cloakroom after school, I stalled putting on my pea coat hoping she'd try again. She didn't. I turned to leave.

A hand shot in and out of my coat pocket. I wheeled around, expecting to find Lester. To my surprise, Alice whizzed past me. Before I could follow, Pete stepped in front of me grinning from ear to ear. He'd been beaming nonstop ever since Cleo's story had awarded him the "Perfect Boy's Smile."

I tried to maneuver around him. He stretched out his arms and blocked me. "Come with me. It's important."

"Later," I muttered, pushing past him.

"No, now!" Pete grabbed the neck of my jacket, almost strangling me.

By now Alice was long gone. I scowled at Pete. "What's so doggone important?"

"You'll see," Pete winked. "Let's go."

We fast-walked to Center and Walnut Street, the heart of downtown. On the way, I slipped my hand into my coat pocket. Feeling Alice's envelope, my curiosity ran wild. "I've really got to get home," I told Pete.

"We're almost there," Pete assured me.

We passed the Garney Bank, Garney Mercantile and the Garney Hotel.

They might as well have named the town "Garneyville." All the buildings were made of red stone, just like our school. The doorways had grey stone arches. The hotel stood out because it had a fancy green and white striped awning, and a doorman in a green uniform with gold braid.

Pete stopped outside of Lambert's Music Store. He pointed to the front window. Inside was a huge poster with Dad's picture and the words: *"Here Now! Al Cook's Columbia Hit, 'Crossbow!'"*

Pete opened the front door. A bell on top tinkled. We entered. The store smelled musky. A squat, unsmiling man leaned on a glass counter sorting records.

"Hey, Mr. Lambert. Guess who this is?" Pete said proudly.

Mr. Lambert glanced up, then went back to his sorting.

"Al Cook's kid!" Pete declared.

Mr. Lambert shrugged and slipped a record into a rack of 78s that lined the wall behind him. "You kids wanna buy something?"

Pete sauntered up to the counter. "So, how's Al's record doing? Making you lots of moola, I'll bet."

"Not bad," Mr. Lambert allowed as he reached into the showcase and pulled out an ornately packaged clarinet. "Him being on the Whiteman show didn't hurt."

Pete put his hand on my shoulder. "Pretty impressive, huh? The son of a star right here in your store."

"Be more impressed if he bought something," the owner grumbled.

I was about to jump out of my skin from wondering what Alice had written. "Pete, I've got to get home." I hurried for the door. "Nice meeting you, Mr. Lambert. Thanks for selling Dad's record."

Pete ran after me. "Wait! You gotta see where my pop cooks. Only take a sec." He nodded next door to a café with a hanging sign:

E
A
T
S

Through the front window, the café looked clean and kempt. Pink counters, white stools, pink walls. A plump henna-haired waitress in a pink and white uniform and a white cap sat on a stool, smoking and thumbing through a copy of *Photoplay*.

Pete rapped on the window. The waitress spun around. Her smile revealed a wide gap between her two front teeth. She called over her shoulder.

A slender dark-skinned man with wavy black hair and a pleasant grin strode from the kitchen. He wore a bright white uniform and exuded confidence. When he spied Pete, he mimed lifting a fork to his mouth and waved for Pete and me to come inside.

Pete grabbed my shoulder. "Come get a free slice of pie! Coconut cream, banana cream, chocolate. Yum!"

The sweets tempted me, but I had to read Alice's note. I backed away. "Maybe some other time." I spun around and ran. Pete called after me, but I pretended I didn't hear him.

A block away from home I slowed down. I reached into my pocket with a shaking hand and took out Alice's note. My name was printed neatly on the front. *"Alice Elizabeth Cody"* and a Scottie were embossed on the back flap.

I pried open the envelope and pulled out a heavy cream-colored card.

DONALD COOK
IS CORDIALLY INVITED TO LUNCH
SATURDAY, MARCH 3, 1945
12:00 PM
CODY RESIDENCE
340 HILL STREET
RSVP CENTRAL 4340
FESTIVE ATTIRE

My heart started thumping. I reread the invitation. Then I read it again. Looking up, I saw a bird soaring high in a sparkling blue sky. I knew just how it felt.

A bunch of letters and magazines stuck out of our mailbox. Mom must have been out, because she always got the mail the instant it arrived. I thumbed through it as I walked around back.

There were the latest issues of *LIFE* and *Coronet*; a letter to Mom from her father, Grandpa Jim; a large, thick envelope for Dad from Columbia Records; a bunch of flyers and, to my dread, four letters addressed to me.

I dropped Mom and Dad's mail on the kitchen table and took the letters to my room. I kicked off my shoes and sagged onto the bed. My hands shook as I opened the first envelope.

The sender—someone with lousy handwriting and even worse spelling—called me every dirty name in the book. The letter was signed with a skull and crossbones.

The next letter came from a lady in Watertown. She said her son didn't get the food or medical care he needed in a German prison camp, and died there. She couldn't understand why we coddled German prisoners here. Or worse, how I could make friends with one.

Her letter got to me. I began to wonder if I'd made a mistake with my story.

The next letter came from a Captain Loeffler. His stationery had an American Eagle and "*The American Legion*" printed at the top. Captain Loeffler said he lost a leg fighting in World War I and was proud to be a soldier. Then he wrote:

Day after day, tens of thousands of men, women and children are killed in this war. To say nothing of the limbs lost, eyes blinded and minds muddled. I have concluded that this is not only abhorrent—it's unnecessary. If countries would take half the money and energy they spend making war and invested it into making peace,

this carnage would end. Congratulations on your courageous arti-
cle. Yes, there are good and bad people everywhere. Hopefully your
article will stir people to make sure the good guys are in control.

I exhaled, buoyed by the Captain's letter.

The return address on the final letter said: "Heartbroken, Farmington, S.D." I opened it hesitantly. Inside were clippings of pictures from *LOOK* magazine. They showed American soldiers just freed from a German prison camp near Munich by the US Forty-Second Rainbow Division.

The Americans smiled, but their smiles held unspeakable sorrow. Their uniforms were little more than rags. Their gaunt eyes bulged out of sunken cheeks. Two smiling young GIs who had liberated the prisoners posed with them. The contrast made me want to cry.

I felt numb from shock. Maybe all Germans were evil. Maybe I made Eric a nice guy because I needed a friend. I felt confused and depressed. Even my excitement over Alice's invitation eked away.

I hardly spoke at dinner, claiming a headache as my excuse. After forcing down my lime Jello and pear desert, I left the table and headed for my room. The telephone rang. I froze in midstep. My insides twisted.

Mom answered. She listened for several seconds then looked at me. "Certainly. He's right here. Please hold on." She held the phone against her chest and whispered, "Senator Garney. For you." She looked awed.

I picked up the phone hesitantly. "Hello?"

"Garney here. I got back into town last night and saw that piece of yours in the paper."

I waited for the axe to fall.

"I think it's terrific."

"You do?" I sputtered. Mom got closer to the receiver, trying to listen in.

"Have you heard about the United Nations confab coming up in San Francisco?"

"No."

"Free nations are all getting together. Want to set up an organization that'll assure peace once the War's over. Your story could set a perfect tone for the meeting. I want to read part of it on my next radio show from the Senate floor, okay?"

An alarm went off inside me. Before today's mail I'd have been thrilled to have him do it. But I couldn't get the pictures of those tortured American prisoners out of my mind.

Mom elbowed me. "Answer him!"

"Donald?" The Senator spoke up. "Did I lose you?"

"Uh, no, sir. I'm very flattered. It's just that I'm having second thoughts about what I wrote."

"What kind of second thoughts?" he asked irritably. "Do you know what an honor this would be?

Mom glared at me.

"I'm very grateful. Honest. But since my story ran a lot of people have pointed out hateful things the Germans have done, especially to American prisoners. I'm all confused. My story might have been a big mistake. If so, I wouldn't want it to become an even bigger one."

"I think you're going off the deep end, son," The Senator sighed. "Sure, the Nazis have done horrid things. But, like you said in your piece, there are good and bad people everywhere. Our only chance for peace is to make sure the good guys come out on top. For the long haul."

My mind felt like it was on a Tilt-A-Whirl. "Senator, I don't know what to think right now. Before I give you an answer, could I see Eric again? Maybe it'll clear things up for me."

"Seems like a waste of time," Garney said with exasperation, "but all right. Be at the camp at noon tomorrow. See Sergeant Atkins."

"What about school?"

"School can wait," he snapped.

"Yes, sir. I'll be there."

He hung up.

"What's wrong with you?" Mom snapped. "You could be passing up the chance of a lifetime!"

I went to my room, gathered up all the letters and pictures I'd received, and showed them to Mom. She stiffened.

"I'm sorry, Mom, but I'm all mixed up. Maybe if I see Eric again I'll know what do."

Mom shook her head and set the pictures face down on the telephone table.

CHAPTER 24

THURSDAY, MARCH 1, 1945

"Sergeant Atkins, please," I said to the GI on the other side of the gate. He had a paunch and none of the spit and polish of an MP. The name on his fatigues read *DINGLE*.

"What fer?" He talked through clenched teeth and had a bulge of chewing tobacco in his right cheek.

"Just tell him Donald Cook's here," I replied politely.

Dingle turned his head and spit a long, brown stream onto the ground. He ambled into the guardhouse, picked up a walkie-talkie and cupped his hand over the mouthpiece. After a brief, static-filled conversation, Dingle returned. "Sarge is on his way."

"Thanks a lot, sir."

He turned his head and shot another stream of tobacco juice out of his mouth. "I ain't no 'sir.'" He sniffed and resumed standing outside the guardhouse.

Sergeant Atkins's Jeep skidded to a halt behind the gate.

Dingle straightened up and clamped his mouth shut. The bulge disappeared from his cheek.

"Well, look who's here," Atkins said icily.

"Hello Sergeant," I replied, surprised by his harsh tone.

He grabbed the top bar on his Jeep and swung to the ground. "What brings you back? Lookin' to stir up more trouble for Eric?"

His words sent a chill through me. "What do you mean?"

Atkins scowled. "That story of yours got around the camp. Some of the Krauts decided Eric was a traitor. Couple of nights ago, a bunch of 'em ambushed him after chow. If a guard hadn't heard the ruckus, well...it wouldn't have been pretty."

"How bad is he?" I braced myself for the worst.

Atkins shrugged. "He'll live. But he took a beating."

"What about the guys who did it?" I asked. "Did you get them?"

"Ran off in all different directions. Pitch dark. Barracks MP couldn't tell who they were."

"Had to have been those SS goons," I reasoned.

"Probably. But we got no proof. And Eric ain't talkin'."

The Sergeant's news made me even more depressed and confused. "That damn story," I muttered ruefully. "It's been nothing but trouble."

Atkins's eyes settled on my chin. He put his finger under it and traced my gash. "So I see."

I pushed his hand away. "Look. A lot has happened to make me all mixed up about things. I've got to see Eric."

Atkins nodded toward the Jeep. "Get your butt in."

To my surprise, we drove past the Quonset hut, the POWs' barracks and the POWs' dining hall. When we reached the end of the camp, the

Sergeant drove onto a flat field.

"Where we going?"

Atkins didn't answer. He made a sharp right toward the river. The field dropped into a steep slope. At the bottom was a one-room building. I recalled seeing a picture of it in our State History book. It was a replica of the first South Dakota State House.

"What are we doing here?" I asked.

"Said you wanted to see Eric, didn't you?"

I nodded. "But what's he doing here?"

Atkins eased out of the Jeep. "Precaution."

A young MP Corporal sat in a white folding chair next to the front door. He leaned back on the rear legs of the chair, one hand on the barrel of his M1 rifle. When he saw us get out of the Jeep, he slammed the chair down and jumped to attention.

"At ease, Taylor," Sergeant Atkins waved. "This here's Cook, the kid who wrote that story about Stiendler"

Taylor gave me a harsh look that I took to mean *what's he doing here?* Atkins herded me to the front door and gave me a harder-than-necessary shove inside.

Sunlight streamed through a window and formed a square spotlight on a round oak table. Dust swirled inside of the bright light. Eric sat in a spindle chair with several open books in front of him.

He looked up at me and distantly muttered, *"Guten morgen."*

I gasped. A thick bandage circled his head. His eyes were swollen with ugly purple bruises.

The MPs headed for the Franklin stove. A blue and white speckled percolator spread the scent of coffee throughout the room.

I gripped a chair back to keep from reeling. An oil painting hanging on the wall of our ruddy, bewigged founding fathers made Eric's battered face seem even more devastating to me.

Atkins poured two cups of coffee: one for Eric, the other for me. The nutty smell was enticing. Mom said I was too young to drink coffee, but right now I needed something pleasant. I took a sip. To my dismay, it burned my tongue and tasted bitter. Still, I managed to force it down.

A voice sputtered from Atkins's walkie-talkie. He went outside to answer it. A moment later, he returned and barked for Taylor to join him. "We've gotta run over to HQ," Atkins said gravely. He thrust a finger at Eric and me. "You stay put with the door locked. Don't let Jesus himself in, hear?" They slammed the door. I heard the lock click.

The only sounds in the room were quiet breathing and my fingers tapping on the chair nervously. I took a sip of coffee, hoping it would calm me down. It just scalded my throat.

Eric knit his hands behind his head.

Finally, I spoke. "I had no idea my story would cause you such grief. I'm sorry." I rested my butt on the edge of the chair seat.

Eric lit a cigarette.

I swallowed to moisten my throat. "Right after my story ran in the paper, we started getting phone calls. Then letters. A lot were nasty. But a few were nice."

Eric's eyes retreated, like they did the first time I saw him.

I reached into my shirt pocket and took out the clippings. "These came in the mail yesterday." I set them on the table. "I've heard a lot lately about how cruel the Germans have been to Jews and people they've conquered. But it all seemed so far away. Then I saw these pictures and read how awful the Germans were to our men.

"I started getting all mixed up. Now I'm worried. Worried that I only saw you the way I wanted to see you because..." My voice trailed off. Eric remained silent.

"Because I wanted a friend." My hands trembled as I held the coffee cup to my cheek, hoping the heat would soothe me.

Eric picked up the clippings. He studied each page without expression. Then he set them down and pushed himself away from the table. He rose, walked to the stove and held up the percolator. "More?"

I shook my head.

"*Ja*, Donald," Eric said icily as he refilled his coffee cup. "Many Germans, they are cruel." He adjusted the bandage on his head with his free hand. "But all Germans, are they like that?"

He sat and turned the book he had been reading toward me. It was open to a painting of white Americans in buckskins riding into an Indian village. With rifles blazing and knives drawn, the whites were brutally slaughtering the unarmed Indians—men, women and children.

I averted my eyes.

Eric reached for another book. He thumbed through several pages and slid it over to my side of the table. A reproduction of a postcard from the 1920s showed two Negroes—a boy and a girl–hanging from a tree. A circle of grinning white people surrounded the tree, applauding the grim spectacle. Printed across the top of the postcard was the greeting: *Sweet Alabama Fruit.*

I felt the same revulsion I had when I saw the clippings of the tortured Americans.

Eric closed the book. "Are all Americans like this, Donald?" Silence drifted over the room.

He reached into his pocket and pulled out a crinkled photo and a yellow telegram. "I have picture, too." He passed them to me. The photo was of a proud, round-faced woman with wire-rimmed glasses and a pretty blonde girl who looked to be around my age.

The telegram read:

GEMEINER ERIC STIENDLER
FARMINGTON, S.D. POW CAMP, USA
PER INQUIRY, NO INFORMATION AVAILABLE ON
SYLVIA STIENDLER AND INGA STIENDLER AFTER RECENT
BOMBING. STOP. AMERICAN RED CROSS.

Any doubts I had about Eric or my story dissolved in my grief. I crossed to Eric and took a deep breath. "Eric, I need to ask you something."

I dialed the Senator's number with my heart in my throat. After two short rings, his secretary picked up. "Marge, this is Donald Cook."

"Yes, Donald."

"The Senator asked me about reading my story in the Senate."

"Yes. Have you made up your mind?"

"Well, I talked it over with Eric, the German soldier I wrote about."

"And?"

"Please tell Senator Garney I'd be honored if he read the story. A couple of things have happened since I wrote it. I'll send an update in a day or so." I took a breath. "Oh, and I have one condition."

"What?" Marge sounded surprised.

I screwed up all my courage. "I'd like Eric to hear the broadcast at my house."

Marge paused. "I'll tell the Senator."

My hand was sopping with sweat as I put down the receiver.

CHAPTER 25

SATURDAY, MARCH 3, 1945

Mom made sure I was dressed in plenty of time for her to pick up flowers and arrive at the Codys at the stroke of twelve. Dad kidded I should make sure that Mr. Cody didn't poison my food. Mom hushed him and said it was quite a compliment for me to be invited.

The day before the luncheon, I tried on my old sport coat. It wouldn't button across my chest, and the sleeves were way too short. Mom rushed me to Penney's and got me a navy blue blazer. She also bought me a white dress shirt and grey trousers. She stayed up late making alterations, so in the morning everything fit perfectly. Dad lent me his blue polka dot tie and tied it for me. Mom slicked down my hair in an attempt to tame my cowlick.

After I was dresed, Mom remarked how grown-up I looked. She sounded sad. Dad tried to make her feel better by saying I got my good looks from her. When I looked in the mirror, I hardly recognized myself. It felt good.

After stopping at the flower shop for a bouquet of white tulips, we arrived at the hill where the Codys lived.

Mom slowed as we approached their house, a sprawling green two-story affair with gables and four chimneys. It had an immense front yard with a box hedge that bordered the sidewalk. I didn't see any doors at the front of the house. Mom noticed they were halfway up the drive, under an overhang supported by white columns. We were still five minutes early, so she drove around some side streets to kill time. At twelve on the nose she pulled into the Cody driveway.

I expected to see cars dropping off other kids, but there were none. Mom stopped under the portico. Three wide cement steps led to a massive set of twin doors made of carved oak and glass. I readied the tulips and got out of the car. My stomach churned as I twisted a winged bronze doorbell. Its chime echoed deep inside the house.

I shifted nervously from foot to foot, almost hoping no one was home. Mom motioned for me to cinch up my tie.

A latch released and one of the doors swung open. A tall reddish-blonde woman with rouged cheeks, bright red lips, brown penciled eyebrows, and a mischievous smile stood in the doorway. She looked over every inch of me, from my slicked-down hair to my oxblood loafers. Mom had made me shine them three times before they passed her inspection.

"Well, don't you look snappy, Donald?" She nodded approvingly and propped her left hand on her hip. She was wearing a silky white blouse with puffy sleeves, yellow slacks and purple velvet slippers with tiny gold tassels. "You're even cuter than Alice said you were."

I blushed.

"I'm Marion Grey Cody," she announced, thrusting out a hand.

"Donald Cook." I shifted the tulips to my left hand and stuck out my right.

"For me, or for Alice?" Mrs. Cody asked slyly.

"Oh, you." I replied quickly and nodded back at Mom. "Mom got them for you."

Mrs. Cody took the bouquet and lifted it to her nose. She closed her eyes and inhaled deeply. "*Lovely.*"

I didn't think tulips smelled.

Mrs. Cody strode over to the Buick. She leaned in the passenger side window. "Oh, how pretty you are, Mrs. Cook! Thank you for bringing Donald by. Alice has been so looking forward to this."

"Oh, it was my pleasure!" Mom replied. Her voice sounded unusually meek.

"Would you care to come in?"

"Oh, no thank you. I, uh, have an appointment."

"Well, maybe another time then? Soon, I hope."

Mom smiled. "What time should I pick up Donnyboy—uh, Donald, this afternoon?"

"*Donnyboy!*" Mrs. Cody exclaimed like she'd just opened a marvelous present. "Is that what you call him?"

"Well, just in the family," I explained with a wince.

Mrs. Cody pinched a dimple on my cheek. "It's perfect." She looked me in the eye. "Do you mind if I call you that?"

I felt trapped. What would Alice think?

"I'm sure he wouldn't mind," Mom answered for me. "He likes it much better than 'Donald.'"

"Excellent!" She turned back to Mom. "Now you needn't worry about picking up Donnyboy. I'll have Douglas drop him off. He's at the station as usual, but he'll be back soon."

"Sure it's not an inconvenience?" Mom looked worried.

"Not at all." Mrs. Cody stepped away from the car. She turned to me and tilted her head. "We better get you inside. Alice is probably having a conniption waiting for us."

"Bye, Mrs. Cody," Mom said as she backed out of the driveway.

Mrs. Cody waved her hand. "Marion Grey, please!"

"And I'm Jane," Mom called.

Mrs. Cody put her arm around my shoulder and led me into the house. The dark wood floors in the entryway shone even brighter than my shoes. I heard tiny feet pattering across the floor. A Scottie dog with a lustrous black coat rushed over to me, jumped up and began pawing at my pant leg. Standing on her hind legs like that, I could see that "it" was a "she." She looked like President Roosevelt's dog, Fala, only much fatter.

"Guess she likes to eat," I commented.

"Coco's pregnant," Mrs. Cody replied.

"Down, Coco!" I heard Alice say firmly. The dog immediately obeyed.

I looked up. Alice strode down a curved staircase, fingers skipping along the carved white banister. "Hi, Donny," she grinned. It was like her teeth shot white sparks as she spoke.

I had to fight for breath. I'd never seen anyone so beautiful. Her blond hair was in Shirley Temple ringlets. Her pink taffeta dress had a wide white ribbon as a belt. She wore white stockings and pink shoes.

I got myself under control enough to speak. "Hi, Alice. You look, uh, very nice."

She smiled graciously. "You, too. I love your jacket and tie."

"Well, kids," interrupted Mrs. Cody. "I think lunch is ready." She nudged me toward the dining room.

I wondered where the other guests were.

We entered a large dining room with an oval table covered by a heavy cream tablecloth. Red and yellow flowers were woven into it. Drapes of the same fabric hung beside floor-to-ceiling glass doors.

A large pewter plate, cloth napkins in silver rings, elegant silverware, and heavy crystal glasses marked each table setting. There were only three: one at the head of the table and two across from each other nearby. I realized with some uneasiness that I was the only guest.

Mrs. Cody stood at the head. I went to pull out her chair like Mom told me to do, but she waved me away. "Give Alice a hand," she insisted.

I hurried around the table and pulled out Alice's chair.

A rail-thin, unsmiling lady entered the dining room carrying a large soup bowl shaped like a duck. Mrs. Cody introduced her as Agna. She greeted me in an accent I'd heard a lot around Farmington. Most of the immigrants in town came from Bohemia, a country near Germany. In fact, WXAX had a popular Bohemian band led by a guy named Lawrence Welk.

Agna wore a black uniform with a collar that looked like two white wings. Her dress had so much starch that it crackled when she bent over to serve the soup.

I took a spoonful. It was cold. Mrs. Cody caught my surprise. "It's vichy-ssoise," she chuckled. "Fancy name for cold potato soup. Give it a try. It's pretty good."

I tasted it. While it didn't exactly knock me out, I finished it out of politeness. Coco lay at my feet under the table. I considered sneaking it to her but didn't dare.

Agna cleared our bowls and set what looked like a wide wine glass on the pewter plate. A third of the glass held a thick red sauce about a third of the way up. A tight circle of peeled shrimp ringed the lip of the glass. I watched Mrs. Cody and Alice dip each shrimp in the sauce, and followed suit. It was delicious.

Mrs. Cody looked at me admiringly. "That was a courageous story you wrote, Donnyboy,"

I glanced at Alice for her reaction. She either didn't hear her mom call me "Donnyboy," or it went right over her head. She smiled silently, just as she had through the soup course.

I nodded in appreciation. "Nice of you to say, Mrs. Cody. But it's caused some problems."

Alice looked up with concern. "What kind?"

"We've gotten a bunch of nasty phone calls and letters. Lots of folks can't fathom how I could make friends with a German after all the horrible things they've done."

Mrs. Cody twisted a cigarette into her long black holder. "And how can you?"

I took a sip of lemonade. "Good question. One letter in particular got me thinking I might have made a big mistake. So I went back to confront Eric about it."

Alice leaned forward. "And?"

"I'm convinced that Eric is as good a person as anyone I know. And the Nazis have been just as horrible to the good Germans as they have to everyone else."

"Bravo!" Mrs. Cody tapped her water glass with a fork. Her lips lifted into a foxy smile. "I understand the Senator is very interested in your story."

I nodded modestly. "I guess he wants to read parts of it during his next broadcast."

Alice looked miffed. "Really? Why didn't I know about this?"

"It just happened," I answered, trying to soothe her feelings.

The conversation stalled until we finished our shrimp. I felt pleasantly full and figured that was it for lunch. But then Agna brought in a big tuna salad, and followed that with strawberry shortcake. I couldn't imagine where Mrs. Cody found fresh strawberries in the winter, but I had a hunch she got pretty much anything she wanted.

Agna gave us each a small bowl with water in it. Mrs. Cody and Alice dipped their fingers in it and wiped them on their napkin. I did the same, trying to make it look like I did it all the time.

Mrs. Cody excused us from the table and Alice asked me to come up to her room.

"Keep your door open, Alice," Mrs. Cody kidded as Alice led me upstairs. "No hanky panky."

"Moth-er!" Alice hissed in exasperation.

Coco followed us into the frilly bedroom and jumped onto a padded green loveseat framed in white gilded wood. Alice settled next to Coco and patted the cushion beside her.

As I eased myself onto the loveseat, my mouth felt dry as chalk. Coco jumped onto my lap. I stroked her tummy. "When is she due?"

"Any time now." Alice joined me in petting Coco. "I'm so sorry about your dog."

I smiled weakly in thanks, hoping she hadn't heard about my foray to the Foleys'.

Alice's deep blue eyes caressed my face. "You know, Miss Morris is having tryouts for *Becky Thatcher* next week."

"Right. Are you trying out?"

Her eyelids dropped. "I probably won't get it, but I'd love to play Becky."

I made a clucking sound. "You're a shoo-in."

She grasped my hand. "You really think so, Donny?"

Every time she called me "Donny," I sizzled. "Positive."

Her fingers snaked up my wrist. "Assuming you're right, who plays Tom Sawyer is *really* important. We have to be a good match."

I almost keeled over. Did she mean *me*? It took a moment for my pulse to stop racing. "Do you have someone in mind?" I squeaked.

She gnawed a fingernail. "Yes. And I need your help."

I pictured myself next to her onstage. "Sure. What do you need me to do?"

"Ask Billy to try out for Tom."

Her words slapped me in the face. I slumped back into the couch.

Alice moved closer. Her eyes reminded me of Bambi's. "He's perfect! But I know he won't do it unless you ask him. You're the only boy he respects."

"I don't know about that," I grumbled.

Her warm, spearmint breath floated up my nose. "Please, Donny. For me?"

My butt squirmed on the thick cushion. "I'd like to, but..."

Alice jumped off the couch beaming. "Oh, thank you! Promise you won't take no for an answer."

I started to protest, but gave in. "I'll try. But no promises."

Alice threw her arms around me. "I knew I could depend on you." She pecked me on the cheek. "Want to play Monopoly or something?"

"No, thanks." I stood and backed toward the door. "I actually have to go."

A frown creased her beautiful brow. "But Daddy's not home yet."

My back touched the door. "That's okay. I need the exercise."

She smiled adoringly. "I'm glad we could spend this time together. It was heaven."

I reached behind me and turned the knob. "If I don't see your mom, tell her thanks. And that I enjoyed meeting her." Not waiting for an answer, I slid out the door, clambered down the staircase, scooted across the entryway and shot out the front door.

Halfway home, I loosened my tie and dabbed my eyes with it.

CHAPTER 26

MONDAY, MARCH 5, 1945

After gym, I cornered Billy in the locker room. "Hey, Billy," I began, trying to sound matter of fact. "Tryouts for *Becky Thatcher* are tomorrow after school. You going?"

He laughed sarcastically. "What are you, nuts or something?"

"You'd make a perfect Tom Sawyer."

Billy walked over to the mirror and started combing his wet hair. "Not in a thousand years."

"Think of your folks. How proud they'd be seeing you up there on the stage."

Billy narrowed his eyes at me in the mirror. "My folks ran off years ago. I live with my Granny. And she's too damn old and tired to go to some dumb play."

I felt lower than a toadstool. "I'm sorry. I didn't know."

"No sweat, Cookie. I take care of myself. Always have. Always will." He raised his eyebrows. "Why are you so hot for me to try out, anyway? Somebody put you up to it?"

I lowered my eyes. "Alice. She's set her mind to playing Becky and thinks you'd be the perfect Tom Sawyer." I looked up at Billy's handsome freckled face and devil-may-care smile. "I have to admit, she's right."

Billy's eyes softened with pity. "Gone sweet on Alice, eh?"

I lifted my hands in frustration. "Yes. No. I don't know. But you playing Tom Sawyer is like a life or death thing for her. And for some dumb reason, I promised her I'd ask you." I looked him square in the eye. "Look, would you at least try out? It'd get me off the hook. And who knows? You might like it."

Billy put his hand on my shoulder. "You poor schmo." Then his eyes sparkled with a devilish glint. "Tell you what. I've been pondering that race we had the other day. Never lost one before, so here's a proposition. Race me one lap around the high school track after school today. If you win, I'll try out for the play. If I win, you owe me a movie, popcorn and soda at Woolworth's. Deal?"

I did the math in my head, and realized I could just cover it with what I'd saved from my allowance. "Okay. But I've never run on a track before. Plus, I don't have the right shoes–you know, spikes."

"Take it or leave it," Billy said as he headed out the door.

"I'll take it," I called after him.

When I told Alice about my deal with Billy, she said she'd come cheer for me. I seized up in fear; the last thing I needed was Alice adding even more pressure on me.

"Thanks, but no thanks," I told her. "I'll call when I get home and let you know how it turned out."

"But—"

"No!"

"Okay."

The high school track team was in Vermillion, so we had the whole quarter-mile oval to ourselves. I wore my gym shorts, a sweatshirt and Converse gym shoes with flat soles. Billy confidently wore a T-shirt and dungarees. But his shoes had spikes.

We did some stretches before Billy led me over to the starting line. "I'll call it," he declared as we crouched on the cinders.

I nodded, leaning so far forward I almost tipped over.

"On your mark...get set...GO!"

Billy took off like a shot. My shoes slipped on the cinders. By the time I got any traction, Billy was leading by a good ten yards. I pounded my feet into the track to get more of a foothold.

We rounded the curve marking the halfway point. Billy stayed glued to the inside lane. I lagged about five yards behind him. His spikes kicked up sharp cinders that peppered my bare legs. I moved outside to avoid the painful splatter.

As I entered the home stretch, the muscles in my legs felt like they were on fire. My lungs gasped for air. By sheer grit, I pulled up alongside Billy.

Less than twenty yards to go.

Suddenly, Billy let out a curse and grabbed his side. He started slowing down.

I willed my legs to churn even faster.

Billy dropped behind me, groaning in pain.

I streaked across the finish line and collapsed on the frozen infield. Billy fell down beside me. Our chests heaved for at least a minute before either of us could speak.

"Well, you did it, you son of a bitch!" he huffed approvingly.

"Only because you got a side splint," I gasped.

Billy hooted. "A side splint? Nah, that was all an act. Truth is, I ran out of steam."

"What?" I fumed. "You just *let* me win?"

Billy scowled. "You know me better than that. I pooped out. Damned if I know why." He kicked at my Converse shoes. "And you in those silly shoes!" He gave me a playful shove and broke out laughing.

I shoved him back and started laughing, too. My chest swelled with a rare warmth. "You know what you just proved, you big dummy?"

Billy shook his head.

"That you'd make a great actor."

After catching our breath and saying goodbye, Billy and I headed off in opposite directions. As I passed the high school field house, I heard a yelp behind me. I turned around. Alice stepped out from behind a high juniper bush and ran toward me, grinning from ear to ear.

"You were stupendous!" she gushed.

"You weren't supposed to watch!" I stormed.

Alice's face turned contrite. "Are you really mad? Don't be. I made sure I couldn't be seen."

I frowned, wanting her to stew in my disapproval.

Alice's eyes glistened adoringly. "I don't know how to thank you, Donny. You...you're the best friend I ever had."

"Thanks," I replied dryly, and turned to walk home. Being her best friend wasn't exactly what I had hoped for.

CHAPTER 27

WEDNESDAY, MARCH 7, 1945

Pete jumped up and down the instant he spied me. The backs of his sandals clopped each time they hit the sidewalk.

"What's the matter?" I asked. "Have to pee?"

"Nah, big news! Say, how come you didn't stick around for the tryouts yesterday?"

I shrugged. "I'm not much of an actor. What's the news?"

Pete rose to his full height. "I'm gonna be the star—'cept maybe for Becky Thatcher."

I stopped in midstep. "Wait, you're Tom Sawyer?"

Pete looked offended. "I said I'm the *star*. Injun Joe!"

I tried hard not to laugh. "Congratulations, you'll be great!"

Pete flashed a toothy grin. "I know."

I tried not to sound too anxious. "Who else got parts?"

"Alice got Becky, of course. Don't know about the others. Had to leave and help Pop at the café. Dishwasher didn't show up again."

The instant Pete and I hit the playground, Alice swept over and led me toward the rear of the building. Pete looked perplexed and started to follow, but I waved him away.

Once we were alone, Alice turned to face me. "Have you heard?" she gushed. "I got chosen for Becky. And Billy—he's playing Tom Sawyer! Isn't that wonderful?"

A stake went through my heart, but I smiled gamely. "Glad everything worked out for you, " I mumbled. "'Scuse me. Got to get to class."

"Toodle-loo," Alice called, her fingers dancing as I clumped away.

Pete came up and poked me in the ribs. "Hey, what was that all about? Something going on between you and Cody?"

"Don't ask."

All morning I wallowed in self-pity. At lunch Billy came over and clapped me on the back. "Hey Cookie, want to thank you."

I looked to see if he was being sarcastic. "For what?"

"For telling me to try out." He pulled back his shoulders and stuck his thumbs in his belt loops. "Have to admit, I wasn't keen on doing it. But it ended up being a piece of cake." He leaned in confidentially. "Morris and Alice, they think I'm a natural."

I scrutinized his happy, cocky face, searching for the tiniest flaw to prove them wrong. I couldn't find one. "Told ya," I agreed, and joined him for a game of kickball.

When I got home from school, Mom and Dad weren't home. As I was reaching for a can of apricots, the phone rang. Hesitantly, I answered. It was Sergeant Atkins. After I hung up the phone, I went to my room and pulled out my story. Half an hour later, I called Marge. "I've got a new ending to my story," I told her. "Would you mind writing it down?'

CHAPTER 28

SATURDAY, MARCH 10, 1945

The Senator's program didn't start until seven o'clock. Mom insisted Eric and his guards come over early for a home-cooked meal. Marge told me the camp commander wanted to nix the whole visit, but the Senator talked him out of it.

Mom's emotions careened all over the place. One minute she was worried that Eric would slit our throats; the next, she was panicked that he wouldn't feel welcome or comfortable.

I followed Dad's advice and stayed out of her way. Fortunately, she ended up spending most of the afternoon at the beauty parlor.

At five o'clock sharp, we heard heavy footsteps on the back stairs followed by a jaunty knock. I bolted for the door, but Mom grabbed my shirt collar and almost strangled me. "Dad first," she ordered.

Dad opened the door to Sergeant Atkins, Corporal Taylor and a nervous-looking Eric. The bandage that had wrapped all the way around his head had been replaced by a large Band-Aid on his temple. His blackened eyes had shrunk into what looked like uneven lines of mascara.

He wore shiny green slacks and a cream sport shirt. Atkins explained the Colonel didn't want Eric leaving the camp in his POW togs, so Taylor had lent him some of his civvies. Aside from being a little flashy, they were at least a size too big for Eric. He looked like a kid playing dress-up.

Dad led everyone into the living room. Mom stood smiling by the coffee table, twisting a handkerchief in her hands. She wore a frilly pink apron over one of her nicest print dresses. Atkins made the introductions. I heard Mom stifle a gasp when she saw Eric's wounds.

Eric and the MPs sat on the couch. Mom brought a tray from the kitchen and set it on the coffee table. It held celery stalks stuffed with cream cheese, potato chips and tiny salami sandwiches.

Dad asked Atkins and Taylor if they'd like a beer. They agreed eagerly. Mom had coffee, while Eric and I had Coca-Cola. Strained chitchat followed for the next half hour. I think we were all relieved when Mom announced that dinner was ready.

We sat at the dining room table, and Mom served a feast: fried chicken, mashed potatoes and gravy, buttermilk biscuits, pear salad with cream cheese and crushed walnuts, cauliflower, and green beans. She topped it off with a devil's food cake with seven-minute icing.

Atkins patted his stomach. "That chicken was so good, it'd bring tears to a glass eye. Gotta be some kinda Southern cookin' I never came across."

Mom didn't say anything for a moment, then spoke up. "Actually, I cooked it in olive oil. That's the way we Greeks do it."

I almost choked on my milk. Mom had never admitted to being Greek in front of people before. I wondered if she felt it would make Eric feel more comfortable.

Eric rose and crossed to her. I noticed his eyes were sparkling. "*Frau* Cook. Most grateful I am for so elaborate a meal you made for us. Even more pleasure to me, is to share with your family and home." He bowed. "*Danke schoen.*"

Mom blushed and said she was pleased to have him.

The Senator's show didn't start for another forty minutes. I asked Mom if Eric and I could listen to records in my room. Mom looked uneasily at Atkins. Atkins smiled and nodded. Mom agreed. "But keep the door open so you can hear us when we call you."

Eric and I sat on the edge of my bed listening to records and not saying much. I played one of my favorites, "Ac-Cent-Tchu-Ate the Positive" by Jonny Mercer. I think he liked it. When I played Dad's new record, "Crossbow," Eric tapped his feet and told me it reminded him of the music in Aachen.

Taylor ambled in every ten minutes on some contrived errand from Mom.

I retrieved one of the Hershey bars Dad had brought me from Chicago and shared it with Eric. Before long, I found myself telling Eric stuff I'd never shared with anyone else. Like how lonely I'd been because we moved around so much. Or how I used to throw up when I got nervous. And the time I almost shot Bo for poisoning Chaplin.

Eric listened quietly.

I told him about my screwy friends, Pete and Billy and David. And about how Miss Morris was my first teacher who ever really encouraged me. I even bragged to him that I'd beat Billy in two races. "But I've yakked way too much," I suddenly realized. "Tell me about you."

He leaned back on his elbows as if contemplating where to begin. "My family, we live in same house in *Vater's* family for over one hundred year."

The more he talked, the more he seemed like any other nice kid I'd ever met. He told me his closest friend was his cousin, Bernie, who lived nearby and was born three months before Eric. They had grown up in the same class at school. Bernie sounded a lot like Billy Rogers: confident, good-natured and fearless.

Eric and Bernie competed with each other at everything, from soccer to their schoolwork. Both loved the outdoors. Bernie often talked Eric into skipping school and going fishing and swimming in the crisp mountain lakes nearby. Their absence always earned them a thrashing from their schoolmaster.

Bernie joined the Luftwaffe shortly before Eric was drafted. A shadow crossed Eric's eyes. "Ve argue the day he leave. I not understand vy he vant to fight. He not understand vy I do not."

"Do you know where he is? How he is?" I asked.

Eric shook his head solemnly.

Our conversation stalled. The topic we'd avoided so far was obviously on both of our minds. I changed the subject. "Do you have a girlfriend?"

Eric's face softened. "*Ja*. Emily."

I pulled up my legs and leaned against the wall behind my bed. "What's she like?"

"She smart. Also stubborn." He made a braying sound.

I laughed. "Sounds like someone I know. Is she pretty?"

Eric nodded. "*Ja. Schön.*"

"Have a picture?"

Eric opened a battered brown wallet. His military ID showed through the window. An eagle with its wings outstretched and its talons clutching a swastika spread across the top of the card. The photo's harsh lighting and Eric's sullen expression made him look menacing—a far cry from the smiling teenager sitting across from me.

Eric slid two fingers behind the ID and pulled out a creased photo. It looked like it was taken at a fair or a penny arcade. It had a pinkish tint and showed a younger Eric with his hair slicked to one side. He wore a striped tie and a blazer with a gold school crest embroidered over his heart. A pretty, round-faced girl with honey-colored hair and a serious smile leaned her head on his shoulder.

Her sureness reminded me of Alice. Only I doubted Emily's finger-nails were chewed to the quick. "Very pretty." My voice grew fearful. "Is she in Aachen?"

"*Nein*. Nuremberg. Study there to be nurse."

I paused, afraid to ask the next question. "Have you heard from her?"

Eric's face tightened. "Not since I am prisoner."

"Maybe she doesn't know where to write. It must take months for let-ters to get here."

Eric's manner indicated he wanted to change the subject. "You have girlfriend, too?"

I started to fidget. "Maybe. I don't know for sure. I think this one girl likes me, but I'm not too crazy about her. Then there's one I *do* like, but I'm afraid it's not mutual."

For the first time since we'd met, Eric actually laughed.

"Hey, cut it out," I tossed my pillow at him. He retaliated. Then I swatted him back. Pretty soon we were in an all-out pillow fight. Our uproarious laughter brought Mom, Dad, Atkins, and Taylor busting into my room. The MPs and Dad laughed at the sight.

Mom didn't think it was so funny. "Enough, you wild Indians. You could open that gash on Eric's head if you're not careful. Besides, it's time for the Senator's show."

The tubes hummed as the radio warmed up. Mom sat in the big chair, while Dad settled on one of its arms. Atkins, Taylor and Eric took the couch. I plopped in my regular spot on the floor and leaned against the chair.

I slipped my hands under my legs, crossed my fingers and hoped I hadn't made a big mistake.

Gene Little's syrupy voice poured from the speakers.

"Today's special program comes to you from the floor of the

United States Senate. Ladies and gentlemen, the Senior Senator from South Dakota, Edwin Garney.”

My heart started to pound.

After a moment of polite applause, the Senator cleared his throat and greeted his colleagues.

“In a little over a month, a conference will take place in San Francisco that may well determine the future of our entire world. It's called the Conference of the United Nations. People from free nations all over the world will meet to lay the foundation for a just and lasting world peace. A peace based on humanity, freedom and forgiveness. It won't be easy. Anyone who has studied history knows people generally prefer war to finding ways to live in peace.”

The Senator paused. You could hear him sip some water.

“Nazi Germany is on the ropes. Japan is reeling. Still, The Sixty-Four-Dollar Question isn't who will win, but how long will peace last? Now, I don't have to tell you forgiveness will be tough to come up with right now. Millions of innocent people have been sacrificed in this horrific struggle. My wife Eliza and I lost our only son at Saipan. Eliza never recovered from this loss. In fact, I'm convinced that she died from grief.”

He lowered his voice so I had to lean in to hear his words.

“But revenge is not the answer.”

Suddenly, his voice rose again. *“It wasn't in 1919, and it won't be in 1945!”*

The Senate erupted in applause.

I glanced at Eric. He stared unblinkingly at the radio.

"The truth is, my fellow Americans, we cannot survive another World War. Our weapons—and those of our enemies—have become so devastating that we would annihilate one another. Which brings me to an extraordinary article I came upon recently, written by an eighth-grade boy."

Every nerve in my body jangled. Eric remained expressionless. Mom clutched Dad's hand and motioned for me to come closer.

"This youngster wrote about an unlikely friendship. A friendship he struck up with a young German prisoner of war. The prisoner had been sent, along with over a hundred other POWs, to the boy's hometown to protect it from floodwaters.

"At first, the boy feared meeting the German. But when he did, he was astounded by how much they had in common. They shared the same dreams of peace; of having a productive career; and of living in a free country."

I heard the crinkle of a paper being unfolded.

"I believe this boy's simple story speaks eloquently for working together to build lasting, sustainable peace after this horrific War ends. I'd like to read the closing words of his article now."

Our living room became so quiet, you'd think everyone had stopped breathing. Each of us stared ahead, caught up in our own thoughts.

"My friendship with Eric has made me realize how lucky I am to live in America. It's also taught me two lessons that will stick with me for the rest of my life. The first lesson is this: Nobody wins a war. We all know of the countless Allied soldiers and civilians that have been killed in this War. But what we may not realize is that

the same thing has happened on the other side. I just learned that Eric's mother and younger sister—along with thousands of other German civilians—were recently killed in their homes by Allied bomb raids."

Mom gasped.

"The second lesson I've learned is this: Sometimes your worst enemy can become your best friend."

For several seconds, the only sound I could hear was my thumping heart. Then a volcano of applause erupted. It was so loud, Dad switched off the radio to keep the speakers from blowing.

Mom and Dad turned to me with shocked expressions. "That ending," Mom said. "It's new."

I looked at Eric. "Eric just got the news. I telephoned the changes to Marge yesterday."

Mom rose, walked over to Eric and hugged him. Dad squeezed Eric's shoulder.

Atkins's walkie-talkie started sputtering his name. The voice on the other end sounded desperate. The Sergeant answered and hurried to the back landing. He returned looking solemn. "Taylor, Stiendler. We've gotta go."

"What's wrong?" I asked.

"Krueger. Son of a bitch ambushed a guard and took his rifle. He and three of his SS buddies are loose."

Mom's hand shot to her mouth. "Do you think they'll come here?"

Atkins shook his head. "Camp's sealed tight as a tick. But I've got a hunch Krueger's looking for Eric." He motioned for Eric to come.

I bolted between them. "Don't go. It's too dangerous!"

Taylor pulled me aside.

Atkins looked at me sympathetically. "Sorry kid, Colonel's orders. Another thing. Don't breathe a word about this, any of you. If the folks in town hear about this, there could be bedlam."

Eric patted my arm. "Is right I go." He held up a finger. "First please, I go to bathroom." He went into my bedroom.

"Make it snappy," Atkins ordered.

Seconds turned into minutes. Atkins paced impatiently, then bellowed, "Come on! The Colonel's sweatin' like a whore in Church." His face reddened when he realized what he'd said. He smiled sheepishly at Mom.

Eric replied that he'd be right out. I heard a toilet flush. He hurried into the living room and apologized for the delay. Taylor grabbed his arm. Eric bowed to Mom and Dad. "Thank you for my happiest day in America." He nodded warmly to me and smiled.

"We'll be in touch," Atkins promised as he and Taylor led Eric away.

I stood at my bedroom window, watching until the Jeep's tail lights faded into the night. Then I crumpled helplessly to the floor.

CHAPTER 29

SUNDAY, MARCH 11, 1945

I ran downstairs in my PJs the instant I heard the newspaper whack the sidewalk. It was so cold that the cream on top of the milk had frozen, forming a thick white cylinder that snaked outside of the bottle. In spite of the frigid morning air, I stood outside and scanned every inch of the *Dakotan* for news about the escape. Not a word. Bob Lyle wrote a piece that praised the Senator's radio show, but there was no mention of Eric or me.

I smelled bacon frying when I came back in. While that smell usually made my mouth water, nothing could have given me an appetite. Mom flitted nervously about the kitchen, setting the table, scrambling eggs and toasting bread in the oven. "Nothing about the escape," I announced drearily. I dropped the *Dakotan* onto the table and slumped into a kitchen chair.

Mom lit a cigarette on the range. "You heard Sergeant Atkins say they needed to keep this hush-hush. Besides, I'm sure they've caught Krueger and the other two by now." Mom's voice was anything but sure.

"They would have let us know."

"I'm sure they've got more important things to do than call us. Now don't sit around moping. Get dressed. And be extra quiet. Your father's stomach gave him fits all night. He's finally sleeping."

Dad got up around eight. He looked pale, but claimed that it was nothing more than too much fried chicken. Mom made him eat soft-boiled eggs and stood over him until he drank a big glass of milk. He insisted on going to the station for the noon show.

I went to my room but couldn't sit still from worrying about Eric. I lay on the bed to read. As I moved my pillow, I found a folded page under it. I opened it gingerly.

> *Donny-boy,*
> *Today was mine happiest day in America. Please to thank your mutter for crunchy chicken which is new to me. Do not to worry about camp. Your story more powerful than hate. So happy we are friends.*
> *Auf Wiedersehen,*
> *Eric*
> *P.S. Hope you not mind I call you Donny-boy. I like.*

"Where are you going?" Mom asked as I slipped into my pea coat.

"I'm antsy. Think I'll run over to Pete's or something."

Mom looked at me suspiciously. "That 'something' better not be going near the camp."

"Mom. I'm not an idiot."

"Sometimes I'm not so sure. But leave me Pete's telephone number so

I can call if we hear anything."

I thought fast. "They don't have a phone. But I'll be back soon. Only an hour or so." Before she could argue I whisked out the door, sprang down the steps and took off running. I zigzagged through a couple of side streets in case Mom decided to follow.

At the edge of Garney Castle I stopped to catch my breath. A field waist-high with dead vegetation separated me from a high metal fence that circled the camp. I bent over and dashed through the weeds to it.

It stood at least twelve feet high, which felt like a mountain to me with my fear of heights. Even if I somehow made to the top, I'd have to climb over rows of sharp concertina wire. I walked alongside the fence, looking for a break in it. Eventually I found a small gap where the ground dipped away from the bottom. I pawed away the dirt until I had just enough room to crawl under the naked prongs.

Inside the camp, nothing moved. The brush waved with an eerie quiet. I dusted off my dungarees and jacket and crouched through the thicket toward the State House. I had a hunch Atkins would take Eric there.

A sound startled me. In the distance to my right, four Jeeps appeared. They drove agonizingly slow. In the lead Jeep, Eric sat next to Taylor in the front seat like a sitting duck. A revolver rested in Eric's hands.

I heard a rustle in front of me. I dropped to the ground and peered through the naked bottoms of the branches. My heart stopped. Krueger and three other POWs were on their bellies not ten yards away from me, their eyes peeled at the oncoming Jeeps.

My stomach knotted. If they saw me, I'd be dead in a minute. If I didn't warn Atkins, they'd kill Eric for sure.

Krueger lifted his stolen rifle. He whispered to the others and rose to a kneeling position. He nestled the rifle stock in his hand and aimed. In seconds Eric would be in front of him. Krueger cocked the bolt.

I jumped up, pointed ahead of me and shouted, "Look out! It's Krueger. He's going to shoot."

Taylor swerved. I dropped to the ground and tried desperately to crawl away. The thicket made it almost impossible.

KAPOW! A bullet kicked up a shower of dirt a foot ahead of me.

KAPOW! KAPOW! Bullets screamed by on either side of me, closer still. I hugged the ground, regretting the sadness I would cause Mom and Dad. I wondered if there really was a heaven, and if they let in dogs.

More shots were fired, but these sounded further away. They had to be for Eric. Keeping my chest to the ground, I turned around slowly. Krueger kept pulling the trigger on his rifle, but all I heard were clicks. He hissed and threw the rifle to the ground.

Taylor's Jeep slammed to a stop right in front of the Nazis. Eric was nowhere in sight. Atkins jumped out and fanned his .45 from side to side like the hero in a Western movie. "Get up, you assholes! Hands behind your heads!"

Three trembling POWs popped up with their hands clamped behind their heads. *"Aufgeben! Aufgeben!"* they cried. Krueger wasn't one of them.

The ground shuddered as three more Jeeps slammed to a stop next to Taylor. MPs piled out and converged on the Germans, rifles and revolvers pointed.

Out of the corner of my eye I saw movement. "Look!" I screamed, pointing at Krueger as he scrambled toward the river.

"Freeze, you worthless turd!" Atkins hollered, firing over Krueger's head.

Krueger kept running.

Atkins took off at lightning speed and tackled Krueger just as he dove into the river. The Nazi writhed and flailed in an effort to escape, but all he ended up doing was gagging on the thick, muddy water. Soon he stopped struggling. Atkins bobbed Krueger's head beneath the surface several times before he finally drug him out.

My heart was in my mouth as I dashed to Taylor's Jeep. "Eric?" I called out. "Where is he?

Taylor slowly lifted his right arm. Seconds later, Eric rose from the bottom of the Jeep where he had been shoved.

"All you all right?" I cried.

Eric smiled. My body went limp with relief.

"Well, look who's here?" a familiar voice chided behind me.

I spun around and went for Atkins, arms flying. "You bastard! You used Eric as bait!"

"Stop!" Eric's voice cracked like a whip. "Idea was mine, not Sergeant's."

I craned my neck back toward Eric. "But you could have been killed!"

Eric shrugged. "Showdown with Krueger coming sooner or later. Better sooner."

Lester's snarling face flashed in my mind, and I knew Eric was right. I apologized to Atkins.

The Sergeant put his arm around my shoulder and called out to Taylor. "Get Eric back to the hut in another vehicle. Stick with him 'til Krueger and them other Krauts are long gone. I'll take our Jeep and drive sonny boy here home."

I shuddered at the thought of Mom greeting us. "I, uh, think we need to come up with a plan."

When Atkins and I pulled into the driveway, Mom was standing at the top of the porch steps. "I knew it," she proclaimed as we stepped down from the Jeep. "You went to the camp."

The Sergeant stepped forward. "Nothing to fret about, Mrs. Cook." His voice oozed Southern charm. "I was on my way to tell you the news when I ran into your boy. Gave him a lift home."

"What news?" Mom asked warily.

Atkins looped his thumbs in his thick white belt. "Krueger and his pals are chained up and on their way to the stockade in Altoona. Eric's back at camp, snug as a bug in a rug."

Excluding a few minor details, it was all true.

Mom's face relaxed for an instant. Then her eyes skewered me. "But you were heading for the camp, weren't you?"

I nodded.

"So you deliberately disobeyed me?"

I lowered my head, figuring the less said, the better.

Mom tilted up my chin and shook her finger in front of my face. "Well, you're getting way too big for your britches. You'd better not make any plans besides school for the next two weeks. No friends. No radio. Nothing. Got it?"

Sergeant Atkins tapped Mom on the arm. "If you don't mind my saying so, I wouldn't be too rough on the boy. You see, he really—"

I kicked him in the ankle and cleared my throat as loudly as I could to cut him off. "Thanks, Sergeant. But Mom's right. I deserve to be punished."

Mom was visibly taken aback by my attitude. She glanced from one of us to the other, trying to decide if we were telling the truth or not. Atkins and I looked at her innocently. Her eyes fell on my pea coat. "How did your coat get torn? And your pants! How did you rip them?"

My mind whirled as I struggled to come up with some halfway believable excuse. Nothing came to me. Just as I was about to confess, Mom threw up her hands. "On second thought, don't tell me. Sometimes it's better not to know."

CHAPTER 30

MONDAY, MARCH 26, 1945

So far, there hadn't been a word about Krueger's attempted escape in the *Dakotan* or anywhere else. Nor had there been any mention of the Senator reading my story during his address. While we did get a couple of nasty phone calls afterwards, we also heard from several people who wanted to congratulate me. The way Dad saw it, most people were so fed up with the War that they just wanted it to end.

Because I was grounded, I couldn't visit Eric for two weeks. Sergeant Atkins called to tell us that they'd put Eric in charge of translating a camp newspaper, and that he was doing fine. I hardly saw much of Pete, Billy or Alice, either. They spent every spare minute at school rehearsing *Becky Thatcher*. It seemed like a lot of effort for a play that would only run for two nights. All the same, everyone seemed really excited about it. I didn't have any plans to go. After all, I didn't exactly relish the idea of seeing Billy and Alice smooching on stage.

"Take this out on your way to school, please," Mom ordered, holding up a smelly bag of garbage. "And don't get it on your new shirt. We're out of clothing stamps."

I held the bag at arm's length as I shuffled down the stairs. The weather had warmed up considerably. The air tasted sweet from things growing.

Halfway to the garage I froze in my tracks.

Trash was scattered all over the yard—newspapers, apple cores, egg-shells, chicken bones, a *Liberty* magazine dripping with coffee grounds. I figured some animal had knocked over our trashcan, but when I checked it was standing straight up.

I pulled off the lid for some clue as to what happened. Inside of the lid was a crude chalk drawing of Adolph Hitler giving a Nazi salute. A balloon coming out of his mouth said *"Heil, Cook."*

I didn't have to be Dr. I.Q. to know this was Lester's handiwork. If Mom saw the mess, she'd go crazy with worry. I had to clean it up—and fast. School started in fifteen minutes.

I slipped out of my shirt and hung it on the garage doorknob. To keep from staining my khaki trousers, I bent all the way over like the Hunch-back of Notre Dame to carry all the junk to the trashcan.

"Donnyboy!" Mom was looking down at me from the upstairs landing. "What in heaven's name are you doing?"

"Uh ... some animal must have knocked over the trash. I'm cleaning it up."

Fortunately, she believed me. "But why aren't you wearing your shirt? You'll catch your death!"

"You said not to get it dirty. Besides, I'm almost done."

"Wash your hands when you're finished," she insisted. Her face turned skeptical. "Had to be a good-sized animal to knock that big can over."

"Might have been a bear," I offered.

Mom rolled her eyes. "We don't have bears in the middle of town." She pondered for a moment, then shrugged and started back into the house. "Most likely a big dog. Hurry before you're late for school."

I stuffed the final pieces into the can and grabbed the Lava Soap from the garage. Turning the outside faucet on full force, I quickly scrubbed away the chalk drawing of Hitler from inside the garbage lid.

The final bell echoed into silence as I ran panting into the classroom. I heard a loud sniff. Then another. Lester spoke up. "Could we open a winder or something?"

"Why?" Miss Morris asked.

"'Cause it smells like garbage in here." He nodded in my direction. "Seems to be comin' from him."

The dam holding back all my rage against Lester crumbled instantly. I balled my fists and stomped toward him. Billy ran over and clamped my arm before I could hit the creep. I tried to pull free, but Billy held me in an iron grip.

Miss Morris jumped up from her desk. "No fighting!"

I trembled with rage. "I'm not putting up with his guff anymore! Lester knocked over our trashcan this morning, and I had to clean it all up!"

"Cool off," Billy said in a low voice, edging between Lester and me. "You're playing right into his hands. Start a ruckus, and you'll get yourself expelled."

What Billy said made perfect sense, but I still strained to get at Lester. It must have taken all of Billy's strength to muscle me back to my seat.

"Sit!" he ordered.

I obeyed reluctantly.

Miss Morris let out a deep breath. "Now, let's all calm down and get to our studies."

Billy spoke up. "Just one more thing, Miss Morris."

"What, Billy?" she asked sternly.

Billy hiked up his pants and strode over to Lester. Lester shrank in his seat fearfully. Billy sniffed. "Son of a gun if Lester ain't right. I smell garbage, too." He leaned in with both hands on Lester's desk. Lester cowered.

Billy's voice became biting. "But it seems to be coming from you, chum. By golly, I think you're smelling yourself!"

The class roared. In spite of my rage, I joined in. Even Miss Morris had to fight back laughter. Finally, she clapped her hands. "That's enough, now. Billy, take your seat." Billy strutted to his desk, grinning from ear to ear.

Lester's eyes swiveled to me, smoldering with hate.

CHAPTER 31

THURSDAY, APRIL 12, 1945

At lunch, Alice ran over to me so fast that I had to grab her to keep from being knocked over. "Sorry!" she apologized breathlessly. Her face became radiant, like Jennifer Jones in *The Song of Bernadette*. "Have you decided what night you're coming to the play? Friday or Saturday?"

I didn't have the heart to confess I might not go. "Gee, I don't know. Does it make a difference?"

"Well, tomorrow's opening night. My mother and father will be there." Her doe eyes drew me in. "I hoped you'd come then, too."

Any doubts I had about going flew out the window. "Sure. Maybe my folks can come, too."

"Perfect." She pursed her lips, made a kissing sound and ran off to rehearsal.

I was the first one in class after lunch. Principal Chester stood next to Miss Morris, looking distressed. Miss Morris held a handkerchief to one eye.

"Sorry," I blurted and started backing toward the door.

"Stay, Donald," Miss Morris said in a quaking voice. "Mr. Chester has an announcement. Sit and wait for the others."

I went to my desk, wondering what could be so awful that it could even upset Chester.

"Kids," the principal said solemnly when everyone got settled. "I've got some bad news. President Roosevelt is dead."

The class gasped. President Roosevelt always made me feel safe when the folks played his Fireside Chats on the radio. Mom and Dad said he was one of our greatest Presidents. The class fired off a volley of questions.

"How?"

"When?"

"Did somebody kill him?"

"Who'll take his place?"

"What'll this mean for the War?"

"Hold it." Chester waved his hand. "I don't have any details other than what I heard on a news flash, but it appears he died naturally. I'm sure we'll know more soon."

The room fell quiet. Miss Morris coughed to clear her throat. "Mr. Chester has decided to called off school for the rest of the day. Please put away your things and go straight home. I'm sure your parents will want you near them."

There was no slamming of desks. No shouts of joy. No pushing and shoving in the cloakroom. One by one, we gathered our things and treaded silently out the door.

CHAPTER 32

FRIDAY, APRIL 13, 1945

After a lot of hemming and hawing, the School Board finally decided that "the show must go on." *Becky Thatcher* would premiere on schedule at seven o'clock in the high school auditorium.

Mom and Dad said they'd go to the play with me. But when Dad came home from the five o'clock show, he was doubled over with terrible stomach pains.

He offered to go to the play anyway, but Mom said absolutely not. When he urged Mom to go with me, she said she needed to stay home and look after him.

As much as I had wanted to go someplace as a family for once, I knew Mom was right. On the bright side, I was now free to sneak out early if I got too bothered by Billy and Alice smooching.

I put on my good navy blue trousers, my white dress shirt and a light jacket, and left the house at ten after six. That gave me nearly an hour to get to the show.

Farmington Elementary didn't have a stage, so the play was held in the high school auditorium. Although lots of people were starting to stream in, it only looked about half full when I arrived.

I chose an aisle seat toward the back so I wouldn't be conspicuous if I left. The folding wooden chair complained as I lowered it. I slid in, scrunched down and shoved my knees against the seatback in front of me.

My watch said six fifty-five. I took a good look around the long, narrow theater. It had red brick walls with lights in the shape of the Farmington High Eagle every fifteen feet or so. I counted forty rows of seats, separated by a center aisle wide enough for two people to walk side by side. A bluish spotlight buzzed on and swept across the plush red curtain. It settled where the two halves met.

"'Scuse me, Cookie." I immediately recognized the heavy gardenia perfume and the crack of spearmint gum.

"Oh, uh ... hi, Cleo," I stammered. She sat next to me. Peggy followed her, giggling as usual. I had to stand so she had enough room to squeeze past me.

"Fancy seeing you here," Cleo cooed. She unbuttoned her scarlet cardigan sweater, revealing a matching sweater beneath that was stretched to the breaking point. Peggy tittered.

My eyes darted around to see if anyone from class noticed us sitting together. None were nearby. I checked my watch. Six fifty-seven. I felt flattered that Cleo wanted to sit by me, but uncomfortable Alice might find out. While she probably didn't care enough to be jealous, I did notice that she always seemed to get uppity the moment Cleo showed me any attention.

A familiar voice sent terror through me. "Why, Donnyboy!"

I bolted up. "Oh, hello, Mrs. Cody. And how do you do, Mr. Cody?"

Mrs. Cody gave me a mischievous smile, while Mr. Cody nodded stiffly. She shrugged her black cloak off her shoulders and handed it to her husband. Her outfit reminded me of Rosalind Russell in the movie, *The Front Page*—a man's suit with a white shirt and tie.

Mrs. Cody arched an eyebrow at me. "I'm so glad that you came opening night. Alice really wanted you to."

"We wouldn't miss it for the world," Cleo replied quickly, grabbing my arm.

My face singed.

Mr. Cody tugged his wife's arm. "Curtain time, Marion Grey."

"Oh, all right," Mrs. Cody huffed. "Now, Donnyboy, don't be a stranger. You hear?"

As they strolled away, I collapsed in my seat. Cleo leaned over. Her lips brushed my ear. "'*Donnyboy*,' huh?"

"Cut it, will you?" I leaned as far away from her as I could. "And for Pete's sake, don't spread it around."

She clucked in amusement.

The curtains parted to reveal what looked like a crude version of a Norman Rockwell cover for *The Saturday Evening Post*. As Becky Thatcher, Alice sat on the front porch steps of a white house. She drew on a tablet while Darrel, in the role of Judge Thatcher, read a book in his rocking chair. Darrel looked like he was drowning in his black suit, which was much too large for him. He took a corncob pipe out of his mouth and declared, "Beautiful evening, Becky."

After some chitchat, Darrel went into the house and a barefoot Billy cartwheeled onto the stage as Tom Sawyer. He faced the audience, looped his thumbs in his red suspenders, winked over his shoulder at Alice, and gave a long, drawn-out wolf whistle.

The audience howled. Billy beamed, gave a slight bow and turned to Alice.

She pretended not to notice him; or at least, that's what we were supposed to think. But something told me Billy's grand entrance bothered her. Billy proceeded to stand on his head, walk on his hands and do all kinds of other show-off stunts. The audience approved enthusiastically. Alice forced a smile.

Billy stuffed his red and white checked shirt into his dungarees and plopped down beside Alice. "Let me draw *you* somethin'," he drawled, grabbing her crayon and tablet.

"You can't draw," Alice said haughtily.

"Sure I can!" Billy insisted.

While Billy scribbled on the tablet, a scrawny pigeon feather rose from behind the porch. As the feather continued its rise, so did the person whose head it was tied to: Pete, in full Injun Joe regalia.

Once upright, Pete flattened his hand above his eyes and scanned the length and breadth of the stage. Not finding what he wanted, he made a face and ducked out of sight.

Billy finished his drawing and held it up to Alice.

"What is it?" she asked skeptically.

"You!" Billy declared proudly. He showed it to the audience. It was a stick figure with curly hair wearing a dress. The audience howled.

"Oh!" Alice exclaimed sourly as she turned her back to Billy.

Long, soft fingers laced their way into mine. I looked at Cleo in surprise. She gave me a smoldering smile. I gulped and turned back to the play.

On stage, Billy was kneeling down on one knee. "Promise me, Becky. Forever and always and ever after this, you ain't *never* going to love anybody but me. Okay?"

My hand started to sweat. It got clammier by the minute. I wanted desperately to wipe it on my pants leg. But I'd never held hands with a girl. I feared that if I took my hand away, Cleo would take hers away for good.

Alice rested her chin on a finger in thought. Suddenly her face turned stormy. "Wait a minute. That's exactly what you made Amy Lawrence promise."

Billy wagged his head guiltily. "Shucks, that didn't mean nothing."

Alice stuck up her nose and slapped Billy on the cheek. The sound was so realistic I winced. Billy looked stunned and touched his cheek. Alice fled from the stage.

"Women!" Billy complained, and shrugged off into the wings.

Darrel rushed out on the porch looking perplexed. "What's all the commotion about?" he blurted. Seeing no one there, he yawned and went back into the house.

All the lights dimmed except a spotlight on the rear of the porch. Pete popped up, made an evil face and gave a whooping war cry as he waved his rubber tomahawk in the air.

The spotlight went out as the curtains closed. Moments later, the house lights came up. As an excuse to slip my hand out of Cleo's, I immediately started clapping. When the crowd began to rise, I mumbled something about going to the bathroom and shot up the aisle, wiping my dripping palms on my pants. I found the boys room and hid in a stall until the lights flickered for the second act.

My escape during intermission did not go well with Cleo. She seemed considerably cooler as I took my seat. I set my hand on my leg, hoping she'd accept the invitation. But she ignored it.

On stage, Billy was hamming it up more than ever. The audience loved it. Alice sulked. Unlike Mark Twain's story, Miss Morris had Injun Joe wanting to scalp Judge Thatcher for sending his father to the pen. As the play drew to a climax, Pete chased the Judge over and under the porch, whooping and wielding his tomahawk.

Cleo seemed enthralled. The tempo of her gum cracking increased as the action on stage intensified.

"Help! Someone please help!" Alice shrieked as she witnessed the attempted scalping.

Billy dashed onto the stage and tackled Pete. They wrestled fiercely. After Billy finally pinned him, Pete grunted "uncle" in some kind of Indian talk.

The audience broke up.

Next came the part I'd been dreading. Billy swaggered over to Alice and took her in his arms.

"My hero," Alice said woodenly. Billy winked at the audience and planted a kiss on Alice's clenched lips.

The audience hooted and stomped its feet. Billy and Alice kept their embrace while the curtain closed. Just before the curtains shielded them, I thought I saw Alice shove Billy away.

When they came out for curtain calls, Alice got polite applause. But the biggest hands went to Billy and Pete.

I started to leave. Cleo tugged my arm. "Wanna go to the Teen Canteen?"

You had to be fourteen to get into the Canteen, and I didn't want Cleo to know I was a year shy. "Thanks, but no." I stretched out my arms and yawned. "I'm a little tired."

"How about taking a walk then?" she asked temptingly.

Electricity shot up the back of my neck. "Well, okay." I looked around and saw the Codys approaching us up the aisle. "But I've got to take care of something first. How about I meet you at the bridge. Ten minutes or so?"

She nodded. I shot up the aisle.

I waited on the dark side of the auditorium for everybody to dribble out. When I heard the front doors lock, I hurried for the bridge. My body tingled. I'd never had a date before. A huge white light bulb of a moon lit up the bridge. It was a short concrete arch that spanned Lynn Creek about ten feet below. Fortunately, this bridge didn't terrorize me.

I looked around. Cleo was nowhere in sight. My excitement faded. They must have gotten tired of waiting and gone to the Canteen. Worse yet, maybe Cleo was just toying with me. I kicked a bridge pillar and started for home, cursing myself for being too chicken to leave with Cleo.

"Psst ... Donnyboy." A loud whisper came from under the bridge.

I stopped cold. "Yeah?"

"We're down here." *Crack.* "C'mon."

I looked down. Cleo and Peggy stood in a spear of moonlight next to the creek.

"What are you doing down there?"

"Come on and see," Cleo purred.

Peggy giggled.

Halfway down the steep bank, my loafers slipped and I had to run to keep from falling. I ended up in the creek, water up to my ankles.

The girls chortled.

I lifted my feet out of the cold, slimy water. "It's not funny."

"Tee hee hee!" Peggy tittered.

"Wow, that was better than anything in the play, *Donnyboy.*" Cleo grinned.

"I asked you not to call me that."

Cleo walked over and kissed me square on the mouth. "There. That make you feel better?"

I stammered unintelligibly and backed away from her.

Cleo came closer. Her finger made a circle on my chest. "What's the matter? You never kissed a girl before?"

"Of course," I said unconvincingly.

Her face turned sultry. "Then you know how to french, right?"

My forehead broke out in a sweat. "Sure."

Cleo moved in until her magnificent chest pressed into mine. "French me," she sighed, closing her eyes and pooching her full scarlet lips together like a goldfish.

I stood there, paralyzed.

"Tee hee hee!" Peggy giggled maniacally.

Cleo opened her eyes, grabbed me by the neck and stuck her tongue all the way in my mouth.

I pulled away gagging.

Cleo planted her hands on her hips in disgust. "I thought you knew how to french!"

Peggy graduated to a full guffaw.

"Doggonit, stop!" I yelled at Peggy, trying to cover up my embarrassment.

Cleo's eyes bore holes into mine.

I lowered my head. "Fine, I lied. Truth is, I never kissed a girl before tonight. Unless you count a peck on my Mom's cheek." I started up the bank. "Sorry to disappoint you."

Cleo grabbed me and spun me around. "Hey, don't take it personally. Gotta be a first time for everything, right?"

I shrugged morosely.

"I betcha he's never really seen a girl, either!" Peggy mocked. "Naked, I mean."

I scowled at Peggy. "You stay out of this!"

"Well, have you?" Cleo teased.

I gulped.

"Uh, well ... that's none of your business!"

Peggy taunted. "Donnyboy's never seen titties. *Real* titties, I mean!"

I tried to escape but Cleo pulled me back. "How'd you like to see mine, Donnyboy?"

Before I could answer, she hiked her sweater clear up to her chin. In the bright moonlight, I could see everything— including the fact that she wasn't wearing a bra.

I fell flat on my butt. My face turned red as a hot plate. I spun around and started clawing up the bank. Sharp rocks tore the knees of my pants.

"What's the matter, Donnyboy?" Cleo laughed. "Didn't ya like what ya saw?"

I reached the top of the bank and took off without looking back. Every time my feet hit the pavement, water from the creek squirted out of my loafers and shot up my leg. Still, I didn't slow down until I was three blocks away from home. Passing under a streetlight, I caught a glimpse of my good pants. The knees were ripped and splattered with mud.

I slowed down, wondering how I could possibly explain this to Mom. But no matter how hard I tried to concentrate, I kept picturing Cleo's proud breasts glowing in the moonlight. And I realized that all those naked natives I'd seen in *National Geographic* magazine didn't hold a candle to Cleo.

By the time I turned onto Pearl, I'd resolved to tell Mom the truth about how my clothes got ruined. To my surprise, Senator Garney's black Lincoln Zephyr was parked in front of our house. A man in a dark uniform sat behind the wheel. All of our upstairs lights were on. I guessed that the Senator had come over to see how Dad was doing.

The back door opened as I started up the stairs. I gritted my teeth, expecting the worst from Mom. Only Mom didn't come out the door. Marge, the Senator's secretary, did—her face creased with worry.

"Donald, thank goodness you're home. I sent the Senator's driver to get you after the play, but he couldn't find you."

"What's wrong? Where are Mom and Dad?" I asked in alarm.

"St. Mary's Hospital. Come inside where we can talk." She gently steered me down the hallway. We stopped in the kitchen.

Marge looked alarmed when she saw my destroyed clothes in the light. "What happened?"

I shook my head. "That's not important. Tell me about Dad."

Marge leaned against the sink cabinet. "A little after seven, your mother called the Senator. She was all upset. Your father had terrible stomach pains and was spitting up blood."

"I should never have gone to that dumb play!" I cried, pounding the kitchen table.

Marge set a comforting hand on my shoulder. "There was nothing you could have done. The Senator was on his way to Washington, so he asked me to call an ambulance and had his car bring me right over." She touched my cheek. "Would you like some milk? Hot chocolate?"

I declined. "How bad is he?"

Marge folded her hands in front of her waist. "The doctor says he has ulcers, which are sores in his stomach. Only they're perforated, which means that they tore open. Your father has lost a lot of blood."

My stomach convulsed, but I swallowed back the bile. "Is he going to die?"

Marge put an arm around me. "I'm sure they'll do everything possible to make him well."

That she didn't answer my question made me more panicked than ever. "Take me to see him. Please."

She smiled. "Nobody can see him now, Donald. He's in a special room. Only doctors and nurses are allowed. Your mother is in the waiting room. She asked me to make sure you got to bed. Hopefully, you can visit him in the morning."

Marge guided me to my bedroom. My PJs were set out on my bunk. "Try to get a good night's sleep, son." She kissed me on the cheek and turned out my bedside lamp.

I folded onto the bed, too devastated to cry. A horrifying vision of Chaplin lying listlessly in the weeds flashed before me. "No, God, *no!*" I kept saying as I pounded the mattress. "Not Dad, too."

CHAPTER 33

SATURDAY, APRIL 14, 1945

The phone rang at six o'clock this morning. I tore into the living room. Marge had already answered it. She looked tired and wrinkled. There were dents on the couch from where she had slept.

Marge held the receiver away from her ear so I could hear, too. Mom said Dad's ulcers were still bleeding. He'd had three blood transfusions, but his blood type, B negative, was rare. The hospital had run out of it.

The Senator told the station to make announcements throughout the day asking for blood donors. Mom said Marge could bring me to the hospital, but that I couldn't stay long.

Mom walked me into Dad's room. He was cranked up in a narrow bed.

A maze of tubes ran in and out of him. His eyes were closed, his face white as marble. Only the rise and fall of his chest gave any sign of life.

I tiptoed over and squeezed his hand. It was cold. He didn't squeeze back.

A bottle of what looked like thick, clear water hung upside down from a bar above Dad's head. A rubber tube ran from the bottle to his right arm. A needle at the end of the tube stuck into his right wrist.

Mom saw the terror in my face. She put her hands on my shoulders. "Dad's going to be *fine*," she said fiercely. "Don't worry."

Everything around me said something different.

A short, plump nun swept into the room, her long black habit flaring behind her. She stopped when she saw me, adjusted her wire rim glasses, scowled, and waggled her finger. "Out, laddie," she barked in a thick Irish accent. "No children."

"You can't make me!" I snapped.

The nun calmly raised her eyebrows. "We'll see about that," she quipped, and advanced on me fearlessly.

Mom got between us. "Please. Can't he stay for a bit, Sister Celia?" She looked at me sympathetically. "He's very worried about his father. And he won't get in the way."

The Sister jutted out her lower lip. "'Tis against my better judgment, but all right. Only for a minute or two." She narrowed her eyes at me. "And no rilin' up yer father, hear?"

I nodded obediently.

For the next five minutes I stood next to Dad in silence, holding his hand. He seemed more like a machine than a person. He breathed in, breathed out. Liquids dripped into him. Urine dripped out of him.

Sister Celia returned. The expression on her face told me there was no use asking for more time. Mom walked me to the door. "Marge is in the waiting room," she reassured me. "She'll take you home."

"No!" I shouted, planting my heels. "If I can't stay in here, I'll wait out there."

"None of that, laddie," Sister Celia growled, and took hold of my arm.

I tried to yank free. But the Sister was much stronger than she looked. "Call me!" I yelled to Mom as Celia dragged me out the door. "Soon as you know anything."

Sister Celia's pointy black shoes were a blur as she towed me down the hallway. Her hand clutched a heavy silver crucifix necklace to keep it from banging against her chest. After a few sharp turns, we stopped in front of a chapel.

I looked at her sourly. "Marge isn't here, is she?"

"Marge can wait. This can't," Sister Celia replied with less steel in her voice. She steered me inside past three rows of wooden pews and stopped at the small alter rail. "Kneel," she ordered, shoving my shoulders down. "Now pray."

"But I'm not Catholic."

"'Tis a pity. But right now, God won't mind."

Sister Celia knelt beside me, folded her hands and closed her eyes. My family didn't go to church that often. And while I'd said my prayers every night for as long as I could remember, I never put a lot of energy or faith into them. Today I did.

Marge drove me home. After I assured her that I'd be all right, she left to change clothes and freshen up. I couldn't believe how empty the house felt.

I hung out by the phone, moving from the couch to the chair to and then back to the couch again. My mind was on fire with worrying about Dad. *Was he in pain? Would he get the blood? Would he die?*

I worried about Mom and me. *If Dad died, where would we live? What would we live on? Would we have to move away from Farmington, from all of my new friends?* I cursed myself, disgusted by my selfishness.

The phone rang just before noon. Lunging for it, I knocked the receiver to the floor. "Sorry," I answered, all out of breath.

"It's Mom." Her voice sounded tense.

I clenched my eyes. "Dad?"

"He's still out. The bleeding's slowed, but it's still a problem." She said a few people had phoned about giving blood, but nobody had showed up yet.

Marge came back around one o'clock. She made me a tuna fish sandwich. I didn't think I could eat it. But once I took a bite, I couldn't stop. I hadn't eaten since last night.

The phone rang. I grabbed it.

Mom sounded almost jovial. She had to talk over a bunch of noise in the background. "Donnyboy, there must be fifty people here to donate blood!"

I thought about Sister Celia and our time in the chapel. "So Dad's okay, then?"

"Not yet. They haven't found a match yet."

"Out of all those people?" I fumed. "The doctors must be making a mistake!"

"Everyone here is knocking themselves out for Dad," Mom scolded. "There are still plenty of people to test. Keep your chin up."

I knelt beside my bed and prayed hard.

The phone rang an hour later. "Find a match?" I asked hopefully.

Mom sounded exhausted but relieved. "Eight. Five were WPAX listeners. You'll never guess where the other three came from."

"Where?"

"The POW camp."

I gasped. "How?"

"When Sergeant Atkins told Eric about Dad needing a rare blood type, Eric reminded him that each prisoner's record said what kind of blood they had. Atkins got Eric the records, and he came up with three matches."

"Was Eric one of them?"

"No, but he talked to the men who were, and they all agreed to donate. Sergeant Atkins drove them right up to Saint Mary's."

"Is Dad still bleeding?"

"A little. But it's slowed down considerably."

Mrs. Cody sent Agna over to our house with a big pot of stew, fresh bread and cookies in the shape of Scottie dogs. She told me that Alice had made the cookies. After dinner, I helped Marge do the dishes.

At eight thirty, Mom called. "The bleeding's stopped," she said in an exhausted whisper. "He's very weak, but he wakes up from time to time. He said to tell you hi."

A tear rolled off my nose and splashed onto the telephone dial.

CHAPTER 34

SUNDAY, APRIL 15, 1945

After the news broke about Dad, all kinds of baked goods started pouring into the station from listeners. Aaron, Senator Garney's driver, delivered a pile of them to the house this morning. Mom asked him not to bring any more, that there was no way we could eat all of them.

"Tell the folks down at the station to take all they want," she suggested.

Mom and I brought a banana cream pie, a chocolate cake and a shoebox full of cookies to the hospital.

"Afraid it will be a while before I can tackle those," Dad chuckled weakly.

Mom nodded. "We thought Sister Celia and the doctors and nurses might like them."

They had moved Dad out of the room with all the machines to a sunny room of his own. He still looked pale, but nowhere near as bad as he had the day before. He fidgeted with the IV tube in his wrist, and was less than pleased about having to use a bedpan. When I asked him how he felt, he said the medicine made him woozy.

Dr. Cabeen entered, a serious, slim man with thinning grey hair and a boyish face. For some reason, he scratched his head whenever he talked. "As long as the bleeding's stopped, Mr. Cook should be fine. But his ulcers can perforate again at any time. The best medicine is to eliminate as much stress in his life as possible."

Mom and I brooded silently the whole car ride home about what Dr. Cabeen had said. Unless things changed drastically at the station, there was no way Dad could avoid getting stressed. That meant we'd have to move—a notion that made my heart sink. I made up my mind to think positive thoughts, like that guy, Norman Vincent Peale, talked about on his radio show.

"Mom!" I nearly shouted. "What if we gave some of the extra goodies to Sergeant Atkins, Eric and the guys in the POW camp who donated their blood?"

Mom pursed her lips in thought, then nodded heartily.

I couldn't believe the abundance of baked goods at the station. Even after Mom and I loaded up the car to the point of bursting, there were still plenty left for the station employees.

Atkins and Taylor helped us carry the treats inside the Quonset hut. I caught each of them downing a cupcake in the process. Taylor rustled up some platters from the mess hall, which Mom filled with an attractive arrangement of cakes, pies, cupcakes, and cookies.

Two MPs led Eric and three other prisoners inside the hut. Their eyes brightened when they saw what was on the table.

"*Gut* to see you, Mrs. Cook," Eric called to Mom. She smiled. I crossed over to him and pumped his hand. "Ach, *mein* brave friend!" he exclaimed. I frantically gave him the nix sign, hoping Mom wouldn't notice. Fortunately, she was busy laying out the rest of the sweets.

Eric nodded that he understood.

Atkins stepped forward. "Let me introduce the guys who gave blood." He crossed to a tall, gangly POW with a bald head and round rimless glasses. "This is Diederick."

The scholarly-looking German bowed his head.

Atkins moved to a short prisoner whose chest and arms were so muscular that they stretched the buttons of his fatigue jacket. "This here's Carsten."

Carsten gave a spry head tilt.

The Sergeant moved to a hulking man with huge hands. "Bamber."

Bamber blinked and averted his eyes. "Hello," he muttered shyly.

Mom and I shook their hands and told them how much we appreciated what they did. Eric asked about Dad.

"Still weak, but much better than yesterday," Mom told him.

Atkins poured coffee and everyone descended on the lavish assortment of sweets. Mom's face darkened when she saw me sipping a cup of coffee, but she didn't say anything.

Talking with Carsten, Bamber and Diederick was a little stiff at first, but Mom just clucked over them until they opened up. Diederick and Carsten spoke decent English. Diederick said he'd been a high school Latin teacher, and that languages came easily to him. Carsten had traveled all around Europe and England as an acrobat in the circus. He had learned bits and pieces of French, Italian and English along the way. "But mostly swear words," he chuckled.

Eric told me about the pieces he'd been writing for the camp newsletter on some of the POWs and their American guards. He said they'd gone a long way to ease tensions between the two groups. I looked around the room and understood why. Take away the accents and uniforms, and I doubted anyone could tell the Germans here from the Americans.

CHAPTER 35

MONDAY, APRIL 16, 1945

Miss Morris stopped me outside the classroom to ask me how Dad was doing. I told her he was much better thanks to all the people who had given blood—including three POWs.

As soon as we were all seated, Miss Morris told the class what I'd told her. Everyone seemed sympathetic except for Lester.

"Nazi blood? Who'd want that?" he hissed.

His words filled me with a burning hot rage. But I counted to ten and let it pass.

Miss Morris congratulated the *Becky Thatcher* cast and introduced them one by one. When Pete stood, the kids broke out in war whoops and stomping. Pete clasped his hands over his head like Joe Lewis after winning a match.

I glanced at Alice. She looked apprehensive.

Miss Morris introduced Billy. The clapping and hooting got even louder. Billy grinned and gave a hearty thumbs up. Cleo stood up and cheered.

"And finally, Alice Cody as Becky Thatcher," Miss Morris announced.

Alice stood and curtsied. The room responded with tepid applause. To make up for it, I clapped so hard my palms stung. The other kids stared at me like I was from Mars. Alice gave me a melancholy smile and returned to her seat.

Billy and I ate lunch together at the edge of the playground. Pete was off basking in the adulation of his fans.

"You really were a terrific Tom Sawyer, Billy."

"Thanks. I loved it. By the way, I'm glad your old man's doing better." He clapped me on the knee. I noticed Alice across the way. She was alone and drawing in her notebook. Our eyes met for an instant, but she looked away.

Darrel Hays ran over, all out of breath and excited. "Hey, you guys heard that new show on WXAX?"

"Which one?" Billy asked.

"Jolly Joe. He talks real hep and plays swell records. 'Caldona,' 'Rum and Coca-Cola,' 'Opus One.' He doesn't come on 'til late, but he's worth staying up for."

"Sounds like it beats the hell out of that hillbilly stuff," Billy allowed.

I kept quiet. For some reason, the news unsettled me.

As we filed into the classroom, Principal Chester stood in front of Miss Morris's desk. I wondered if somebody else important had died.

Chester cleared his throat and put on the closest thing to a smile he could muster. "Kids, it's only a matter of time before Germany surrenders. And the Chamber of Commerce is planning a big victory parade.

The theme is 'Fight for Peace.'"

I didn't know whether to laugh or applaud.

Chester hooked his thumbs into the straps of his suspenders. "The Chamber of Commerce wants the school to have a float. And based on the bang-up play you all put on this weekend, I'm giving your class the honor of making it."

The honor was met with little enthusiasm—and in some cases, groans.

Chester scowled. "Miss Morris will organize everything. I expect you to make Farmington Elementary proud." He stomped out.

The teacher looked a little delirious. "Well, that's a surprise. I guess the first thing we ought to do is come up with an idea for the float." She scanned the room. "Who'd like to volunteer for the planning committee?"

No response.

"Come on, kids, it's a parade. Think of how much fun it'll be."

An arm lifted. Mine.

"That's the spirit!" Miss Morris exclaimed. "But Donald can't do it alone. Who'll help him?"

Lester made a farting sound with his hands.

Miss Morris got red in the face. "That's rude, Lester. Do it again and you'll be headed straight for Mr. Chester's office."

Lester crossed his arms and slumped in his desk.

I pretended to look straight ahead, but my eyeballs flitted back and forth checking out my classmates. Cleo stared at her fingernails. Pete picked at some invisible lint on his billowy black shirt. Billy pretended to be asleep. Maybe he actually was.

"Kids?" Miss Morris implored.

Slowly another arm went up. Alice's.

Several boys guffawed. Cleo snorted.

"Marvelous!" Miss Morris turned to Alice and me. "I heard on the news this morning that Berlin could fall at any time. So put on your thinking caps and meet me before class this Wednesday with ideas."

"That's kind of fast," I said.

"Knowing you two," Miss Morris purred, "I'm sure it'll be plenty of time."

The class giggled.

Miss Morris shook her finger. "As for the rest of you, don't think you're getting off scot-free. There'll be plenty of building to do and costumes to make. Everyone needs to pitch in."

On our way out of the cloakroom, Alice came up to me. "You were so courageous to volunteer, Donny."

"Thank goodness you bailed me out," I laughed. "I was about to panic, thinking I'd have to come up with an idea all by myself. With your imagination, I know we'll be okay."

She started to raise a finger to her mouth but pulled it back. "I was afraid you wouldn't want my help. I mean, I was such a bust in the play."

"What do you mean?" I asked. "Look, you were great. Anybody who says otherwise is just plain jealous."

Her face returned to its normal, confident expression. "We'll make a great team," she said, squeezing my arm. She fluttered her eyelids, turned and strode away with her head held high.

I leaned against the cloakroom wall to keep from swooning.

CHAPTER 36

TUESDAY, APRIL 17, 1945

Dr. Cabeen said Dad could come home tomorrow. Mom took me to the hospital this afternoon to see Dad and say goodbye to Sister Celia.

Dad seemed like his old self, only better. His skin had a rosy glow to it. I didn't hear him belch once. His way of kidding people made him a hit with the other patients. You could tell he'd formed a special friendship with Sister Celia, even though she always nagged him to eat his food and not smoke.

Dad asked Mom to bring a dozen copies of his new record. He autographed one for each person who'd helped him during his stay.

Sister Celia corralled Mom and me in the hall on our way out. She told us how close Dad had come to dying, and warned us that we had to make sure he ate right, got plenty of rest and stayed as stress-free as possible.

CHAPTER 37

WEDNESDAY, APRIL 18, 1945.

I entered the classroom with a dark cloud hanging over my head. I'd struck out trying to come up with an idea for the victory float. Miss Morris sat on the edge of her desk. Alice stood next to her looking almost as distressed as me.

"Let's get started," Miss Morris said cheerfully.

"You start, Donny," Alice said eagerly.

I rubbed my chin hoping for divine inspiration. None came. I shifted from foot to foot. "To tell the truth, I've been pretty wrapped up with Dad being in the hospital. I tried hard to come up with something, but..." I threw up my hands. "Maybe somebody should take my place."

"No," Alice declared. "Your father has to come first."

"Thanks," I said with relief. "Oh, please tell your mom we loved the stew. And your cookies were the best ever."

Alice smiled magnanimously.

Miss Morris cleared her throat. "Sorry to interrupt you two, but time's a-wasting. Alice, how about your idea?"

Alice gnawed at an invisible fingernail. "I'm afraid I don't have anything, either."

Miss Morris took off her glasses and gnawed on one of the temples. "Hmmm."

Deadly silence.

"I—I had this one idea," I stammered. "But it's probably dumb."

"Tell us," Miss Morris urged.

I shuffled my feet. "It's actually a dream I had last night. It only lasted for a second or so."

"What was it?" Alice asked anxiously.

"It was all kind of fuzzy," I began, "but I saw a big platform with red, white and blue bunting all around the bottom. In the middle was a kid in an Uncle Sam suit and a girl dressed up like the Statue of Liberty."

I closed my eyes, straining to remember.

"Oh yeah, and Uncle Sam was shaking hands with a kid dressed in those shorts with suspenders—you know, like Germans wear?"

"I believe they're called *lederhosen*," Miss Morris interrupted.

"That's right, *lederhosen*. And there were a bunch of other kids dressed up like people from all over the world. They were standing in line to shake hands with Uncle Sam and the Statue of Liberty."

I opened my eyes and looked up sheepishly. "Dumb, huh?"

"It's wonderful!" Alice exclaimed.

Miss Morris agreed. "Although including a German could be a problem," she added, screwing her mouth up to one side.

"No, it's perfect," Alice insisted. "It's just like what Donny wrote. If we want peace, everyone has to get along."

A red flag went up in my mind. Was I getting myself—and the people I cared about—into another mess?

Alice grabbed a notebook and a pencil from her desk. She started sketching so fast that her hand almost blurred. In a matter of minutes, she proudly held out her drawing.

Stylized stick figure renditions of Uncle Sam, the Statue of Liberty and a crowd of kids waved from a parade float, just as I'd described a moment before. A banner arching over the float read *Peace, Let's Shake On It.*

"Wow!" I exclaimed.

Miss Morris nodded cautiously. "Very nice. But we have to get Mr. Chester's okay first. And that can't happen 'til Friday, when he's back from a coach's conference."

I figured Chester would kill the idea for sure, which would save me a lot of grief. But the fact that Alice was excited made me want to fight for it.

As soon as I got home, I went right in to see Dad. He was sitting up in bed, wearing blue PJs with silver piping and smoking a cigarette. The drapes shut out the afternoon sun. The warm light from his bedside lamp lent a deceptively healthy glow to his face.

He set his cigarette in a black, horseshoe-shaped ashtray on his bed-side table. Stamped across it in white letters was *The LaSalle Hotel Moline.* That's where he and Mom met, back when he played with Paul Whiteman. As soon as the band finished its run there, the two of them ran off and got married.

I sat in a chair beside him. "Dad, I need to talk to you about something."

"Sounds serious."

"It is," I said, rubbing my hands together nervously. "I don't really know you."

Dad looked baffled. "What do you mean?"

"You never talk about your family. I have no idea what you were like growing up. The only thing I do know is that you're related to some famous Scottish poet named Robbie Burns. And I only know that because Mom told me."

Dad grimaced. He picked up a glass of chalky-looking liquid on the nightstand, held his nose and took a sip. "There's really nothing to tell," he said sorrowfully.

I jumped up, sensing that I'd crossed a line. "I didn't mean to upset you."

"That's okay," he nodded.

I backed toward the door. "I'll let you get some rest."

"I am a little tired," he sighed. His voice sounded far away.

I turned to the door and heard the scratch of a match. A whiff of sulfur stung the inside of my nose.

At dinner I picked at my spareribs and sauerkraut. I hated sauerkraut. Mom said it was good for me.

"Why so glum?" she asked.

"I think I upset Dad. I told him he seemed like a stranger. I don't really know anything about his life other than the times we've spent together. And it seems like he's always left raising me to you."

Mom stared past me for a long moment. "It's very painful for Dad to talk about his childhood."

"Why?"

Mom cleared our plates. She poured a cup of coffee, lit a cigarette and sat across from me. "Dad's father, Porter, had a drinking problem and never spent any time with him. Dad worshiped his mother, Viola, but she got TB and died when Dad was twelve."

"How come nobody ever told me?"

Mom took a drag on her cigarette, held the smoke in her lungs, then turned her head away and slowly exhaled. "Like I said, it's too painful for him. After Viola died, Porter started drinking more than ever. He lost his job playing piano for the silent movies. Lost most of his music students, too."

She sipped her coffee and cleared her throat. "Your Dad was pretty much left on his own. Got to the point where the only time he saw his father was when Porter gave him violin lessons."

I sat there mesmerized.

Mom snuffed out her cigarette in the beanbag ashtray. "After a year or so, Porter met this widow, Eunice, and they got married. Eunice never wanted kids, and she made things pretty tough for your Dad. Also, your Dad hated her for taking his mother's place."

Mom got up and rinsed her coffee cup. "Things went from bad to worse between Eunice and your Dad. Finally, Porter packed Dad off to live with Viola's folks, the Smitleys, in Gilman, Iowa."

I followed Mom to the sink and rinsed my glass. "How was that?"

"Dad won't say. What I do know is he ran off to Kansas City the day after he graduated high school. He was determined to join a jazz band."

"What happened then?" I asked.

Mom's voice quavered. "I think he had the time of his life."

CHAPTER 38

THURSDAY, APRIL 19, 1945

Alice and I sat on pins and needles all day at school. Miss Morris made us promise not to tell anyone about our float idea until she talked to Chester. And that was still a day away. Billy and Pete kept trying to pump me for information, but I kept mum.

When I came home from school, Dad was napping. I went to my room. Mom came to my doorway. "Someone's here to see you."

"Who?" I asked, hoping it might be Alice.

"David."

"Be right out," I said, jumping off my bunk and sliding into my loafers.

David sat on the couch in the living room. I took the chair. Mom asked us to keep our voices low so we wouldn't wake Dad. "There's some Nehi grape soda in the fridge and oatmeal cookies in the jar," she added, slipping on a ruby cardigan sweater. "I'm running to the Rexall to pick up Dad's prescription. Be back soon."

David and I went into the kitchen. I ran hot water over an ice cube tray to loosen some cubes. David blocked the lip of his glass with his hand.

"I'd prefer a beer," he said with a wink.

He'd obviously seen the bottles of Pabst Blue Ribbon when I opened the fridge, so I couldn't say we didn't have any. But if I gave him some and Mom found out, she'd go into a tizzy.

I handed him a bottle. "Drink it fast before Mom comes back."

He nodded, popped the cap and took a huge gulp. We went into the living room. David sat on the edge of the couch. As he unbuttoned his Ike jacket, the dog tags he wore around his neck fell loose and clanked. His expression grew serious. "Need a favor."

"What?"

"You know the *Major Bowes' Original Amateur Hour*?"

"Yeah. It's pretty corny."

"I know. But that's where Frank Sinatra started. And guess what? Auditions for new contestants are gonna be held at your pop's radio station."

"I had no idea."

David fidgeted. "Could you put in a good word about me tryin' out?"

I took a sip of my grape soda and grimaced from the carbonation. "I can ask. But I'm not sure Dad has anything to do with it. Mr. Cody likes to run everything."

"Maybe so. But from what I hear, your pop's the Senator's favorite."

"I'll ask Dad when he wakes up. How do I get in touch with you?"

David aimed a finger at me, squeezed it and made a popping sound. "Don't worry about that. I'll be in touch with you."

I wrote down our number on a pad and gave it to David.

"Good," he grinned, draining the last of his beer. He slipped the bottle into his jacked pocket and patted it. "I'll stash this someplace far away."

"Thanks."

"Hey, if I do get to audition," David began timidly, "would you come? For moral support n' all that?"

"Sure, if I can make it. How about your Mom and Ben?"

He waved his hand. "They'll be too busy."

The phone rang around seven o'clock. "Cook residence," I answered.

"Cookie, it's me." David's voice sounded anxious.

"If you're calling about the auditions, I asked Dad."

"And?"

"He called the station and got your name on the list. Just show up next Wednesday a little before four o'clock."

"You're a real ace, Cookie. Give your pop a big thanks for me." His voice lost its brashness. "And you'll be there, right? If you can make it, I mean."

"Bet on it."

I heard the first few lyrics of "Happy Days Are Here Again" as he hung up.

The sound of my bedroom door opening jarred me awake. A slash of yellow light fell across my bed. Dad's silhouette walked toward me. My Big Ben clock read eleven thirteen.

I bolted upright. "Dad! You okay?"

"Shush," he whispered, nudging me over with his hand until he had enough room to sit. "Mom told me about your little talk. Apparently I've kept my life a big secret from her, too." He eased himself into a laying position and put an arm behind his head. "I filled her in on everything, and decided I owed you the same."

I moved onto my side and leaned my head in my hand.

Dad stared straight ahead as though in a reverie. "Bloomington was small. But a metropolis compared to Gilman, where my father sent me to live with the Smitleys."

"How old were you?"

"Almost fourteen. My father and Eunice had been married just over a year. That year was pure hell for me."

"What were your grandparents like?"

"Old, in their sixties. The last thing they needed was a moody teenager. Grandpa Dan worked as a blacksmith, shoeing horses and stuff like that. He didn't talk much and when he did, he beefed. Cars were getting popular, so fewer and fewer folks needed a blacksmith.

"Grandma Ethel made sure I had enough to eat and my clothes were clean. But neither one of 'em spent much time with me. I felt like a boarder."

"How about your father? Did he come see you?"

Dad snorted. "Porter made it maybe twice the whole time I lived there. And when he did come, he spent most of his time in the local tavern."

"Did you have many friends?"

"None to speak of. Most of the kids were from farms. We didn't have a lot in common." He turned to me. "I'm happy you've fit in so well here."

A warmth spread across my stomach.

"The first week I arrived in Gilman, I decided I'd get out as soon as I finished school. My dream was to join a band. I spent all my spare time practicing the fiddle or working. Depending on the season, I pulled cockleburs, detasseled corn, raked leaves, shoveled snow—anything to make enough money for my getaway. At night, I listened to the jazz bands on the radio and played along with them."

My neck started to hurt, so I sat up and crossed my legs Indian-style.

"Before sunrise on the day after I graduated high school, I threw my things into one of Grandma's empty feed sacks and hopped a train to Kansas City. I left the Smitleys a note thanking them. I knew they'd be relieved to be free of me.

"I couldn't believe it when I walked out of Union Station in K.C. There were so many people, and they were all in a hurry and dressed up in fancy suits and hats. The streets were jammed with flashy new automobiles and bright green streetcars. Horns honked. Bells clanged. I'd never seen anything like it."

"Were you scared?" I asked, entranced by his story.

"Nope. I was probably too dumb to be," he laughed. "My biggest fear was how long my money would last. I'd managed to save exactly fifty-nine dollars. My train ticket cost eleven dollars. I didn't have much of a cushion."

I couldn't imagine Dad being so carefree.

"I got the cheapest room I could find, which was fifty cents a night. Lived on a lot of 'special' tomato soup: hot water and ketchup. Night after night, I hung around outside the jazz clubs on Twelfth Street with my fiddle, trying to get one of the bands to hear me play. The bands were mostly colored and only a few had fiddle players, so I didn't have much luck."

He took out a pack of cigarettes from his pajama pocket and lit one. He picked up one of my loafers to use as an ashtray. "You had to be twenty-one to play in the clubs, and I was barely eighteen. To look older, I grew a mustache and slicked back my hair. I also plunked down twenty dollars at Monkey Wards on black shoes, a pin collar shirt and tie, and a grey pinstriped suit."

"Like you're wearing in the picture Mom has of you in your bedroom."

He laughed self-consciously. "I guess so. Well, it didn't take long before I was nearly broke. I hated the thought of going back to Gilman, but I didn't have any other options. The night before I was set to leave K.C., a band leader I'd been pestering named Cozy Cole said he'd let me sit in with his men for one tune after his club closed."

I leaned forward.

"Well, the second they closed the club, I ran through the back door and clambered up to the bandstand. Cozy asked what I wanted to play. I didn't want him to think that I only knew one or two songs. So I took out my fiddle and said, 'You call it.'

"Cozy nodded to his men. The drummer did a four-beat countdown, and they swung into 'Honeysuckle Rose.'"

Dad paused to puff on his cigarette. "I knew the song from playing along with the bands on the radio. I eased in, just keeping a nice soft pad to their rhythm. But then Cozy nodded for me to solo.

"I knew this would probably be my first and only chance to get a job playing music. I closed my eyes, and for the next three minutes I played runs and voices and harmonies like you wouldn't believe. Where they came from, I had no idea.

"One by one, the other musicians stopped playing and gaped. When I finished, there was an eerie silence. Then Cozy walked over to me and said, 'Son, you're one helluva hot cat. You've got yourself a job!'"

I broke out clapping. Dad grabbed my hands to silence me. "Shush. You'll wake Mom."

"Wow! That must have been the happiest day of your life!"

"Uh-huh," he answered. The smile on his face made him look like a teenager.

Dad rose slowly and shuffled into my bathroom. I heard him tap my shoe against the toilet bowl and flush. He came out, lay my loafer on the floor and headed for the door. "Get some sleep, DB."

"Dad."

"Yeah?"

"Cozy Cole was right. You really are a helluva hot cat."

Dad's eyes glistened in the dim light. "Well, thanks, son. So are you."

CHAPTER 39

FRIDAY, APRIL 20, 1945

Just before lunch, Blue Hair brought Miss Morris a note from Mr. Chester. She read it without expression and slid it inside a drawer in her desk. When the bell rang, she asked Alice and me to stay. We exchanged ominous looks and walked to the front of the classroom.

"I'm sorry, kids," Miss Morris said with a sigh, "but Mr. Chester nixed your idea for the float."

"Is that final?" I inquired, looking from Miss Morris to Alice.

"Afraid so," Miss Morris responded.

"Oh, I don't think so," Alice snapped, her eyes blazing.

Miss Morris frowned. "He's the principal, Alice."

"But we know someone higher up," Alice said defiantly. She turned to me. "Right, Donny?"

"We do?" I wondered if she meant God.

Alice rolled her eyes at me and announced that we would ask her grandfather, Senator Garney, to overrule Chester.

The "we" made my stomach churn.

Miss Morris held up her hand. "Now you know I can't be a part of this. But what you choose to do outside of the classroom is none of my business." She peered at us over her glasses. "But be warned. If this works, Mr. Chester will want your scalps."

I followed Alice to the cloakroom. "When can you see him?" she asked eagerly.

I looked at her incredulously. "Me? But you're his granddaughter. He's way more likely to do what you ask."

Her mouth turned down. "Not true. He thinks I'm spoiled." She brightened up. "But he loves you! He raves about your story all the time." She glanced from side to side and lowered her voice. "What I'm about to tell you is *very* confidential."

I tilted my ear close to her mouth.

"You can't tell anyone, not even your parents. Promise?"

"Sure, sure," I whispered.

"Well, grandfather got so much good publicity for reading your story in the Senate, President Truman is about to nominate him for a big job."

"Wow. What's the job?"

"He won't say. But it's b-i-g big." She took a step closer to me and raised her eyebrows. "So when can you ask him?"

I felt like I'd just fallen through a trapdoor. "Well, I guess I could call Marge this afternoon and see if he'll meet with me."

Alice plucked her white cotton cardigan from its hook and slipped it on. It had a tiny black Scottie over her heart. "You're wonderful," she purred.

My mouth turned dry as chalk. I accidently knocked my windbreaker to the floor. Alice and I bent to retrieve it at the same time. We ended up chest-to-chest, lips inches apart.

There was the click of high heels outside the cloakroom. Miss Morris leaned in. "You kids still here?"

I swept my windbreaker off the floor and popped up. Alice stood and strode out of the cloakroom. "Just leaving," she called, and waggled her fingers at us over her shoulder. Miss Morris chuckled and followed Alice out of the classroom.

I leaned against the cloakroom wall, savoring the memory of what had just happened. The flowery scent of Alice's hair. Her minty breath. The warm softness of her chest. Her sweaters may not have been as tight, but Alice was every bit as grown-up as Cleo.

When I got home, no one was there. There was a note from Mom saying she took Dad to Dr. Cabeen for a checkup. I dialed Marge's number. She greeted me cheerfully. When I asked if I might see the Senator, she went off the line for a moment. She came back on and said the Senator had to leave town soon, but if I came right over he could see me. I felt a pull in my stomach, but I ignored it and told Marge I was on my way.

The Senator looked up from his desk. "What can I do for you, son?"

"It's about our class float for the Farmington victory parade. Alice and I came up with an idea for it, but we've run into a problem."

A small, ornate gold clock on the Senator's desk chimed four times. By the Senator's reaction, I could see that I didn't have much time. I unrolled Alice's drawing and explained our idea as rapidly as I could.

"Looks fine to me," Garney grunted. "What's the problem?"

I pointed to the figure wearing *lederhosen*. "This is supposed to be a German. Mr. Chester thought that'd stir up a hornet's nest, so he killed the idea."

I could almost hear the gears turning inside the Senator's head. "You're looking for me to change his mind?"

"Yes, sir."

The Senator hitched up his pants. "As you know, Donald, I've been preaching forgive and forget." He smiled in self-satisfaction. "And thanks to a bit of help from you, it's worked quite well—as you'll be hearing soon." He paused and tapped a silver letter opener on his desk. "The way I see it, Chester's a sad excuse for a principal. But that doesn't mean I have the authority to overrule him."

My hopes were dashed.

The Senator leaned forward to look at me. His face stretched into a sly smile. "Be that as it may, a call to Mrs. Chaney, the head of the School Board, just might do the trick."

"That would be fantastic, Senator."

He rolled back from his desk and rose. "I'll try to reach her before I go."

I grasped his hand in both of mine and pumped. "Thank you, sir. Thank you so much."

The Senator's eyebrows knit into one furry line. "I hope you two know what you could be getting yourselves into."

I swallowed. "Yes, sir. I do."

When I stepped outside Garney Castle, a cold wind was whipping at scudding grey clouds. Thunder rumbled on the heels of jagged white lightning. I ran for home at top speed.

Half a block from our house, I saw a blinding flash and heard an ear-splitting crack. Smoke seeped from the giant limb of an oak tree as it sunk to the ground. Fat, cold rain bombs pelted me. Within seconds, my windbreaker, flannel shirt, T-shirt, and trousers were soaked.

Mom rushed to the back door when I burst in. "Thank heavens you're home," she cried. "All that lightning had me worried. Where have you been, anyway?"

"It's kind of a long story," I answered through chattering teeth.

"Well, get out of those sopping clothes and tell me."

Mom turned white as a ghost when I told her about the float and why

I saw the Senator. "What in the world were you thinking?" she nearly screamed. "A German shaking hands with Uncle Sam is bound to make a lot of people in this town go berserk. And because everybody here knows about you and your article, they'll know you're the one behind it. What if they decide to take it out on your Dad? You know what that kind of stress could do to him."

When Dad came home, I told him about the float. I said I was afraid it could backfire and create a lot of stress for him. "Tomorrow I'm going to tell Miss Morris I can't be a part of it," I promised.

Dad looked like he was going to blow his top. "Now wait a minute! Didn't we just have a talk about you needing to take risks?"

"Yes, but—"

"But nothing," Dad growled. "Don't use me as an excuse for chickening out."

His words filled me with shame. I felt caught in the middle of a tug of war. It seemed like only a matter of time before I'd end up split in two.

CHAPTER 40

MONDAY, APRIL 23, 1945

The rain continued harder than ever today. Mom drove me and Pete to school. Shortly after class started, Blue Hair clomped in and dropped a note on Miss Morris's desk.

Miss Morris read it and looked up with a surprised expression. "Well, what do you know? The School Board has approved our float."

Alice gasped with pleasure and beamed at me. I smiled weakly and shrank down in my seat.

"Things have changed a bit," Miss Morris continued. "Officially, the float's now being sponsored by Senator Garney. But it'll still be our idea."

Lester narrowed his eyes. "What idea you talkin' about?" Miss Morris nodded at Alice and me. "Why don't you two tell everyone?"

A tremor ran through me. I looked straight ahead, glued to my seat. Alice shot me a baffled look and stood. She unrolled her drawing and held it up for the class. She got halfway through explaining the idea when Lester interrupted.

"What's that guy in Nazi shorts doin' there?"

Alice glared at him with disgust. "They're not 'Nazi' shorts. They're *lederhosen*. Germans wear them on holidays."

"You're glorifying killers!" Lester exclaimed. A few others mumbled their disapproval.

Alice looked at me for help.

I lowered my head.

Miss Morris stepped forward. "Let's just calm down. Obviously, some of you aren't comfortable with this idea. But it's very much the same message Donald had in his article. And most of you said you agreed with him."

Billy and Pete cheered their approval.

Miss Morris held up a finger. "Tell you what, let's vote on it."

"It's already approved!" Alice cried in exasperation.

"But not by the class," Miss Morris reasoned. "Everyone, tear off a scrap from your tablet. Those in favor of the float, write 'Yes.' Those opposed, 'No.' When you're finished, fold your paper and drop it in the basket on my desk. Majority rules."

Alice looked at me apprehensively. I avoided her gaze and set pencil to paper.

The final ballot dropped into the basket. Miss Morris carried it to the blackboard and started tallying. The first four votes were against our idea.

Lester cheered.

Next came four votes in favor of it.

"What's wrong with you guys?" Lester chided.

Soon the tally was up to eight each. Miss Morris pulled out the final slips of paper and read them aloud. "Yes, no, no, yes."

It was tied at ten apiece. Miss Morris looked perplexed and counted the class. "We have twenty ballots and there are twenty-one of you here today. Someone didn't vote."

While the others looked around the room, Alice zeroed in on me.

In spite of my humiliation, I stood. "Guess that's me." I walked slowly over to Miss Morris and handed her my ballot. She read it and made a mark. "There you go. Eleven in favor, ten against."

Lester kicked his desk. Billy booed him. Miss Morris ignored the ruckus. "Now, we all have a lot to do in just a little time." She scanned the class. "Who can do what?"

Melvin Rosner, a spare, ruddy-faced farm boy, raised his hand. "Pa's got a flatbed for haulin' hay. Bet we can use it for the float." I'd never heard him speak up in class before.

Shirley Elkman, a petite girl the kids called "Goggles" because of her Coke bottle glasses, waved her hand. "I kin pull Mel's flatbed with our tractor."

Laughter swept the room.

"What's so funny?" Shirley huffed indignantly. "You ain't never seen me drive!"

"We could use the $25 our class won in the scrap drive for the bunting," suggested Peggy.

I could sense the enthusiasm growing.

"Dad belongs to the American Legion," Darrel said. "They've got an Uncle Sam suit he wears in the Fourth of July parade every year. I betcha we could borrow it."

"Excellent." Miss Morris made a note.

"I'll be the Statue of Liberty," Alice proclaimed. "We've already started on the costume." She turned to me. "And you'll be Uncle Sam, right?"

My face flamed. "Uh... "

"Great!" said Alice, cutting me off with a smile.

Cleo raised her hand. "I'll be a Spanish señorita," she purred sexily.

Billy gave a soft wolf whistle.

"Looks like we're off to a good start," Miss Morris said, glancing at the

Regulator clock. It read three forty-four. "We'll fill all the other parts tomorrow. Then everyone can begin working on their costumes."

The final bell sounded and set off the usual pandemonium. Miss Morris asked me and Alice to stay. Reluctantly, I joined Alice beside the teacher's desk.

"You certainly didn't seem very excited about your own idea," Miss Morris commented.

"I'm sorry, it's just that this whole thing is tearing me up inside. Mom's convinced folks will get mad all over again when they see me on the float. She says they'll take it out on Dad, which could make his ulcers start bleeding again and put him back in the hospital. Meanwhile, Dad thinks I'll be a coward if I *don't* do it."

"Oh," said Alice softly. She looked chagrined. Suddenly, she brightened up. "But you don't have anything to worry about, Donny!"

"Why's that?" I asked suspiciously.

"Because everybody's going to love the float!"

I hoped she was right.

Miss Morris broke in. "Look, you two. I have to go. Is there anything we're missing?"

Alice's face lit up. "Yes, there is. I saw it in a vision last night."

"Spill it," Miss Morris said impatiently.

Alice's face took on a dreamy expression. "I saw dozens of white doves. They kept circling the Statue of Liberty."

CHAPTER 41

WEDNESDAY, APRIL 25, 1945

Dad slowed in front of the entrance to Garney Castle. His wipers slapped back and forth in a blur, but couldn't keep the windshield clear of the sheeting rain. "See you upstairs," he said.

"You can't take the fire escape," I protested. "It'll be slick as glass. Besides, it's your first day back. You're still weak."

Before Dad could object, I reached across, turned off the engine and pulled the keys out of the ignition. "Sorry, Dad," I said. "I won't let you chance it."

"Give me the keys," Dad ordered.

I folded my arms across my chest and clenched the keys.

Dad sighed and gave in. "Okay, DB."

After we got out of the elevator, Dad headed straight for the studio. I went to the auditorium. As I strolled up the aisle looking for David, I saw about thirty people—old timers to little kids—milling about. A rumble of talking, singing and out-of-tune instruments bombarded my ears.

A set of five-year-old triplets with sausage curls dressed in blue and white sailor suits practiced a tap routine in the aisle. Just past them sat a rail-thin old man with bushy hair and a huge salt-and-pepper beard. He wore an old Army uniform larded with ribbons and medals. As I stepped over his outstretched legs, my eyes watered from mothball fumes. They didn't seem to bother him in the slightest.

I heard a hiss, squinted and saw a familiar face in the back row. David wore his usual outfit–Ike jacket and fatigues—but his cocky smile looked forced. I waved and hurried over to him.

As I settled in beside him, he tapped my arm with his fist.

"You alone?" I asked, looking around.

David shrugged. We stared ahead in silence. Not that there was much to look at; like most radio studios, this one was pretty drab.

The *Major Bowes' Original Amateur Hour* was a popular show even though its host, the Major, had a dull, dreary voice. Whenever he didn't like an act, he would bang a gong—at which point the humiliated performer was hustled offstage.

The audience loved it. I thought it was cruel.

Mr. Cody entered the studio accompanied by a short man with wavy black hair and a blue pinstriped suit. They crossed to a microphone, where Mr. Cody introduced the man as Ted Mack. He explained that Mr. Mack was there to judge the contestants.

Everyone clapped enthusiastically. Mr. Mack bowed modestly and sat next to Mr. Cody on a folding chair in the rear of the studio.

Dad's group plus Jim and Tessie Mae and Jennie the Colorado Cowgal were all there to back up the contestants. Dad said the hillbillies would hurt more than help, but he didn't want to get into an argument with Cody.

Jennie was six gorgeous feet tall. Tessie Mae, on the other hand, was short and dumpy. Her eyes and nose seemed too small for her face. She kept giving Jennie sour looks.

Tessie Mae's husband, Jim, had the ruddy good looks of a roughneck. One side of his mouth was always hitched up in a smirk that seemed to say, "Hey, girls! Look at me!" And from what I overheard Dad tell Mom, many did—which infuriated Tessie Mae to no end.

David fidgeted in his seat.

Dad had a short conversation with Mr. Cody and Mr. Mack, and walked over to the microphone. The audience hushed. "Thanks for coming, folks. Mr. Mack has asked me to remind you that all winners will be invited to New York to be on the *Amateur Hour*, all expenses paid."

Mr. Mack waved. The studio windows rattled from all the applause. Mr. Cody puffed up like a powder pigeon. Mr. Mack took out a fountain pen and rested a yellow tablet on his crossed legs. I felt David's body grow tense in his seat.

The old soldier tried out first. His specialty was whistling. He warbled away to "Let's All Sing Like the Birdies Sing." He actually sounded good; but halfway through the song, his false teeth flew out of his mouth and he couldn't finish.

A lady streetcar conductor from Sioux City followed. She carried a glass of water and announced she'd sing "Indian Love Call." Every time she got to the yodeling part, she took a sip of water and gargle-sang.

I tried my best not to laugh, but failed. Mr. Cody twitched uncomfortably in his seat. Mr. Mack tapped his pen on his pad and looked pained.

Finally, they called David. He strutted into the studio standing as tall as his short body would stretch. He crossed to Dad and whispered something in his ear. Dad nodded and said something to his men. David tugged the bottom of his Ike jacket, flashed a toothy smile and strolled up to the mike.

I crossed my fingers.

David tapped a four-beat countdown with his foot. Dad's group swung into a short intro. David turned to the audience and cradled the mike in his hands.

> *"You got to ac-cent-tchu-ate the positive,*
> *E-lim-in-ate the negative..."*

With Dad's group behind him, David sounded incredible. His voice was bold and brash, but sweet as honey, too. When he began snapping his fingers, the audience joined in. Dad and his men took turns improvising jazz riffs behind him.

David built up to a sassy finish. "No, don't mess with Mister In-Betweeeeeeeeen!"

The audience went wild. I clapped so hard my hands ached.

David and I suffered through the rest of the auditions. The triplet Shirley Temples went last, with an embarrassing version of "The Good Ship Lollipop."

Mr. Cody walked pompously to the microphone. "On behalf of WXAX and Mr. Mack, we'd like to thank all of you for trying out today. We wish we could pick all of you." He feigned disappointment. "But competition for the *Amateur Hour* is steep. I'm happy to announce that Mr. Mack has chosen one contestant to appear on the show."

Mr. Cody paused for dramatic effect. I could hear David's heart thumping.

"Let's give a big hand to...David Bacton!"

David jumped up with clenched fists held high in the air. I clapped with all my might. Even the disappointed contestants gave him a hearty round of applause.

At dinner, Dad raved about David. I glanced at Mom. I could tell by the look on her face that she sensed the envy in Dad's voice, too.

Around midnight, a tremendous clap of thunder shook my bed and woke me. Rain pummeled the roof with such fury I feared the ceiling might fall. It took me a while, but eventually I was able to go back to sleep.

CHAPTER 42

FRIDAY, APRIL 27, 1945

Mom and I were listening to Dad's show during breakfast when Gene Little broke in.

"We interrupt this program for an important announcement. The caissons supporting the Meredith Bridge are being eroded by torrential rain and flooding. It is in imminent danger of collapsing.

"An emergency crew of around a hundred Army Corps of Engineers and German POW volunteers are working feverishly to shore up the bank and divert the raging Missouri. If the bridge falls, it will block barge shipments of grain for months. Grain vital to the War effort. All schools will be closed today. Able-bodied men *are urged to report to the bridge to lend a hand.*

"Wait. This just in. A German POW working at the bridge site
has been swept away by the roiling waters..."

Fear gripped my stomach. I bolted up and ran out of the room.

Mom chased after me. "Where are you're going?" she demanded as I slipped on my yellow slicker and galoshes.

"I've got to see if Eric's there. Besides, they need help." Before she could stop me, I flew out the back door.

"Donnyboy!" Mom called. "Come back here this instant!"

Grasping the railing with both hands, I edged down the slippery back stairs.

"Please!" Mom screamed from the landing as I sped around the corner of the house.

I didn't reply.

Rushing water spilled over the curb and flooded the sidewalk. I felt awful about upsetting Mom, but I had to find out about Eric. I knew Mom would call Dad and have him try to intercept me, so I zigzagged through backstreets and alleyways.

Every time my feet hit the pavement, they squished like a washing machine. A fierce wind hurled stinging water darts at my face. I paused at the corner of West Fourth and Walnut. Looking toward the river, I could barely make out the bridge that was two blocks away.

Heading for the bridge, I noticed that all of the stores were closed. Only an occasional car or Army truck forded the flooded streets. As I slogged on, my thoughts were flooded by worries. *What would I do when I got to the river? What if Eric had drowned?*

The closer I got to the river, the more the wind whipped my slicker. The frigid rain poured under my hood and drenched my flannel shirt.

By the time I reached the bridge, I could see that huge chunks of concrete had broken away from the caissons—exposing the narrow iron skeletons inside.

At least a dozen Army trucks and Jeeps were scattered haphazardly on the street. Their flashing red lights reminded me of the first time I saw Eric, when his convoy had passed us on Pearl Street. While it had only been three months, it seemed like a lifetime ago.

I threaded my way through the vehicles.

Snatches of frantic conversations burst from the walkie-talkies in the MPs' hands. The MPs either didn't notice me or were too busy to bother.

At the crest of the riverbank, I stopped and looked out. Everything looked like liquid pewter. Only the jagged silhouette of trees on the Nebraska side of the river kept the water and the sky from blending together completely.

Ear-splitting sounds assaulted me from all sides. The howl of the wind. The clatter of the rain. The roar of the river. Pile drivers clanged away, beating posts into the river bottom. On the bank below, teams of POWs in grey ponchos tied wood slats together and stretched them along the riverbank to stop the earth from eroding.

I tried to pick out Eric. But between the blistering rain and the hoods shrouding their faces, they all looked like shimmering grey ghosts. I felt helpless and scared.

"Hey, kid!" a voice shouted.

I spun around. A black slicker with a big MP emblazoned on the chest plodded toward me. The rain was so thick, it took me several seconds before I recognized the man inside.

"Sergeant Atkins!" I waved, my spirits rising.

"You outta your gawdam mind?" the Sergeant yelled hoarsely. A miniature Niagara Falls cascaded from his hood. "This is one helluva bad cloud."

"Eric? Is he here?" I shouted.

Atkins nodded.

My heart almost stopped beating. "He wasn't...he didn't drown, did he?"

Atkins looked grim. "No. Was a guy named Ziggy. But the way things are going, it could be any one of 'em–anytime."

"Where's Eric?"

Atkins wiped the rain from his eyes and pointed to a team of POWs below. "There."

I started down the bank.

"Hold on!" Atkins grabbed my shoulder. "They ain't makin' mud pies down there, son. Those timbers are heavy as lead and full of splinters. To make matters worse, the bank's slicker than snot on a doorknob."

"I'll be careful."

"It's too risky. If the current picks up any more, that whole damn bridge could snap and tumble down on everybody here."

"I don't care!" I screamed. I wrestled free of Atkins's grasp and took off down the bank.

The Sergeant shook his head and called after me. "It's your funeral."

When I got to him, Eric was on his knees looping a thick rope around four heavy planks. He looked up at me in surprise. "Donnyboy!"

"I came to help."

Eric shook his head. "*Nein*. Much danger here." He tried to shoo me away with his hand.

A loud crack rifled through the air. I turned and saw one of the huge caissons supporting the bridge start to buckle.

"You need help," I shouted, pointing to the bridge.

Again, Eric waved me away. The three Germans who had donated blood—Diederick, Carsten and Bamber—trudged over to us.

"I'm not going," I announced stubbornly. "So you might as well tell me how I can help."

Reluctantly, Eric nodded. He explained they were riprapping—weaving timbers into flexible mats that would prevent the bank from been eaten away entirely. He decided the safest job for me was helping Diederick braid the planks together.

I watched as Diederick swiftly formed a slipknot between each timber. This allowed the mats to bend along with any bumps in the riverbank. When six planks were woven together, Diederick tied everything off with a double bowline.

"*Verstehen?*" Diederick asked.

"Think so," I responded warily. "But I'll need a little help at first."

Diederick patiently showed me how to weave the tough rope around the timbers and knot them off. I gave it a try. Splinters from the wood speared my hands. The sisal rope had knife-sharp threads that slashed my fingers. In spite of the burning pain in my hands, the pummeling rain, and the quicksand mud that sucked at my feet, I eventually got the hang of it. Soon all discomfort was eclipsed by the pride I felt from working with the other men. Whenever Diederick and I finished weaving a mat, Eric and the others came over to help slide it down the bank.

An hour passed. Then two. I shivered from the cold and dampness. Eric and the others had been working since six o'clock this morning. Their smiles faded from exhaustion. Fatigue shrouded their eyes.

Eric, Bamber and Carsten sloshed over to get the mat we'd just finished weaving. The mud sucked it down and it wouldn't budge. Diederick and I lined up to help. For leverage, I snaked my left hand around a rope loop and pressed my other hand against the timbers.

"*Ein...zwei...drei!*" Bamber grunted as we heaved against the mat. It barely moved an inch. We bent over and pushed twice as hard as before. This time the mat moved nearly a foot. We all took a deep breath and strained against it with all our might. It broke free and started sliding pell-mell toward the river's edge—dragging me with it.

"Let go!" Eric screamed.

"I can't!" I yelled back. My left hand was caught in the rope. Mud splashed into my eyes. I tried shoving my free hand into the muck as a brake, but it only skidded across the surface. I looked up. The heaving river rushed toward me.

Eight feet.

Five feet.

Three feet.

At the edge of the eroded bank, I spied a lone tree branch. I thrust out my free hand with all my might and grabbed it. My other hand jerked free from the rope and I skidded to a halt. The mat rocketed into the river and immediately sank with a baleful gurgle.

I grabbed the branch with both hands and heard a loud snap. I watched in dread as its stringy innards separated and broke one by one. Once again, I began slipping toward the water. I clawed at the mud, trying desperately to summon the energy to move up the bank. But the harder I fought to put some distance between myself and the river, the closer I got to the water. My chin dropped in the mud, and I prepared myself for the end.

Just as I was being sucked in, someone grabbed my arm just above the wrist. I looked up. Carsten! He lay flat on his belly. His outstretched arm gripped mine like a vise.

Behind him was Eric, also lying flat and holding onto Carsten's legs. Grasping Eric's legs was Diederick, whom Bamber had by the left foot. Bamber's other musclebound arm wrapped around a thick tree.

Slowly, the former acrobat inched our human chain toward him. His face turned purple. The veins in his neck became so swollen that I feared they might pop at any second.

Up, up Bamber pulled us. I felt the earth beneath me grow firmer. Eventually, I pressed my free hand into the ground and rose to my knees. Carsten smiled and let go of my arm. I crawled for several yards on my hands and knees, and slowly rose to my feet.

"*Danke, danke,*" I panted to my saviors. Carsten, Eric and Diederick sat on the ground straining to catch their breath. Bamber unwrapped himself from the tree trunk. His hands were raw and bleeding, but he gave me a big grin.

"Donnyboy! What in the name of God–?" I looked up and saw Dad bellowing down at me. I prayed he hadn't seen what had just happened.

Sergeant Atkins and Bob Lyle stood next to Dad. Lyle held a big press camera in one hand and gave us a thumbs up with the other. Rain gushed off the broad brim of Dad's cowboy hat. His boots were ankle deep in mud.

I waved meekly.

As we set off for home, a blinding white sun shone through holes in the clouds. Caught in the light, the river glistened like a giant mirror. Only occasional drops of rain fell from the trees. Wisps of steam floated up from my filthy, drenched clothing. Still, I couldn't remember a time when I'd felt happier.

Mom met us at the back door. When she saw me, she let out a scream and slapped my face. She'd never hit me before.

Suddenly, Mom's body went completely slack. She buckled to her knees, then hugged me so tightly I could hardly breathe. After what seemed like forever, her tears stopped. Her breathing slowed. She dropped her arms and rose. "Leave those filthy clothes here in the hallway," she sniffed, dabbing her eyes with the bottom of her apron. "I'll draw you a bath."

CHAPTER 43

SATURDAY, APRIL 28, 1945

When I sat down for breakfast, the newspaper was lying next to my cereal bowl. Bob Lyle had the lead story: *ENGINEERS, POWS, VOLUNTEERS SAVE BRIDGE.* Smack in the middle of the page was a photo of Eric, Diederick, Carsten, Bamber, and me. I don't know when Lyle snuck the shot. In his story, he made a big deal out of the five of us working together.

Fortunately, he didn't mention that I'd nearly drowned. Dad had scrawled *WOW!* next to the photo before he left for work.

Mom sat across from me smoking a cigarette and sipping her coffee. I could tell something was bothering her. She coughed nervously and said, "I'm sorry I slapped you."

"That's okay, Mom. I understand."

"You're growing up so fast."

I squeezed her hand.

"Even though you were foolish and could have been killed, I'm very proud of you." She flicked the corner of her eye with a finger. "However," she resumed her normal Mom tone and pointed under the sink. "Even heroes have to empty the trash."

I gave her a quick hug and got the wastebasket out from under the kitchen sink. I opened the back door and slapped a hand over my mouth to smother a scream.

A dead rat dangled from a cord tacked to the top doorjamb. The corpse had a bullet hole through its head and a swastika carved on its belly. Holding the rat by the cord, I took it down and closed the door quickly so Mom wouldn't see.

I dropped the poor animal into the wastebasket and carried it to the vacant lot. Finding a spot far away from Chaplin's grave, I dug a shallow hole and buried it.

A strange calmness came over me. Lester was asking for it. And I knew it wouldn't be long before we finally had it out.

"And now, live from Radio City Music Hall in New York, CBS presents the Amateur Hour with Major Edward Bowes."

The Major's monotone welcomed all the contestants and radio listeners.

"Tonight we have a shining array of talent. A plump plumber from Peoria who plumbs a mean trombone. A classy lassie from New Jersey who orchestrates a shipyard crane for a living and clinks water glasses to music for fun. And a diminutive young crooner from a small town with a sophisticated, big city voice."

I sat on the floor next to the radio. Mom and Dad leaned forward on the couch.

The Major spun the Wheel of Fortune. *"Now who'll be first? Round and round she goes, and where she stops nobody knows..."*

Click-click-click...click...click...click...

The wheel stopped.

"Miss Amelia Montrose, the Queen of Clinks."

I groaned.

The band started up and Miss Montrose clinked water glasses to "I'm Looking Over a Four Leaf Clover." Everything sounded fine for a while, but for some reason the band started speeding up. Miss Montrose raced to keep up with them. Her clinks became clangs, and the clangs gave way to the shattering of glasses—followed by the whoosh of running water.

The Major gonged Miss Montrose to a halt. The audience roared. I could just make out her sobs as she was led off the stage. I swore I'd never listen to another Major Bowes show again.

David was next. I lay on the floor with my chin resting on my hands. I could feel my pulse pounding as the Major asked David to name his favorite singer.

"That's easy, Major Bowes. It's 'The Voice,' Frank Sinatra. He's my idol." He sounded like a puppet.

"Well, David," the Major crowed, *"The Voice' got his big break right here on this very show—as have so many of today's most celebrated performers."*

"Gee, I hope it works for me too, Major."

I knitted my eyebrows. "That doesn't sound like David at all."

"He's reading a script," Dad said. "And a bad one at that."

"Well, I hope they didn't script his singing," said Mom.

The orchestra played a sweeping intro. David began in a voice so low I had to strain to hear him.

"If...I...loved...you,
Time and again I would try to say..."

Dad shot me a knowing smile. "Hold on. I think he's got something in mind."

David's voice grew stronger, hypnotic—almost drawing me inside the radio. As the song continued, his voice soared way out in front of the band—commanding, yet tender and sweet. Mom's eyes filled. Dad sat with his hands folded, a faraway look on his face.

David and the orchestra soared to a thrilling crescendo. Shivers danced up my back. Abruptly, the musicians stopped playing. My heart caught in my chest.

In the sweetest voice I'd ever heard, David finished all alone in a whisper:

"How I loved you,
If...I...loved...you."

The radio fell silent. None of us spoke.

Just as I started to worry that the audience didn't like David, they exploded with cheers and applause. Mom and I clapped along with them. Dad just sat there, his lips crinkled up in a funny smile. I looked at him expectantly. He didn't look back.

After what seemed like an eternity, Dad turned to me. "You know, DB."

"What, Dad?"

"That David's one helluva hot cat."

I burst out laughing.

Mom frowned. "Is this some kind of inside joke?"

Neither of us replied.

CHAPTER 44

SUNDAY, APRIL 29, 1945

Alice called this morning and asked if I could come over and see her costume. I said there might be a problem, but I'd check with Mom and call her back. Mom had grounded me for a week because I went to the river.

It took a lot of cajoling, but Mom finally gave in. "Put on your good blue trousers and white dress shirt," she said, raising her hands in exasperation. "I'll drop you off."

I rang the Codys' intimidating front door bell. After several seconds, the door opened. I gulped. Mrs. Cody stood in the doorway dressed like Madame Chiang Kai-shek. "Donnyboy!" she spread her arms. "The hero arrives."

My face burned. "If you're talking about the story in the paper, it really exaggerated things."

"Don't be modest." She took the vase of white tulips Mom had armed me with. "Oh, how lovely! Come in."

Walking behind Mrs. Cody, I noticed two shiny black sticks poking out of her red hair. Her white silk jacket had an ornate dragon embroidered across the back in gold thread.

"Mom said to say hello."

"Such a lovely woman. Do thank her for me." Her wide black pants billowed as she strode across the marble floor, revealing glittering gold slippers on her feet.

I stopped. "Mrs. Cody, am I intruding? Are you getting ready for a party or something?"

"No, no," Mrs. Cody laughed. She turned around and gave me a smile generally saved for idiots or very small children. "Why?"

"Oh," I swallowed. "It's just that you look so nice and all..."

She waved her cigarette holder. "Just a lazy Sunday at home."

The conversation ended in an awkward silence.

Coco, Alice's black Scottie, scampered across the marble floor, stopped at my feet and rolled over onto her back. I bent over and rubbed her distended tummy. "When are the puppies due?"

Mrs. Cody set the vase down on a glass table. "Any minute now."

"I bet you're excited."

"Alice is," she replied dryly.

"Alice wanted to show me her Statue of Liberty costume."

"Dame Liberty is waiting upstairs in the library." Mrs. Cody pointed her cigarette holder at the curved staircase. "Please hurry up before her arm drops off from holding her torch."

I knocked at the library door.

"Just a minute," Alice called out.

I heard the rustling of fabric. The scrape of a chair. "All right," she called breathlessly. "Come in."

The heavy door swung open slowly. At the far end of the room, bright white sunlight streamed through sheer white curtains. It illuminated Alice in a heavenly glow.

Head held high, she stood perfectly still on a spindleback chair. A silky white toga flowed in pleats from her shoulders. It clung teasingly to her breasts and hips and pooled at her feet. Her right hand hoisted a *papier-mâché* torch with a red cellophane flame.

The sight took my breath away.

The statue shifted uneasily. "What do you think?"

"I...you...it's amazing," I gasped.

Alice relaxed and lifted the hem of her skirt. "Come here and help me down." I rushed to the chair and grasped her hand as she stepped to the floor. We ended up inches from one another. Her right hand lingered on my shoulder.

Neither of us moved. A thousand butterflies fluttered inside my stomach. My mouth became too dry to risk talking. Slowly, she circled both of her arms around my neck and pressed against me. Her breath had the sweet scent of Juicy Fruit gum.

My heart raced. I hardly risked breathing. The only thought in my mind was that I wanted to stand like this forever.

After a long moment, she stepped back and led me over to the couch. Once we were seated, she lifted her eyes to mine and gazed at me adoringly. "I saw the paper yesterday. You were so brave."

"Not really. Eric and the other POWs did all the tough stuff."

"I don't believe you," she chided, pulling out the folds in her dress. "Do you think I look too fat in this? Agna insisted on using tons of material. Honestly, you'd think she runs things around here."

"Gosh, no," I assured her. "You look like that statue of Venus, only with arms and a head."

She made a face. "You're making fun of me."

I insisted that I wasn't. After an agonizing silence, I cleared my throat. "Alice. There's something I need to talk to you about."

She looked fearful. "About us?"

I felt my face flush. "No, about Lester."

"He's a cretin."

"Yeah. But he might be dangerous."

"Nonsense."

I told her about everything he'd done, from painting the swastika on our driveway to hanging the dead rat over our back door. "Having somebody play a German on the float might send him over the edge."

Alice looked alarmed. "I couldn't stand it if something happened to you."

I shook my head. "It's not me I'm worried about. It's you."

"Oh, Donny. You're so gallant." She wrinkled her nose. "But don't worry about Lester. He's all bark and no bite."

"I'm not so sure."

Alice sat up straight. "Gosh, I just realized something. We still don't have anyone to play the German."

"There's still time. I'm sure someone will step up."

"Don't bet on it." Alice played with the folds in her dress. "And since Germany's supposed to surrender any second now, there's a good chance we'll run out of time." Alice's eyes twinkled. "But I have an idea." She tapped a finger on my chest. "Who would be the ideal person to play a German?"

"I don't know. Who?"

"A *real* German, of course!"

"But we don't have any real Germans in class."

"Forget the class." Alice's eyes grew wide with excitement. "I'm talking about Eric!"

I almost choked. "That's impossible. The School Board would never go for that. Neither would the Army, or even Eric himself."

Alice folded her hands confidently. "Grandfather can handle the

School Board and the Army. As far as Eric goes, I'm sure he'll do it if *you* ask him."

"Hold on," I protested, and edged back against the couch arm. "I could never just put him on the spot like that."

Her face slackened in despair.

Suddenly, I was struck by a foolproof way out. "Tell you what," I said, scooching closer to Alice. "If you can talk the Senator into clearing the way with the School Board and the Army, I'll ask Eric."

Alice protested. I held firm.

"Well, okay," she surrendered.

CHAPTER 45

MONDAY, APRIL 30, 1945

It seemed like progress was being made on the float. Billy grew tired of me badgering him, and finally agreed to participate. When the class heard that, everyone who had held out agreed to take part. Everyone, that is, except Lester and his cronies.

Just before the final bell rang, Miss Morris walked over to Lester's desk. "Wouldn't you like to do something on the float?" she asked.

"Sure," Lester scowled at me. "Line up all the dirty Krauts and their buddies here, and mow 'em all down. Just like they did my brother."

His words felt like bullets. So that's why he had it in for me. The combination of Lester's revelation and the worry I already felt about having to ask Eric to participate left me in a sour mood. I avoided everyone after class was dismissed and went straight home. No one was there. Mom had her weekly Bridge game at Darrel's house.

I poured a glass of milk, got two oatmeal raisin cookies out of the cookie jar and turned on the radio. I thought listening to *Jack Armstrong* might take my mind off things. But instead of a harrowing adventure about "the All-American Boy," I heard the smoky voice of Edward R. Murrow.

> *"...I repeat, it is now confirmed that Chancellor Adolph Hitler of Germany is dead."*

I spewed milk all over myself.

> *"He and his wife of one day, Eva Braun, committed suicide in a bunker below the Reich Chancellery at approximately three thirty this afternoon Berlin time. The cause of death is thought to be a gunshot wound to the head or possibly cyanide poisoning. Soviet forces are battling their way to the center of the city where the Chancellery is located. The cheering you hear in the background is taking place everywhere here in the streets of London..."*

I slumped into the chair feeling shell-shocked. When the news finally sunk in, I should have started jumping up and down. But I couldn't. All I could see were images of tortured American soldiers and Eric's dead mother and sister.

CHAPTER 46

TUESDAY, MAY 1, 1945

I said goodbye to Mom and was about to bound down the porch steps when I saw it. Perfectly balanced on the top railing was a woven paper basket overflowing with orange marigolds, purple pansies and butter yellow daffodils. My nose filled with airy, sweet perfume. Whoever made the basket must have spent hours on it. Every strip of pink and lavender construction paper matched precisely, and there were no paste stains anywhere.

A folded yellow card on a red cord hung from the basket's handle. "*To D.C.*" was printed on the outside. I flipped the card open.

HAPPY MAY DAY!
GUESS WHO?

It was the same flowery handwriting that was on my Valentine's Day card.

"Cleo?" I mused with vague disappointment.

To avoid getting the third degree from Mom, I hid the basket in the garage. I'd decide what to do with it after school.

At school, everyone was jubilant over Hitler's death. Especially Lester.

"Even though the War's not quite over, I'm told we can start decorating this Friday outside Garney Castle," Miss Morris announced. "Melvin, do you think your father can drop off his flatbed then?"

Melvin nodded.

"Shirley, can you get your tractor there, too?"

"Think so. I'll check with Pa," she replied.

"Great. Everyone who's taking part, let's meet right after school Friday by the fire escape."

Lester rolled his eyes and shrank down in his seat.

All day I kept glancing at Cleo, searching for some sign that she'd left me the basket. Nothing. She kept checking her lipstick and hair in her compact and gazing adoringly at Billy. It boggled my mind. Cleo must have left the basket. Was her display of affection for Billy just a cover-up?

Alice and I stayed after class with Miss Morris to double-check all the things we'd need for Friday. Pencil and tablet at the ready, Alice suggested we write down all the things we knew we had.

"Agna and I picked up all the bunting," she began.

"Senator Garney's having the banner made," Miss Morris added.

"Darrel's getting me the Uncle Sam costume," I said.

We ended up with a long list. "I think that covers everything," Miss Morris said, "except someone to play the German."

Alice spoke up confidently. "Donny and I are working on that. I'm sure we'll have someone real soon." Earlier, Alice had told me her grandfather would be back from Washington on Friday. She said she'd talk to him then. I felt grateful for the reprieve.

Miss Morris turned to me. "Do you have someone in mind?"

Sweat poured from under my arms. "We can't say just yet," I hedged. "But we'll know soon."

Miss Morris raised her eyebrows. "If you say so. But if you can't come up with someone soon, we'll just have to go without a German."

I nodded and started to leave.

Alice grabbed my arm. "Wait. We still haven't discussed my idea."

"What idea?" Miss Morris asked, conspicuously eyeing the clock.

"The white doves," Alice said, closing her eyes. "You know, circling around my torch."

I started to rub my chin as though I were contemplating her idea. In reality, I was just trying to hide my grin.

"It's an interesting idea," Miss Morris said politely, "but I'm afraid it wouldn't work."

Alice stuck out her lower lip. "Why not?"

"First of all, where would we get them?" Miss Morris tapped her fingers impatiently. "And even if we could, how would we keep them from flying away?"

Alice fell silent.

"Darrel's got some trained pigeons," I offered. "Maybe those could work?"

Alice rolled her eyes.

I vowed never to open my mouth again.

Miss Morris started clearing her desk. "Look," she said sympathetically. "If you find a way to make it work, I'm all for it." She held out her hand. "Can I have your notes?"

Alice tore the page from her tablet. But instead of giving it to Miss Morris, she held it up to me. "Want to check it, Donny?"

I was still smarting from my *faux pas* about the pigeons, so I just shook my head. Alice thrust the paper right under my nose. "Check it! Can't you read my *handwriting*?"

I certainly could. And it made me realize what an idiot I'd been. "Criminey!" I nearly shouted.

Miss Morris's head jerked back. "What is it?"

"Uh, nothing," I stammered. "Something just hit me, that's all."

Out of the corner of my eye, I could see Alice looking smug. Miss Morris took out her compact and waved us away. "Skedaddle you two, I've got a date. And Happy May Day."

Alice and I walked down the empty hallway in silence. Just before we reached the front doors, I pulled her into the shadows beneath the staircase. "I never, ever dreamed it was you."

"What do you mean?" she teased.

I scuffed my shoe on the floor. "The Valentine. And the May Basket this morning."

A ray of golden sunlight splashed across her face.

"I thought they were from Cleo," I said morosely.

"I figured," Alice said with a snort.

I took her soft hands in mine and squeezed them. "But I'm so glad they're from you. They're the best presents I've ever had. I never dreamed you'd send them to me. I—I thought you hated me."

Her face softened. "You're right, but wrong at the same time." She took a breath. "From the first day we met, you scared me."

I cringed. "No wonder. I threw up on you."

She shook her head. "Not because of that. You see, until you came along I was pretty much the best at everything. Best student. Best manners. Best dressed."

"You still are."

"No," she said plaintively. "You're way smarter. You've lived in all kinds of interesting places. And you even dress swell."

I grimaced. "Except for those short pants."

Alice laughed. "They showed off your nice legs." She turned serious. "But the thing that scared me the most was how sweet and open you were. I've never let myself be that way."

I put my arms around her waist, just below her breasts. "You've got lots of things better than me."

She blushed. Electricity crackled between us. She tilted her head back. Her moist Cupid's bow mouth beckoned like a magnet.

I closed my eyes and leaned in.

"'Night, kids!" Miss Morris's cheery voice stopped me cold. "'Night, Miss Morris," Alice replied.

The front doors opened. They creaked closed.

We kissed.

CHAPTER 53

FRIDAY, MAY 4, 1945

We all met beside the fire escape at Garney Castle. As expected, every eighth grader showed up except for Lester and his hangers-on. Agna drove up in the Codys' Lincoln Continental. Alice got out of the passenger side and asked for help unloading the bunting. I made a beeline for the car.

In spite of her thick glasses, Shirley did a masterful job of threading her red Farmall tractor and Mel's flatbed through a maze of other floats in the field.

"Wow! Imagine how great you'd be if you could actually *see*?" Billy shouted.

Shirley gave him a hex sign.

The air was suddenly heavy with the scent of gardenias. With a deafening gum crack, Cleo slinked toward us in a low-cut red dress and matching red high heels. Her dress was slit up the side, revealing black fishnet stockings. A black comb with rhinestones held her thick brown hair in a high pile. Her face looked like a Technicolor movie.

She strode right past me and sidled up to Billy. He let out a low wolf whistle. Pete crowded next to them. Miss Morris walked over. "Ahem," she coughed. "I assume this is your costume for the float?"

Cleo fluttered her long fake eyelashes. "Uh-huh."

Miss Morris nodded. "Well, we're here to decorate—and your costume could get trashed. I hope you brought some regular clothes?"

Cleo reluctantly held up a Mode O'Day bag.

Miss Morris looked relieved. "Does anyone know if there's a ladies room around here?"

I pointed to the top floor. "The station has one. Cleo can go around front and take the elevator."

"What's wrong with the fire escape?" Billy asked. Someone from the station had just scuttled up it.

I shook my head. "It's pretty rickety. I wouldn't chance it."

Billy took Cleo's arm. "That makes it more fun," he chuckled, guiding her toward the structure. "You game?"

Cleo nodded enthusiastically.

"You'd be safer going around front," Miss Morris called after them.

Cleo slipped off her high heels and quick-stepped up the fire escape stairs with Billy. I closed my eyes. Every rattle sent shivers through me. When I opened my eyes, they were entering the studio door.

It took about an hour and a half to put up all the bunting. The red, white and blue scallops made Melvin's beat-up flatbed look almost presidential. Alice and I worked side by side as often as we could without making it look like we were trying to.

Walking home, I felt content. The other kids were excited about the float. Alice seemed to like me. Life was good. When I turned onto Pearl Street, something whizzed by my ear and clattered to the sidewalk. A rock.

Two others whooshed past. Then one hit me hard in the middle of the back.

I spun around.

Lester's head bobbed down behind a tall hedge. He wasn't alone. Another head dropped down right after his. This one had carrot red hair. It took all the strength I had, but I swallowed my anger and continued home.

I didn't say anything to Mom and Dad about the episode with Lester and Bo. No sense in worrying them. At nine thirty, after we'd listened to *Suspense* and *This Is Your FBI*, I yawned and said goodnight.

The phone rang.

Dad answered. "It's for you," he said, pointing at me.

"Hello?"

"Donny!" Alice said excitedly. "Grandfather *loves* the idea!"

The news hit me like an electric shock.

"He said it fit right in with the big job he's being nominated for."

"Did he tell you what it was?"

Alice hesitated. "No. But it sounds very, very important."

I lowered my voice to a whisper. "He still has to clear it with the School Board and the Army, you know."

"He says he'll handle that tomorrow."

My shoulders sagged under a gargantuan weight. "Well, I guess it comes down to me now."

"Marge will arrange a meeting with Eric right after school Monday."

I went mute.

"Aren't you excited?"

"Yeah, sure. It's just...everything's happening so fast."

"Oh, and one other thing. Be sure and listen to Jolly Joe tonight."

"Why?"

"Just listen."

Click.

Mom gave me the third degree about Alice's phone call. I told her it was all just float-related and escaped to my room.

Jolly Joe didn't come on until after the eleven o'clock news. I considered sleeping until then, but feared I wouldn't wake up. To keep the folks from suspecting anything, I switched off my light.

As it turned out, I couldn't have slept if I wanted to. Just when everything seemed to be going right, all kinds of problems were popping up. Dealing with Lester was bad enough. But now Bo was back in the picture. And I had no idea how I could convince Eric to be a sitting duck on our float.

I checked my Big Ben clock. The radium dials glowed ten twenty-eight. Kicking off my covers, I tiptoed to the door and peered through the keyhole. Dad was asleep on the couch, his head in Mom's lap. Mom was reading one of her *Reader's Digest Condensed Books.*

I had to get my mind off my worries. But with Mom up, I didn't dare turn on my lamp. By chance, a bright splash of moonlight shone through my window, forming a well-lit pool on my floor.

I scoured my bookshelf, and finally pulled out an old *Action Comics.* Sprawling on the floor, I devoured the parts I usually skipped—like the short, short story in the middle and all the mouseprint ads.

I learned that I could make big money in my spare time by selling birdseed. And that I could keep Bo from kicking sand in my face at the beach by sending away for a Charles Atlas course. I flexed my arm to check my muscle. The tiny bulge confirmed that I could use Mr. Atlas's help. I made a mental note to see if I had enough money saved to order the course.

The moon was enveloped by a cluster of black clouds, and the room went dark. I glanced up at the clock: ten forty-one. I started doing push-ups in anticipation of taking on Lester and Bo. At fifteen, my arms turned to rubber.

The clock finally crept up to eleven o'clock. I turned on my combination radio-record player, keeping the sound real low. WXAX news came on. German troops in Italy had surrendered to the Allies. Most of the remaining German soldiers in Berlin had surrendered to the Soviets. But there were still pockets of Nazis who refused to give up.

"Now stay tuned for our sensational new record show, Jolly Joe!" the announcer said at the end of the newscast.

I leaned into the speaker.

Jolly Joe's lively introduction was sung over Glenn Miller's recording of the "American Patrol" march.

"It's Jolly Joe at five-seven-oh
And eleven-oh-five each night!"

The music faded and Joe's voice came on, all breezy and syncopated. His huskiness suggested something forbidden—and fun.

"Hi, all you cats and gals. Jolly Joe here, and what I really wanna know is, are you ready to swing? Clear everything out of the way, cause we're gonna get the joint jumpin' with 'Juke Box Saturday Night.'"

Joe followed with "Take the 'A' Train," "Perdido" and "Straighten Up And Fly Right." I checked the clock. Eleven thirty-five.

I started to wonder if Alice had just been teasing me. Or maybe something had gone wrong. Either way, my exhaustion began to get the better of me. I reached for the off switch.

Joe's voice stopped me. *"Now here's a special dedication from an infatuated lass to her shy boyfriend, who's got the softest lips in Farmington."*

My fingers dropped from the knob.

Joe made a loud kissing sound. *"A wants D to know it had to be you."*

I fell into a blissful trance as the intro to "It Had To Be You" poured out of the speakers. When the song ended, I switched off the radio and floated to my bed.

My reverie was cut short by a blinding flash of lightning right outside my window. Thunder immediately rattled the bed. All of my fears about Bo and Lester and my impending meeting with Eric came rushing back like the rain bombarding my window.

CHAPTER 54

SATURDAY, MAY 5, 1945

David called from New York this morning. By the tone of his voice, I could tell he'd won. He said he got so many votes that the Major hired him to join one of his traveling shows right away.

Happy as I was for him, the news left me a little blue. "Will I get to see you before you go?" I asked hesitantly.

"You betcha," he reassured me. "I have to come back to get my things and tie up some loose ends. 'Cause I'm not quite sixteen, Ma's got to sign a paper sayin' it's okay for me to travel on my own. Ben won't let her do it unless I pay her. But what the heck."

"Can't wait to see you."

"Same here. Oh, and be sure to tell your pop thanks for all the help, okay?"

Dad was at work. Mom had gone shopping. I went outside looking for something to do. The Dakota delivery boy cycled by and tossed a paper onto the front walk. "It's an extra," he called out when he saw my surprised expression. I read the headline and almost keeled over: *TRU-MAN NOMINATES GARNEY FOR FRENCH AMBASSADOR*. Underneath was a picture of the Senator shaking hands with the President.

The story said it wasn't a sure thing for the Senator. He had to be confirmed by the Senate, and many Senators didn't believe he had enough experience for the job. Garney's scoffing response: *Bring them on!*

I laughed as it sounded just like the feisty Senator. But my mirth quickly faded as I read the last line of the story:

Garney confirmed his appointment could force him to sell radio station WXAX.

The instant Dad came through the door, I peppered him with questions about the possible sale. Mom joined in my concern.

Dad pooh-poohed us. "The station makes so much money, whoever buys it would be nuts to change things."

That seemed to relieve Mom. Not me.

CHAPTER 55

MONDAY, MAY 7, 1945

Marge called just before I left for school this morning. My meeting with Eric was set for four o'clock.

Mom asked why Marge called and I told her. Her eyes widened and she set her jaw. "Why didn't you talk this over with us? Why do you keep going off half-cocked?"

"I didn't go off half-cocked!" I protested. "Having Eric play the German was Alice's idea. She's had the Senator clear the way with the School Board and the Army. But nothing's set in stone yet. I still have to ask Eric if he'll do it, and I doubt he will."

Mom threw up her hands in surrender. "Since you're going, I might as well bake some cookies for Eric and his friends. Stop by before you head over."

I ran all the way to school, anxious to see Alice before class started. I didn't get there until a minute before the morning bell. I caught up with her outside the classroom and told her Marge had set up my meeting with Eric. She bubbled over with glee. I told her not to get her hopes up since I couldn't imagine why Eric would want to do it. She patted my cheek and said she knew I could convince him.

Darrel brought the Uncle Sam costume to class. It was made of worn red, white and blue satin. There were a few moth holes in the pants, but Miss Morris said no one would see them from a distance. The costume included a flattened star-spangled top hat and a scraggly white beard.

Miss Morris asked me to try it on. I tried to refuse, but everyone insisted. I took the costume to the boys room, praying it would be empty. It was.

I was shocked by how well the costume fit. The sleeves were a little long and the waist had to be taken in, but Mom could easily fix that. I slipped on the beard, popped open the top hat and glanced in the mirror. I looked like a sorry version of Uncle Sam in the "I Want You" poster.

I peeked out the door to make sure the coast was clear, and darted back to the classroom. To my surprise, the other kids applauded when they saw me. And I don't think they were just being polite.

Outside, the temperature had climbed into the seventies. Billy, Pete and I sat on the ground with our backs against the wall of the schoolhouse and ate our lunches. Alice and I kept looking at each other from across the schoolyard. I wished Billy and Pete would go play kickball or something so I could talk to her about the Jolly Joe show, but they didn't budge.

I approached the guardhouse with a tin full of cookies and a stomach full of dread. Sergeant Atkins and Corporal Taylor sat in their Jeep just inside the gate. I climbed aboard.

"What's in the tin?" Atkins nodded at the round red container in my lap.

"Cookies for Eric."

Atkins pried off the top with his thumb and took one. "Chocolate chip! My favorite. Have one, Taylor."

"Just one each," I admonished, snapping the lid shut.

We entered a Quonset hut stuffed with soldiers and POWs milling around two lines of desks that went at least five-deep. The place hummed with the ringing of telephones, the clicking of typewriters and the shouts of MPs shuttling paperwork between desks. For the first time, I saw wrinkles in the MPs' uniforms. Some had even loosened their ties.

I looked at Atkins. "What's up?"

"Big things in Berlin."

Eric sat at a desk wearing earphones and pecking at a drab, olive-colored typewriter. When Atkins and I approached, he stopped and lifted the earphones off his head. I noticed bags under his eyes and blond stubble on his face.

He smiled, rose stiffly and extended his hand.

What small nerve I had mustered flew right out the window. "You look real busy. Maybe I'd better come back another time."

Atkins shook his head. "Eric's been at it forty-eight hours straight. He could use a break."

I held the tin out to Eric. "Mom baked you and your friends some cookies."

Eric took them gratefully. He pried off the lid and offered the tin to Atkins and Taylor. In spite of my dirty look, they helped themselves. Eric took one, put the tin down and called out in a loud voice: "Home-baked cookies here from *Frau* Cook!"

The soldiers descended like a pack of starving wolves. Several men crammed one cookie in their mouth and stuffed another in their pocket.

I slid my hand over the open tin. "That's enough. Leave some for Eric and his friends." The men backed off unhappily.

Only the bottom layer of cookies and a few broken pieces remained.

"Sorry," I said, handing the tin back to Eric.

Eric smiled. "Still plenty for me and the others. Everyone here exhausted. Deserve cookie."

"Be back here in fifteen minutes," Atkins barked. As he nudged us toward the door, he shamelessly snagged a broken piece from the tin in Eric's hands.

Outside, a warm breeze bathed us in its sweet, heady scent. Eric sniffed the air. I led him to a bush with tiny white blossoms. "It's jasmine. Smells like perfume, but only lasts a couple of weeks."

Eric pushed his nose into the petals and inhaled deeply. His face eased. We strolled down a dirt path. He laced his fingers together and stretched his arms high over his head.

"I guess the War's almost over," I said, breaking the silence.

He nodded.

"I guess that means you'll be going home soon, right?"

His eyes dropped. "*Nein.* Today message come. One, maybe two years before prisoners go back."

"So you'll be here longer?" I tried to keep the hope out of my voice.

He shook his head. "Bridge now safe. Soon ve go to big camp at Altoona. There ve vait."

We stopped at a bench and sat. I screwed up my courage. "I need a favor, Eric. A big one."

Eric looked at me receptively.

I pulled Alice's drawing out of my pocket. "Farmington is having a victory parade. This drawing shows our class float. Alice drew it."

Eric chuckled.

I reddened and pointed to the drawing. "The idea is to have kids dressed up like people from all over the world. They'll move in a continuous circle to shake hands with Uncle Sam and the Statue of Liberty. It's hard to read, but that banner says *Peace, Let's Shake On It.*"

Eric nodded his approval.

My finger moved to the left. "This guy in the *lederhosen* is supposed to be a German." I took a quick breath. "We thought it would be keen if a real German played him." I swallowed. "You."

Eric looked stunned.

"Senator Garney's cleared it with the Army and the School Board." I tried to garner up Alice's enthusiasm. "You'd be perfect!"

Eric stared into space for a long time. Then he sighed and laid a hand on my shoulder. "Your idea is *gut*. I like. But me, I vould feel like monkey with organ grinder. You, your friends, all much younger. Surely someone could play German."

I shook my head morosely. "Nope. We tried everything. You're our only hope."

"*Attention! Achtung!*" A raspy voice boomed from the camp loud-speakers, piercing our eardrums. Eric and I jerked our heads toward the sound. The voice spoke in English first, then German.

"*Allied HQ European Theater reports the German government has surrendered. Repeat, Germany has surrendered. General Alfred Jodl, Chief of the Operations Staff for the German High Command, has signed unconditional surrender documents. All forces under German control must cease operations by twenty-three hundred hours Central European Time tomorrow. The War in Europe is over.*"

A shock wave hit the camp. Scarcely a sound was heard for nearly a minute. Then all hell broke loose among the GIs. They hooted and hollered and honked their car horns. Men on KP streamed out of the mess hall, banging on pots and pans.

Not twenty yards from us, a POW work party stood paralyzed. Some looked crushed, others perplexed. I glanced at Eric. His face betrayed a host of conflicting emotions. I heard mumbled prayers. Muted curses.

Sighs of relief.

To my surprise, one of the POWs began to quietly clap. Then another. Soon the entire work crew. It didn't sound like the raucous clapping of approval. Nor was it the bitter applause of defiance. Rather, it was the sound of gratitude—gratitude for the end of suffering, and the hope of better things to come.

I shared their feelings. A hand gently touched my shoulder. I looked up. Eric's eyes were blurred with tears. "I vill join you on float."

CHAPTER 56

TUESDAY, MAY 8, 1945

Alice and I told Miss Morris before school that Eric had agreed to play the German.

She turned ghostly white. "Mr. Chester will have apoplexy," she groaned.

Alice reminded her that the Senator was now sponsoring the float, and had cleared everything with the School Board and the Army. When the color came back to Miss Morris's cheeks, she said it was a very courageous idea. But she suggested we don't tell anyone until the day of the parade.

Afraid of what Lester might do when he heard the news, I convinced Alice to agree.

Everyone was too jubilant to get much schoolwork done. Even Lester seemed happy. Again, Miss Morris asked him to be on the float. He bragged that he had a more important job helping the Veterans of Foreign Wars stage their fireworks display after the parade.

Alice slipped me a note telling me to meet her after school for a surprise at Seratoma Park.

Just before lunch, Mr. Chester announced we were dismissed for the day. Everyone cheered and cleared the classroom. Chester shot me his usual sour look. I shivered, imagining how enraged he'd become once he got the news about Eric.

Billy and Pete corralled me in the cloakroom and asked me to come fool around with them. I declined, offering some lame excuse about having to help Mom wash windows. They called me a mama's boy, but I held my ground. Finally, they left me alone.

I stalled until Alice left. Then I stealthily made my way to the park. Alice stood at the entrance, her notebook clutched to her breast and an angelic smile on her lips. My heart careened against my ribs. "What's your surprise?" I panted.

She snuggled her arm in mine. "Agna's baked a German chocolate cake. Have you ever tried it?"

"No."

"It's out of this world." She pulled on my arm. "Let's go. Hurry!"

"Hey, Cookie!" A familiar voice sent shivers down my spine. I spun around and saw Billy and Pete sidling up to where Alice and I were standing.

"Thought you had to get home and help your poor Ma wash windows?" Billy mocked.

Pete joined in, guffawing. "Don't wanna be late!"

My face turned scarlet. "Cut it, will you?" I searched for a suitable excuse. "I, uh, just remembered I had to tell Alice something and..."

"Don't pay any attention to those ignoramuses," Alice snapped, tugging on my arm.

"Ooo, don't let us get between you and the ole ball and chain," Billy smirked.

"Yeah!" Pete added.

I tugged my arm free from Alice. "Look, there's nothing going on between us, so—"

"Donny!" Alice's lower lip trembled at my betrayal.

"It had to be yoooouuuuu!" Pete crooned, hugging himself and making googly eyes.

"We're just friends!" I whined.

Alice's eyes blazed. "Are you going to come home with me or not?"

"Well, I did tell my Mom I'd help her," I lied unconvincingly.

"Fine!" she cut me short. "And just so you know, *Donnyboy* Cook, I *hate* you!" She stormed off.

I called after her, but she only started running.

From the way her body trembled, I could see that she was sobbing.

"Damn it!" I hissed, pounding my thighs and feeling like Benedict Arnold.

"Hey, we were just kidding," Billy said contritely.

"Yeah, it was only a joke," Pete chimed in.

"Well, it sure didn't sound like one," I snapped. "With friends like you, who needs enemies?" I waved them off in disgust and started to head home.

"Don't be sore, Cookie!" Billy called after me. "I didn't know you liked her so much."

I didn't know either, until now.

CHAPTER 57

WEDNESDAY, MAY 9, 1945

Ever since Monday, Alice had acted like I was dead to her. I telephoned three times to apologize, but she wouldn't take my calls. I avoided Pete and Billy like the plague. I felt as lonely and alone as I did when I first came to Farmington.

The second school ended, I headed for home. Billy and Pete ran up to me. "C'mon, Cookie. We got a surprise for you."

"You spoiled my last surprise. Alice was gonna give me German chocolate cake."

Billy punched my arm. "You need to let bygones be bygones," he cajoled. "You'll get over her. Plenty of fish in the sea."

Pete jiggled his eyebrows. "I think Cleo likes you."

I gave him a dirty look. "Open your eyes, Pete. She's moved on to Billy."

Billy snorted. "Broads are a dime a dozen. Come on. This'll cheer you up."

I didn't have the will to argue anymore, so I tagged along.

We entered Seratoma Park. A line of grey cement picnic tables hugged the ground like giant turtles. In the middle of the park was a wide dirt playground with swings and teeter-totters.

Looming over the park was the new Farmington water tower. It looked like a big white egg held up by four spindly, fifty-foot legs. In the center of the egg was a blue triangle with *CD* painted in white. The initials stood for "Civil Defense."

Billy stopped beside a skinny metal ladder at the base of one of the legs and shook it. The only support was a brace at the bottom and one at the top. It gave me the wimwams.

Billy tilted back his head. "See that plank running around the bottom of the tank? That's for CD Wardens so they can look for enemy planes." He uttered a derisive laugh. "Enemy planes in Farmington?"

Pete doubled over laughing. In spite of my foul mood, I couldn't help laughing, too. Billy grabbed a rung on the ladder and hoisted himself up. "C'mon, let's check it out."

My legs turned to jelly. "No thanks."

"The view's stupendous," Billy urged. "You can make it. It's easier than that dumb rope climb at gym class."

I lowered my head.

He turned to Pete. "How about you, Prince?"

Pete held up the palms of his hands. "I'd love to. But alas, I cannot take the risk. I owe myself to Persia."

Billy rolled his eyes. "Fine, be that way. *Adios, amigos.*" He glided up the ladder like a cat climbing a tree. In no time at all he was at the top. He leaned out and looked down at us. We waved. As he waved back, he took his hand off a rung and lost his balance.

"Billy!" Pete and I screamed together.

Just as he started to topple over the edge, Billy grabbed hold of the ladder and jerked to a stop. "Help!" he hollered, dangling from one arm.

I turned to Pete. "You've got to help him. You know I can't stand heights."

Pete started trembling and backed away.

"Hurry!" Billy cried.

My stomach lurched as I started up the ladder. Each vibration sent shivers through me. Up, up I went. Fifteen feet. Twenty. My dry throat rasped with every breath I took. My hands sweat so much they could barely grip the rungs.

"Hurry, Cookie," Billy pleaded.

I made the mistake of looking down. A powerful force pulled at me, and I felt the urge to jump. Sweat stung my eyes. My head whirled. I didn't dare move.

All of a sudden, Billy pounded his chest with his free hand, yodeled like Tarzan and started to laugh maniacally.

I felt so shocked that I almost forgot about my fear of heights. Almost.

"So this was all a joke?" I shouted.

Billy nodded in delight.

Grasping the ladder for dear life, I gingerly backed down. Once I reached the bottom, every fiber in my body shook. Billy slid down effortlessly and bounced onto the pavement. He patted me on the shoulder. "You gotta feel great. You made it better than half way up."

The only thing I felt was humiliation. If Billy really had been in danger, I doubted I could have saved him. Another thing kept gnawing at me. Ever since the rock attack, I'd seen neither hide nor hair of Bo. And Lester had kept a suspiciously low profile lately. Something told me they were gearing up for something big.

CHAPTER 58

FRIDAY, MAY 11, 1945

Everything had gone to hell. Alice hated me. I was disgusted with myself for being a coward at the water tower. I fretted about the radio station being sold. But most of all, I was worried something might happen to Eric for agreeing to be on our float.

The phone rang as I was sitting down to breakfast. I picked up and grumbled, "Hello."

"Cookie," a distant voice said.

"David? Where are you?"

"LaGuardia Airport. Coming back home for a couple days."

"When do you get in?"

"Not 'til late tonight. Have to fly to Chicago first, then change planes to

Sioux City. From there, I'll take a car."

"Tomorrow's the big victory parade in town. Our class has a float. Can you make it?"

"Oh, I'll be there. The Senator asked me to sing 'America' to kick off the festivities."

"Wow. Can we get together afterwards?"

"Sure thing. Hey, folks are starting to get on the plane. Gotta go."

I started down the back stairs just as our plump mail lady came puffing up. She held up a large envelope. "Special delivery for your pop. He home?" It had the round Columbia Records insignia in the corner.

"No, but Mom is."

"That'll do," she wheezed.

I opened the door. "Mom, special delivery."

"Coming," Mom called.

The envelope sure looked fat. I wondered if it was full of checks for Dad's record.

We met in the parking lot in front of Garney Castle for a final rehearsal. Alice stood beside me, but she might as well have been a million miles away. I kept trying to strike up a conversation with her, but she just stuck her nose in the air and ignored me. Finally I gave up.

During a break, I asked Miss Morris if she shouldn't tell the class about Eric now. She said she'd rather wait until right before the parade. I shared my concern that the surprise might discombobulate some people, but she insisted it would be fine.

At three o'clock we were dismissed. Miss Morris told everyone to be in costume and meet at the bottom of Central Street tomorrow morning at nine o'clock sharp.

As everyone dispersed, a huge Garney seed truck full of men wearing coveralls drove up. Emblazoned on the front of the men's coveralls was the motto *The Color of Corn Is Green.* Garney and his driver parked right behind the truck in the Senator's Lincoln. The men unloaded the banner, which they strung up between two towering poles mounted on either side of the decorated flatbed. Dark blue words on a yellow background proclaimed:

SENATOR EDMOND GARNEY
PRESENTS FARMINGTON ELEMENTARY EIGHTH GRADE
IN PEACE, LET'S SHAKE ON IT!

Senator Garney crossed over to me wearing a self-satisfied grin. "Well, what do you think, son?"

"It's swell. Thanks for making all of this possible."

The Senator patted the golden ear of corn on his bolo tie. "Can't deny I had my reasons. Guess you've heard about my nomination?"

"Congratulations."

His thick salt-and-pepper eyebrows furrowed. "A few Senators are giving me a lot of heat. Say I'm a hick without the faintest idea how to make France and Germany get along."

"I think they're dead wrong, sir."

"You bet they are. And your idea about having that German soldier on your float was a stroke of genius. A great way to show how I can bring enemies together."

I flushed. "Thanks for the compliment, but it was actually Alice's idea."

He shrugged. "Don't matter. The point is, it's perfect." The Senator took a final admiring look at the banner and clapped me on the back. "Practice your smile, son. All the big newsreels, networks and newspapers will be here tomorrow." He turned to leave.

I grabbed his arm. "Excuse me, Senator, but I read you might be selling the radio station. Is it true?"

"Absolutely not."

I exhaled in relief.

He closed one eye and tapped his nose. "Fact is, it's already sold. Signed the papers this morning." Garney winked and waddled to his limousine, whistling "Don't Fence Me In."

I ran straight home and burst into the living room. "Mom! Dad! The Senator sold the station!"

"So I heard," Dad said indifferently.

I looked at Mom. She appeared unruffled. "Aren't you worried?"

She shrugged. "Everything will work out fine."

"But Dad could lose his job. We might have to move."

They smiled serenely and told me not to agonize over it.

I went to my room with the uneasy feeling that they weren't telling me something. And I bet it had a lot to do with that special delivery letter from Columbia Records.

CHAPTER 59

SATURDAY, MAY 12, 1945

Dad had to report directly to the WXAX float after his morning show. He put on his cowboy outfit and left before I got up.

Mom smoothed the red lapels of my Uncle Sam jacket. "You make a perfect Uncle Sam," she gushed, then crinkled her nose. "But those fumes. You poor thing!" She picked up her Brownie camera. "Hold still. I'll take your picture."

"Mom, I look like a freak."

As usual, she ignored my protest and steered me to a patch of sunlight slanting through the dining room window. "Say cheese."

The instant I heard a click, I streaked past her and out the door before she could take another.

As I approached the parade starting point, I was greeted by a deafening tumult—bands tuning up, people laughing and shouting, tires squealing, tractors rumbling. Throngs of people had spilled off the sidewalks and filled the street. I weaved through them with my head down, hoping no one would pay any attention to my silly getup.

Soldiers, sailors and marines strolled through the crowd, joking, smoking and eyeing the ladies. Their uniforms had perfect creases, and their shoes were so shiny you could see your reflection in them. Pert girls in short, gold-striped white skirts with big bass drums strapped to their shoulders leaned against buildings to keep from falling over.

Aunt Jemima stood in front of a tent with a banner promising *FREE AUNT JEMIMA PANCAKES*. With her white neck scarf, yellow bandana and red and white blouse, she looked just like the lady on the pancake box–only not as plump.

I finally reached Center Street, where I checked my watch and panicked. Ten minutes late. Standing on my tiptoes, I saw our float across the sea of people. We were first in a long line waiting to join the parade.

I caught glimpses of Miss Morris shepherding my classmates up a small stepladder. As they climbed aboard, they laughed and giggled at each other's costumes. Most of the costumes were surprisingly good.

Alice stepped onto the float looking like a Greek goddess. Her flowing white toga clung to her body like a sculpture. My heart ached.

"Well, look who's here!" Billy shouted as I approached. Some of the kids gave me wolf whistles. I burned with embarrassment.

Billy wore a tight blue and white striped T-shirt and snug black sailor pants. A thin painted moustache curled on his upper lip, and a black beret tipped rakishly over his left eye. He clapped me on the back, then stepped back hastily. "P-U, you smell like a mothball factory!"

"Tell me something I don't already know."

Billy fanned his face. "Hey, where's the guy who's supposed to play the German?"

I turned around in a full circle looking for Eric, but there was no sign of him. I didn't know if I was upset or relieved. "Guess he's running a little late."

"Why all the mystery?"

"It's no mystery. It's just..." my voice trailed off as I heard a car honking and backfiring. An old Nash coughing plumes of smoke edged past the floats and approached us. With a final sputter, the car stopped.

The back passenger-side door opened. A brown foot cradled by an ornate gold sandal dropped beneath the door. Then another.

The top strap of each sandal was encrusted with an emerald as big as a fifty-cent piece that shimmered like lime green Jell-O. As the sandals touched the ground, I spied the bottoms of knife-creased, yellow silk trousers the color of sunshine.

The car door closed.

The class caught its breath.

Pete tugged on his long tunic, tailored from the same luxurious fabric as his pants. He looked older and regal. The high collar of his tunic framed his face in a warm yellow glow. He tapped the blood red ruby in the middle of his sky blue turban. Something glinted on his chest.

His medallion.

Pete's father popped out of the car wearing a dapper black suit. "Sorry for the delay, everyone. Streets were jammed."

Miss Morris told him he was just in time. Pete strode over to his father, placed his palms together like he was praying, and bowed. Mr. Flavorian returned the bow, then threw his arms around Pete in a proud embrace.

I whispered to Billy. "Maybe he is a Prince."

"Who'd have believed it?"

Soon everyone had taken their places on the float. Everyone except Eric.

A stuffy-looking lady with a clipboard and a nametag that read "Parade Official" swept over to Miss Morris and told her they were ready for us to move out. Miss Morris nodded, then turned to me and mouthed, "Where is he?"

I hiked my shoulders. *Had Eric backed out?*

I got my answer a few seconds later. Corporal Taylor roared up in his Jeep, siren blaring, red light flashing. Atkins sat next to him, hollering for people to clear the way. Taylor squealed to a stop by the float. Eric sat in the rear seat wearing a white embroidered shirt and grey *lederhosen*. He looked uneasy. Next to him sat a frowning GI clutching a rifle.

I groaned as I rushed to greet them. "You really had me worried. I pointed at the grumpy soldier. "What's he ...""

"Ran into a problem," interrupted Atkins. "Guy supposed to guard Eric got some kind of stomach crud." He nodded at Dingle. "Had to replace him, pronto."

I made a face.

Atkins shrugged.

I motioned for Miss Morris to introduce Eric. She shook her head and pointed to me. My stomach plummeted. I swallowed and rustled up a big smile. "This is Eric, my German friend," I announced unevenly. "Senator Garney arranged for him to be on the float with us. Private Dingle here is going to ride along," I added, trying to sound nonchalant. "Army procedure."

Miss Morris bustled over and nudged Eric, Dingle and me onto the float.

Some of the kids looked stunned. Others, enthusiastic. For the first time in days, Alice grinned. To make Dingle look like he belonged on the float, Atkins ordered him to stand in the rear at parade rest.

As I scrambled up the ladder, I spotted Mr. Chester standing on the curb. His eyes blazed. Thank goodness school ended in a week.

"America! America! God shed His grace on thee,
And crown thy good with brotherhood
From sea to shining sea!"

Speakers carried David's voice to us from the reviewing stand in front of Garney Castle. The orchestra accompanying him built to a stirring crescendo that left me with chills. People clapped for what seemed like five minutes.

After a short silence, I heard the suspenseful roll of snare drums followed by the boom of a cannon. The parade began.

Senator Garney led the way, waving from the back of a gleaming black Cadillac convertible. Trailing him were a string of Packard and Lincoln convertibles carrying The Lone Ranger, Jack Benny, Fred Allen, and other celebrity look-alikes.

Shriners in red Fezzes driving miniature cars came next. They whipped around one another like kids driving bumper cars—scarcely missing the people who had spilled into the street.

The WXAX float rolled by next, featuring Dad's group, the hillbillies, The Neighbor Lady, Farmer Frank, and other station personalities.

The lady with the clipboard waved and shouted for us to go next. Wearing a Dutch milkmaid costume and a yellow mop for hair, Shirley revved up the tractor and jerked us onto Center Street.

I took my place beside Alice, awed by her beauty. She smiled radiantly at the crowd. I might as well have been on Mars.

Eric sat on the top row of hay bales on the left side of the float. Even though he was short, he stood out over the kids on either side of him. As we moved into the crowd, my apprehension about putting Eric in such a tight spot turned into raw fear.

CRASH! I jerked my head to the right. Two of the miniature Shriner cars had collided.

Shirley hit the brakes. Our float lurched to a stop. Alice started to topple over. I reached out and caught her. She looked up at me, eyes wide with fear. Realizing this might be my only chance, I took it.

"I'm so sorry," I said in a rush. "I-should-never-have- turned-my-back-on-you. I've-been-miserable-ever-since! I-I *love* you, Alice!"

The edges of her Cupid's bow mouth slowly lifted. "You do?"

"Honest!"

"Well," Alice nodded, "I guess we could be...friends."

"Anything you say."

By this time the Shriners had picked up the wrecked cars and dropped them by the curb. Our float jerked forward. Everyone resumed their places. Alice smoothed her toga. "Do I look all right?"

"Heavenly," I sighed.

She sighed back.

As we rolled down the street, kids straddled their parents' shoulders and waved flags. Folks leaned dangerously out of upstairs windows laughing and clapping. To my relief people either didn't realize who Eric was or didn't care.

The class formed two lines and started shaking hands with me, then Alice. Before long, Eric approached. The crowd went eerily quiet. Every nerve in my body prickled.

Someone shouted, "Hey! That's a Kraut. Get him outta here." Other voices grumbled their agreement.

A guy in a Corps of Engineers uniform stepped into the street and held up his arms. "Can it, you cretins. He's one of the guys who saved your precious bridge."

The crowd hushed. Eric stopped in front of me and held out his hand. His upper lip beaded with sweat.

The terror that had knotted up inside of me unwound like a toy plane propeller on a twisted rubber band. Grinning, I grasped Eric's hand in both of mine and pumped. He squeezed my shoulder.

The crowd buzzed back to life. One person clapped. Followed by another. And another.

Eric nodded politely to the audience and crossed to Alice. Whistles and cheers began to mix in with the applause.

Cleo strutted up with one hand on her hip, her chest thrust out and her gum cracking like a whip. Instead of shaking my hand, she gave me a token wave, spun in a circle and swept right past Alice without so much as a hello.

I heard a chorus of appreciative hoots and whistles from the men in the crowd. Alice gnashed her teeth.

Billy shook my hand, winked at the audience and pretended to twist his penciled moustache. All the girls twittered and cheered.

Pete came next and bowed to the crowd. They roared their approval. Just as I gave him a hearty slap on the back, I spotted Lester.

He was standing in an apartment house doorway, his beady eyes darting back and forth. A burly man in a Veterans of Foreign Wars cap approached him. He slammed a brown bag into Lester's arms and slinked off. Seconds later, Lester vanished into the crowd. While I had no idea what the bag held, something told me it wasn't good.

As we turned onto Front Street, I saw Mom standing at the curb and waving excitedly. I snuck a little wave back. She snapped my picture.

We approached Garney Castle and the reviewing stand. Every landing and step on the fire escape overflowed with onlookers. The stairs shuddered as people stomped in time with the band music. I could swear I saw the fire escape pull away from the wall.

Senator Garney jumped out of his limousine and clambered up to the reviewing stand. He passed the "Meet Your Navy" band and a platform holding a dozen photographers and newsreel cameramen. Garney called to the press people and pointed to our float. Movie cameras panned and started whirling. Flash bulbs popped.

The Senator motioned for David to join him. Instead of his usual fatigue pants and Ike jacket, David wore a double-breasted blue suit and neon blue tie. His dark hair was slicked into a pompadour like Frank Sinatra's.

Garney whispered something in David's ear. David reached for the microphone. His coat sleeves pulled back to reveal French cuffs with gold cufflinks that twinkled in the sunlight. "Ladies and gentlemen," David said dramatically, "let's give a big hand to Senator Garney's float,

'Peace, Let's Shake On It,' presented by the Farmington Elementary eighth grade."

There were a few scattered boos. But the cheers far outweighed them. Senator Garney clasped his hands over his head.

The Navy band broke into Woody Herman's "Woodchopper's Ball." The crowd started dancing in the street. Cleo kicked off her skyscraper heels, grabbed Billy's arm and started jitterbugging.

The floats that were ahead of ours started veering off into the empty field where the parade ended.

SCREECH! Shirley slammed on the brakes. Kids fell over one another. I grabbed Alice, barely managing to keep us both from toppling.

Looking up, I saw that four of the Shriners' tiny cars had collided. Steam spewed from cracked radiators. Mortally wounded engines sputtered and popped. With faces as red as their fezzes, the drivers climbed out of their cars and started cursing one another.

It may not have been a photo finish, but the parade was finally over. I wanted to jump for joy. Having Eric aboard had gone off more or less without a hitch.

The Navy band kept playing. More couples joined the dancing. Photographers and newsreel cameramen split up to cover the dancers and the midget car mayhem.

Pete let out an Injun Joe victory whoop, grabbed Peggy and started dancing. Other kids joined in. I saw many shake Eric's hand and pat him on the back. Dingle kept his stance like a toy soldier at the back of the float, looking edgy and confused.

I tore off my scraggly beard and hugged Alice.

BANG! A firecracker exploded. Close by.

POW! I jumped back as a cherry bomb exploded only a few feet in front of me. The blast singed my Uncle Sam trousers. Alice screamed. I shielded her with my body and craned around to find the source of the fireworks.

Lester marched toward us with a hateful grin. He was carrying the brown bag in one hand, and a glowing punk stick in the other. Holding the punk stick in his teeth, he pulled three cherry bombs out of the bag. He lit their fuses and tossed them at us one at a time.

"Get her out of here!" I shouted, shoving Alice toward Eric. He lifted her in his arms and carried her toward the back of the float.

A cherry bomb landed at my feet and exploded. I hopped away just in time, my ears ringing from the blast. My stomach started burbling like a witches brew, but I forced it back down.

Billy ran up to me. "What the hell's goin' on?" he yelled. I pointed to Lester.

Two more explosions barely missed us. Billy prepared to jump off the float. "I'll take care of him."

"No!" I grabbed the neck of Billy's tight T-shirt. It choked him, stopping him cold. "This is between Lester and me."

"What's goin' on?" Dingle called to me. He hoisted his rifle to his shoulder.

"Nothing," I replied with forced calm. There was no telling what Dingle would do if he panicked.

Eric lowered Alice to the ground. The other kids poured off the float around him.

"*Kommen!*" Eric called, waving urgently for me and Billy to join him at the back and flee.

I didn't move. Billy remained at my side.

Lester stood in front of the float and narrowed his eyes. "Nazi lover!" he snarled, and lobbed a three-incher at me.

The explosion ripped my pants leg to the knee. An ugly, raw burn ran up my shin. I stifled a cry, not wanting to give Lester the satisfaction of knowing he'd hurt me.

Eric rushed over, ripped a piece of fabric from my torn pant leg and wrapped it around my bleeding shin.

Dingle stepped forward and leveled his rifle at Eric. "Hey, Kraut! Get back here."

Eric ignored him. Dingle aimed. Billy stepped in front of Eric, blocking Dingle's shot. "You moron! Eric's trying to help him."

Dingle cursed and bellowed at Billy to get out of the way. Billy didn't budge. Flustered, Dingle lowered his weapon.

A couple of men in the crowd noticed Lester menacing us and rushed toward him, fists balled. Lester lit a skyrocket and waved it at them. They scattered. Lester spun around and aimed the rocket at me. I was so scared I couldn't move.

"That's goin' too damn far!" I heard a husky voice cry. A streaking hulk in faded fatigues and carrot red hair tackled Lester at the knees. Lester crumpled like a puppet without strings. Bo scrambled on top and pinned Lester's arms to the concrete.

"Lemme go, you sombitch!" Lester bucked and writhed, but managed to keep hold of the sputtering rocket.

Sweat poured from Bo's forehead as he struggled to hold Lester down. He hunched a shoulder to wipe the sweat from his eyes. Lester wiggled his arm loose and pointed the sputtering rocket at Bo.

Bo ducked. The missile whizzed by him, but left a shower of searing sparks in its wake. Bo's shirt caught on fire. He let go of Lester and tried to smother the flames by rolling back and forth on the street.

Lester scrambled to his feet shaking his right hand painfully. The explosion must have burned it. Undaunted, he pulled a cherry bomb out of the bag, lit the fuse and hurled it at me. It came as such a surprise that I didn't have time to dodge it.

From out of nowhere, Eric leaped between me and Lester. The cherry bomb exploded a foot from his face. He bellowed and clasped a hand over his right eye. Blood seeped through his fingers.

"Oh, my God!" I cried. I turned to the back of the float and called to Alice. "Get help. Quick!"

Alice picked up the fabric of her toga and raced for the reviewing stand with Cleo and Peggy right behind her.

Eric sank to the floor moaning. I knelt beside him and pressed my handkerchief against his eye, hoping to stem the bleeding. "I'm so sorry," I whispered breathlessly.

Billy stopped staring down Dingle and dropped beside me. He nudged me out of the way and held the handkerchief to Eric's eye. "I'll watch Eric. You take care of Lester."

Lester stood rooted in a daze, his face contorted in hate and fear.

I rolled off the float and landed hard on my right ankle. It shot a bolt of white-hot pain up my leg. Picking myself up, I hobbled toward Lester with my fists clenched. Every step felt like an electric shock.

Lester turned on his heels and ran. I willed myself after him. Lester pulled ahead. In spite of the excruciating pain, I churned my legs faster.

He burst through a covey of dazed spectators and picked up even more speed. When I saw where he was heading, my heart jumped into my throat.

"Stop him! Stop him!" I shouted at the few people remaining on the fire escape.

Lester lit a cherry bomb and flung it at them. They scampered for safety.

He leaped onto the fire escape, dropped his bag and scuttled up the stairs on all fours like a rat. I reached the staircase seconds later and screeched to a stop. Lester looked down at me and jeered.

Waves of nausea crashed in my stomach. Every second I hesitated, the closer he got to escaping. I grabbed the railing and started up. Bolts popped out of the wall. The metal skeleton started swaying. My temples pounded, but I kept climbing.

Lester swept past the first landing. I hobbled behind him, not daring to look down. The stairs clanked and groaned. He cleared the second landing. More bolts pulled from the building.

Bile surged up my throat. I swallowed it back and kept climbing. Lester passed the third landing just before I reached the second. He paused, pumping his fist at me and cackling.

Seconds later, Lester reached the top landing and the door to the studio. I grabbed the railings with both hands, too pained and exhausted to take another step. My shoulders slumped in defeat. Tears of humiliation filled my eyes.

Just as Lester reached for the studio door, the top landing came loose and swayed away from the building. Lester lurched desperately for the doorknob, but missed.

The staircase picked up speed, tumbling toward the ground. Lester screamed and clawed at the air. I felt like Alice falling down the rabbit hole. Then a comforting silence came over me. I looked down and saw Mom, Dad and others waving frantically. I smiled and waved back. A huge tree rushed toward me, its heavy branches spread in a wide embrace.

I awoke with a start. Mom and Dad hovered over me.

"Thank God," Mom cried.

"Eric. How's Eric?" I demanded groggily.

"The Senator sent him straight to Sioux City in an ambulance. There's a great eye specialist there," Dad said soothingly.

"He won't be blind will he?"

Mom forced a smile. "They'll do everything they can for him." Her face clouded. "How do you feel?"

"Woozy."

Dad nodded. "They gave you a shot in the ambulance."

"Where am I?"

"Saint Mary's." Mom whispered, stroking my forehead.

I tried to adjust my position. "Yeow!" Needle-sharp pains shot through my chest and shoulder.

"Careful!" Mom exclaimed. "You broke two ribs."

"And your collarbone," Dad added.

My lungs felt like they were on fire. "What about my lungs? It hurts when I breathe."

"A rib punctured one of your lungs," Mom said sympathetically. "It collapsed, but the Doctor says it'll fill up soon."

I groaned.

"It could have been a lot worse," Dad said brightly. "The tree broke your fall. Lester didn't fare so well."

"Was he...? Did he...?"

Dad shook his head. "He's here. But pretty banged up."

Mom snapped off my bedside lamp. "Now quit fretting and get some sleep. Dad and I will be right here."

I heard someone shuffle into the room. "No ya won't," barked a familiar voice. "Ya been here too long already. Off with ya, now."

Mom tried to protest, but Sister Celia held firm.

Mom bent over and kissed me on the cheek. "Sleep tight, Donnyboy."

The Sister shook a finger at me. "An' don't be forgettin' yer prayers!"

CHAPTER 60

MONDAY, MAY 14, 1945

It had to be a dream but it seemed so real. Explosions all around me. Alice screaming. Eric moaning and clasping a hand to his bleeding eye. Lester cackling. Falling, falling. I forced myself to wake up. My sheets were all pulled out, blankets on the floor. I was soaked in sweat and every inch of me hurt.

Sister Celia chided me for tearing up my bed, but remade it quickly without jarring me. She wheeled in a tray with oatmeal, orange juice and a tiny cup holding yellow, green and white pills. When I told her I didn't like oatmeal, she gave me a disapproving look. "Eat it anyway."

The Sister cranked up the bed to move me closer to the tray. My shoulder bandage felt like a straitjacket. She handed me a spoon and hovered over me as I forced down the sticky, tasteless gruel. Hoping she'd let me quit eating, I told her how much pain I was in.

"You should be grateful God saved ya," she sniffed. "And yer gonna eat every bite a that."

A dour-looking man with yellowish-grey hair, silver-rimmed glasses and a protruding lower lip entered the room. Celia greeted Dr. Adamson and stepped to one side.

He did all the regular things doctors do when you get a checkup, with a lot of humming and clucking. When he pulled down the top of my faded hospital gown, I saw an ugly amoeba-shaped bruise on my ribs. "How come you didn't tape my ribs like you did my shoulder?" I asked him.

"Lungs need to expand," he grumped. "That is, if you want to breathe."

I didn't ask any more questions.

The doctor crossed to the front of my bed and jotted something on a chart. Without another word, he left.

Mom arrived around nine in the morning to spend the day with me. Dad dropped by between shows. They did their best to cheer me up. But I couldn't help worrying about Eric and whether or not I'd ever heal.

The folks promised to let me know about Eric as soon as they heard anything. Mom said Dr. Adamson told her I was coming along just fine, which was news to me after the way he'd acted. Sister Celia shooed Mom and Dad out just before the clock struck nine.

After they left, the Sister gave me a pill that was so big I had trouble swallowing it. It left a bitter taste in my mouth and made me feel like I was floating away from my body. I dozed off recalling how soft Alice felt in my arms.

CHAPTER 61

WEDNESDAY, MAY 16, 1945

Mom and Dad couldn't come to the hospital until lunchtime today. The family we rent from, the Koenigs, were in town, and had asked to meet with the folks this morning. I asked Mom what about. She said she didn't know, which made me nervous. Maybe they were moving back and we'd have to leave.

Sister Celia made sure I ate every bite of my breakfast. Oatmeal again. As she cleared away my tray, Dr. Adamson glided into the room.

Without a word, he stuck an ice-cold stethoscope to my chest. "Big breaths," he grunted.

I drew in a small breath.

"Deeper."

I took in more air. It felt like someone stabbing me in the ribs. "Ow!"

"Hmmm," he mused.

"What's wrong?"

"Nothing. Lung's filled up just fine."

"How come it hurt when I took a deep breath?"

"That's your ribs, not your lungs. They'll take some time to heal."

"When can I go home?"

He pursed his lips. "Couple days maybe. But you'll have to stay still. Those ribs have to knit."

I asked if he had heard anything about Eric. He strolled to my chart and made some notes. I thought he was ignoring me. But when he finished writing, he leaned on the bed and told me Eric had gotten plastic surgery under his eye and that it had gone fine. As far as his vision was concerned, it was too soon to tell. They'd know more after they took his bandages off in a week. The doctor got up to leave.

"Oh, and one more thing," I said hesitantly. "Lester, the other kid on the fire escape? How's he doing?"

The doctor shook his head. "Nasty breaks on his arms and legs. Plus a pretty scorched hand."

To my surprise, the news didn't make me feel all that great. But it didn't make me hate him any less.

Mom arrived around one in the afternoon. She seemed distracted.

"What did the Koenigs want?"

"Nothing that concerns you." She quickly changed the subject. "Dr. Adamson says you can go home Friday. But you've got to rest. Understand?"

"He told me. But what about the Koenigs?"

Sister Celia bustled into the room. "Seems you've got some company," she clucked, and started cranking up my bed.

Miss Morris peeked into the room. "Hi Donald. Some of the kids and I thought you'd like a little company. Is that okay?"

I grabbed the hand mirror from my bedside table. Aside from some scratches on my face from the fall, I looked fairly normal.

"That'd be great," I answered.

Miss Morris smiled. "I'll bring them in."

"Just a wee minute, Miss," Sister Celia interrupted. "I'll be handlin' this." She took Miss Morris by the elbow and led her into the hall. "Line up me beauties—and no shenanigans. I'll allow one a you in at a time, with a one-minute time limit. Any questions?"

Silence.

Sister Celia positioned Miss Morris at the doorway and told her to time each kid.

Cleo wobbled in on high heels and dropped a pack of Black Jack gum on my nightstand. She winked, leaned over and kissed me on the cheek. I think I felt a tongue flick.

Pete strode in nervously and launched into an elaborate explanation of why he'd bolted off the float so fast. I told him not to worry, that it was very brave of him to put his country first. I meant it. Ever since I'd gotten a load of him in his Persian finery, I'd started to wonder if his fantastic claims to the throne weren't so fantastic after all.

Darrel brought me a new *Plastic Man* comic book. Peggy giggled in, handed me a flowery "Get Well" card, and giggled out.

There was a pause, and it looked like I'd seen the last of my visitors. I tried not to look disappointed. Then Alice floated through the door.

Her white dress was covered in tiny violets, and billowed with every step she took. In her arms was a bouquet of fresh cut spring flowers. "You were so brave after the parade, Donny," she said as she approached my bedside. Her eyes misted. "You probably saved my life."

It took me several seconds to trust myself to speak. "I don't know about that, but thanks for the flowers."

"You like them?"

"They're perfect."

"Good," she brightened up. "I chose them myself."

"I can tell."

We locked eyes, and no longer needed words.

"Time's up," Miss Morris called out.

"Wait!" Alice exclaimed. She set the flowers on my bedside table and leaned over. "I love you, Donnyboy," she whispered, and kissed me on the lips. Then she dashed out of the room.

My heart raced after her. The rest of the day was a blur.

A finger poked me in the chest. I awoke with a start. *"Ouch!* Hey, what the—?"

"It's me, Cookie," David said in a loud whisper.

I could just make him out in the pale blue moonlight. He was wearing the shirt and suit jacket he had on at the Parade, but no necktie. "How are you?" I whispered.

"Top of the world. Question is, how are you?"

"Oh, I'll be fine. But I'm worried about Eric."

David nodded. "Tough break."

We looked at each other silently for a moment. "It's great seeing you," I murmured, looking around nervously. "But if Sister Celia catches you, she'll skin you alive."

"Had to risk it, Cookie. Leavin' tomorrow morning. Wanted to say goodbye."

His news jarred me. "So soon?"

"They need me on the *Amateur Hour* tour right away."

"How long will you be gone?"

"Forever, I hope. I'm in no hurry to see Mom or that son of a bitch, Ben, again. Had to fork over half my prize money to those two just so they'd okay me to go on the road."

"That's crappy."

He shrugged. "Yeah, but worth it."

I lowered my eyes. "It won't be the same around here without you. Think you could write every now and then?"

"Count on it." He paused. "Well, gotta fly, Cookie." He clapped me on the shoulder. I didn't let on how much it hurt.

"Good luck," I said.

David winked. I felt a bittersweet joy for him as he tiptoed out the door and out of my life forever.

CHAPTER 62

FRIDAY, MAY 18, 1945

I set my internal alarm clock for five in the morning—an hour before Celia went on duty. I awoke right on time and eased out of bed. My ankle panged if I put too much weight on it, so I took a metal cane out of the closet, draped a blanket over my shoulders to cover my gaping hospital gown, and limped to the doorway.

I peeked out. No one in sight. I turned left, away from the bright lights of the nurse's station.

Each patient's name appeared in a slot by the door. Sliding my feet to muffle my footsteps, I moved slowly from door to door. I'd nearly looped around to the nurse's station before I found him.

His door was ajar. The room was bathed in the cold, pewter light of dawn. My heart raced. I stepped inside and clenched my fists.

Lester was sleeping with his mouth open. Every time he exhaled, he moaned softly. His entire right leg was encased in a white plaster cast that extended from foot to hip. A thick bandage covered his right hand. Another cast covered his left arm all the way from the wrist to just below the shoulder. Blood-soaked bandages swathed his head like a helmet.

I was so shocked at the sight of him that I involuntarily banged against the door.

Lester's eyes shot open, full of rage, fear and pain. "Who is it?" he cried.

"Guess," I growled.

His right hand grabbed a metal water jug and waved it menacingly. "What you want?"

The resolve I'd built up started to crack. "I came here to get even. But now I'm not so sure I want to."

"Even?" He sniffed. "Look at me. I got the worst of it."

His tone infuriated me. "Eric will probably be blind in one eye because of you."

Lester squirmed. "It's his own fault. He shouldn't have jumped up in front of you like that."

"Bastard!" I raised my fists and moved toward his bed.

Lester's hand trembled as he waved the water jug at me. "Don't come any closer. I'll bean you."

I paused, not from fear but indecision.

Lester sensed my hesitancy. "Listen. It just wasn't right putting a Nazi up on a pedestal like that. Not after all they done."

"I keep telling you," I whispered through clenched teeth. "Eric's *not* a Nazi." I stepped closer.

Lester pulled the jug back to throw it and knocked over a framed picture on his bedside table. It crashed to the floor but landed right-side up. Through the cracked glass I saw what looked like an older, happier version of Lester in a GI uniform with his arm around a smiling, younger

Lester. It occurred to me that I'd never seen Lester smile before.

My fists uncurled and my shoulders slumped. I felt sorrow and disgust—not with Lester, but with myself for wanting to harm him.

Lester stared at me like a deer caught in the headlights and brandished the jug. "Don't come any closer," he hissed pathetically.

Feeling utterly spent, I backed away from him. As I turned to leave, I heard a whoosh of air behind me and ducked. The water jug whizzed over my head and clattered into the hallway.

Celia got me dressed and into a wheelchair. "I hope I don't see another Cook around here anytime soon," she said with mock exasperation.

"I hope not, too," I replied solemnly. "But that doesn't mean I won't miss you."

Her face reddened as she leaned over to adjust the blanket tucked around my legs. When she finally straightened up, she reached into the pocket of her black habit and handed me a tiny silver cross on a slender silver chain.

I was flabbergasted. "For me?"

She clasped it around my neck. "Aye. Always wear it, ya hear? It'll protect ya. And heaven knows ya need protectin'!"

The thought of wearing jewelry, especially a cross, made me feel self-conscious. But I gave the Sister my word that I'd never take it off.

After she wheeled me out to my folks' car, I stretched up and hugged her. "Thanks, Sister Celia. I won't ever forget you."

She squeezed me hard for a brief moment, then pulled away. A finger flicked to her eye as she walked back toward the hospital entrance.

CHAPTER 63

FRIDAY, MAY 25, 1945

Mom broke the news at breakfast. "We're moving." It felt like someone had hit me in the head with a sledgehammer. "No!" I pounded the table with both fists. Coffee and cereal went flying.

"Now simmer down," Dad said. "Let me explain."

My body was in such turmoil that I had to fight for breath. "I don't want any explanation. We're staying." I sprung up from the table and landed hard on my sore angle. "Ouch!"

Dad grabbed my arm and forced me back into my chair. "Now look, DB. I know this really upsets you, but it's not like the other times we've moved. This time we've got no choice."

Mom leaned in and stroked my hand. "The new station owners are firing all the musicians. They're changing to a new kind of programming that's really popular—guys talking and playing pop records. Like the Jolly Joe show that you and your chums like so much."

"But couldn't the Senator get Dad another job here?" I reasoned. "I could go to work."

"There's something else you need to know," Dad said, taking a sip from his coffee cup. "The Koenigs are moving back from San Diego. Their son gets out of the hospital in a couple weeks. He fell in love with a nurse, and they're getting married. The newlyweds are going to need the upstairs."

I rubbed my temples, trying to erase the pain inside. "There's got to be other places to rent in Farmington. I'm sure we could find one."

"That wouldn't solve anything," Dad said with a shrug. "And as far as the Senator's concerned, he's leaving for France any day now. The Senate confirmed him yesterday."

"But where will we go? What will you do?"

Mom smiled and held up the special delivery envelope. "You see these?" she asked, pulling out a pile of yellow papers. "They're royalty statements for Dad's record. They arrived last week with a very hefty check."

Dad's face lit up. "And I've been offered a contract to record the kind of music I like."

A vise tightened around my heart.

Mom put her arm around me. "I know this is a blow, honey. You've made so many great friends here. And Lord knows you've become your own person. But what you have inside of you now won't go away."

"So where are we moving?" I asked, fighting back tears.

"Kansas City," Mom answered. "We know lots of families with kids your age there. And there'll be so much more for you to do."

Dad looked excited. "Columbia has a great studio in K.C., Donnyboy. And there are a ton of jazz clubs where I can play."

"But you promised we'd stay here for good," I said numbly.

Mom nodded sympathetically. "I know. But nothing lasts forever."

The rest of the conversation came to me through a fog. My mind was on Alice and Eric and Billy and Pete, and how unfair it was that I had to be torn away from them. All I remembered hearing was that we had to be gone in two weeks when the Koenigs returned.

I stood. "May I please be excused?"

"Finish your breakfast," Mom said. "Please."

"Not hungry." I drifted out the back door and wandered onto the vacant lot. Kneeling, I scraped away the dirt that held Chaplin's cross in place. Once it was free, I brushed the cross off and carried it up to my room.

CHAPTER 64

SATURDAY, MAY 26, 1945

I'd been holed up in my room ever since I got the news about moving. Mom insisted on bringing me food, but I barely even picked at it. Billy and Pete came by to celebrate school ending, but I didn't want to see them. I couldn't even talk to Alice when she called.

Dr. Adamson came by. Except for being slightly tender, my ribs and shoulder were fine. I could almost put my full weight on my ankle. And the burn on my shin was almost healed.

Later that afternoon, Mom came in to tell me Miss Morris had dropped by with my final report card. I said I wasn't interested.

Mom had to drag me into the living room, which made Miss Morris uncomfortable and embarrassed me to no end. I apologized for being rude. Miss Morris smiled and handed me my report card.

Mom read over my shoulder as I studied it. At first glance, it looked like I'd gotten all A's and one B. The B was for Arithmetic, my worst subject. Then came a shock: I'd gotten an F in Gym.

"That's not fair!" I cried. "Chester did it for spite."

Miss Morris held up her hand. "Believe me, I know. That's why I took it upon myself to talk to Mrs. Chaney, the head of the School Board. I told her how you and Mr. Chester had butted heads over your story about Eric. She was aware that you'd missed the last week of school because of your bravery at the parade, and agreed to change the F to an incomplete."

Mom looked concerned. "Won't that make trouble for you with Mr. Chester?"

Miss Morris grinned. "Well, it seems Mr. Chester is retiring." She tried—in vain—to suppress a tiny giggle. "The former principal, Mr. Van Ness, no longer thinks he's a Christmas tree, and will resume his position this fall."

Mom gave each of us a perplexed look.

"I'll tell you about it later," I said, and turned back to Miss Morris. "Thanks for going to bat for me, although I don't think it'll make much of a difference. I just found out that we're moving to Kansas City."

Miss Morris grew wide-eyed. "Really? We're moving, too. I mean, Bob Lyle and me." She flushed. "Bob asked me to marry him, and we're moving to Des Moines. He just got a wonderful new job at the *Des Moines Register*."

"That's fabulous!" Mom exclaimed.

"Wow, congratulations," I added with a nod.

While Miss Morris told Mom all the details about her wedding, I was hit by a staggering realization. First David left. And now, Miss Morris. Maybe my idea of Farmington as a comfortable, dependable and permanent place wasn't so accurate after all.

CHAPTER 65

SUNDAY, MAY 27, 1945

I heard a siren in the distance. It was the same pulsing wail that I'd heard the day we arrived in Farmington—and the first time I saw Eric.

I looked out my bedroom window. Corporal Taylor squealed to a stop in front of our house. Next to him, Sergeant Atkins puffed on a thick cigar. In the back of the Jeep was Eric, clinging to the Sergeant's seat to keep from flying out.

My face blanched. Eric had a black patch over his right eye. I hurried downstairs as fast as my tender ankle would allow.

When I reached the bottom of the porch steps, Atkins and Eric were standing at the curb. Eric's right cheek looked red and raw like he had a bad sunburn, but there was no sign of a scar. I could barely make out a short row of tiny stitches just below his eye patch.

"Want to come in for a soda or something?" I asked eagerly.

Atkins took the cigar out of his mouth, "Can't. All we got time for is to say goodbye."

"Wait, you mean you're leaving? Now?"

"Yep."

I looked at Eric desperately. "You, too?"

He nodded slowly.

"But Eric just got out of the hospital!" I yelled, advancing on the Sergeant. "What the hell's going on?"

Atkins pushed me back gently. "Relax, son. Everything's fine. Garney fixed it so the POWs in Farmington would be on the first boat back to Germany. His way of sayin' thanks for helping with the flood. And for Eric being on your float and all."

I looked at Eric through bleary eyes. "That patch. Are you...?" I couldn't say the word.

"Blind?" Eric finished for me. "Maybe. Maybe not. Vill take some time to know."

My head slumped. "It's all my fault."

"*Nein.*" Eric put his hand under my chin and jerked it up. "No one's fault. *Verstehen?*"

My mind was so mixed up I didn't know what to think. We stared at each other in aching silence.

"Gotta go, fellas," Atkins said gruffly, and motioned for Eric to board the Jeep.

I stepped between them and held out my hand to Eric. "I—I'll really miss you." Hard as I tried not to, I broke down crying. "Sorry," I sniffed. "I'm such a baby."

Eric wrapped an arm gently around my shoulders. "I vill miss you, too, Donnyboy. Strange. Have you ever felt happy and sad all at same time?"

"No," I croaked.

"Von day, maybe, you vill."

Atkins tapped Eric's back and jerked a thumb toward the Jeep. "Sorry to break this up, but the Colonel will have my ass on a plate if we don't get right back to camp."

Eric reached into his pants pocket and handed me a scrap of paper. "Please to write me. Address of *mein* uncle."

"I will," I promised.

Eric settled in the back seat and turned around to look at me.

I remembered the same face from four months before. Mysterious. Forlorn. Withdrawn.

Today, his perfect features seemed older and more battered than before. But they glowed with a newfound sense of hope and happy anticipation.

CHAPTER 66

MONDAY MAY 28, 1945

"Anyone home?" I called from the knoll on the edge of the Foleys' compound. Thanks to a lush vegetable garden and lots of bright yellow sunflowers, it looked much cheerier than it did the last time I was there.

I hollered again.

Pa Foley exited the house with his usual sour demeanor. "Whatcha want?" He wore the same ragged bib overalls and faded red underwear shirt I'd seen him in before.

"Came to see Bo," I shouted.

"Not here."

"Coming back soon?"

"Why you askin'?"

"It's kind of personal."

Two red-haired Foley kids slipped out of the doorway and clung to their Pa. "Well, he ain't here." Mr. Foley shook the kids from his legs and started back into the house.

"Is Bo in the Army?"

Pa Foley looked over his shoulder. "Was. But lied 'bout his age and they kicked him out." He waved me off like a gnat. "Now git." He herded the kids into the house and slammed the door.

Disappointed, I pushed through the overgrown brush that led to the stockyards and the road home. Something plopped against my back. I glanced down. A small pinecone bounced on the ground. I figured it fell from a tree.

Then another hit me. And another. I spun around, nostrils flared.

Bo leaned against a fir tree, grinning and juggling pinecones. I grinned back. "Just the fella I wanted to see."

"What fer?"

"To thank you."

Bo looked wary.

"For going after Lester. You saved a lot of people from getting really hurt. Myself included."

Though Bo tried to seem nonplussed, I could tell he was pleased.

I started to back away. "Just wanted you to know I appreciate it."

He laughed. "Guess I owed ya one fer not shootin' me."

I winced. "Sorry about that. But you did poison my dog."

Bo scratched his head. "What makes you so sure?"

"Are you trying to say you didn't? How dare you!" I began self-righteously. Suddenly, I remembered something David had said. "Wait a second! David told me he heard you arguing with someone the day Chaplin disappeared, but when he got to the backyard you were the only one there." I pounded my forehead. "Lester. He was with you. He was the one who poisoned Chaplin!"

Bo's lips tilted into a self-satisfied smile.

CHAPTER 67

FRIDAY, JUNE 1, 1945

"**L**ook, Mom." She almost fell over when I showed her the ad.

J. C. PENNEY
MEN'S SHORT PANTS SALE
$3.79 A PAIR!

"I thought you never wanted to wear short pants again?" she asked in confusion.

"Not in the winter. And not to school," I justified myself. "But it's hotter than Hades outside."

Mom found her wallet, pulled out a ten and handed it to me. "Here you go. Might as well get a new T-shirt and tennis shoes while you're at it."

"What about ration stamps? I thought we were out."

"We are. But we don't need them anymore."

I didn't know if it had something to do with David and Miss Morris leaving or my dumb mistake about Bo, but I'd finally accepted that we were moving. Tomorrow would be our last day in Farmington.

After I got home, I laced up my new white Converse sneakers, slipped on my new white T-shirt and stepped into my new tan shorts. I looked in the bureau mirror. I'd filled out a lot in just a few months. I even noticed some peach fuzz on my upper lip.

Ever since I'd avoided her calls, Alice hadn't tried to get in touch with me. Yesterday I finally called her back. She sounded friendly enough, but when I asked if I could see her, she said they were up to their ears getting the Senator ready to move. She promised to call if she got a free moment.

I decided she'd forgotten about the "I love you" in the hospital.

Just after lunch, there was a knock at the back door. My heart skipped like a jump rope. Maybe it was Alice. "I'll get it," I shouted.

I opened the door and found myself face to face with Billy and Pete. "Hear you're movin' tomorrow," Billy said.

"Yep," I sighed, and invited them in.

Mom took a break from scrubbing the apartment and made us lemonade. Even though most of our food was packed, she still managed to come up with a with a package of Lorna Doone cookies. We sat around the breakfast table and devoured them.

The phone rang. I wanted to answer it, but didn't for fear of being rude to my friends.

Mom hastily dried her hands on a dish towel. "I'll get it."

I strained to hear what she said on the phone, but Billy and Pete were yakking so much I couldn't concentrate. They said they were sorry to see me go, but that I was a "lucky dog" to be moving to such a big city.

Billy made me promise to write him with our new address. He said he'd probably hitchhike to Kansas City this summer for a visit.

I said I hoped he would.

Pete confided he'd probably be going back to Persia, now called Iraq, any day now. His relatives had written that the Shah was a British puppet who was losing his grip on the country. The time had come for Pete's clan to reclaim the throne.

Mom hung up the phone.

"Who was it?" I asked casually.

"Nobody special."

Dejected, I went back to listening to my friends until they ran out of things to say. We filed onto the back landing and looked at each other awkwardly. "Well, it's been great knowing you," I said, trying not to get all choked up.

For an instant, Billy's cockiness was replaced by a long submerged hurt. "I've heard that one before," he said bitterly. "You'll forget us the minute you hit K.C."

I realized he was referring to his folks who deserted him. I grabbed his shoulders and locked eyes with him. "You're wrong, Billy. I'll never forget you. And if you don't come see me, I'll find a way to come see you. And that's a promise."

Billy looked stunned. It took a while, but slowly his mouth relaxed into a grin. "Well, if you say so, Cookie."

Pete stared at his sandaled feet. "Here's something you can count on. When I'm on the throne, I'll bring you over first thing. Both of you. And nothing will be too good for you."

"I'll hold you to it, Pete," I laughed, squeezing his brown arm.

There was nothing more to say. Heads down, they tromped down the stairs and disappeared around the house.

After they left, I moped from room to room.

"Look," Mom said sharply, "it's beautiful outside. Make yourself useful." She wet a rag, and handed me a can of Old Dutch Cleanser. "Go clean the porch swing."

"I don't feel like it."

She slapped the rag in my hand and pointed to the back door. "Clean the swing."

I hesitated.

"Now."

It took just a few minutes to clean the swing, but the air was so warm and sweet that I decided to stay outside. I sat on the front steps with my elbows on my knees and my chin in my hands, and allowed my eyes to close.

The warmth of the sun nearly lulled me to sleep. Only my aching for Alice kept me from dozing off.

A car drove up and stopped. My eyes crept open. It was the Codys' Lincoln Continental. My heart did a somersault.

Mrs. Cody leaned out of the driver's side window and waved. Alice opened the passenger door and got out, looking picture perfect in a lemon yellow sundress.

I jumped up to greet her. Mrs. Cody told Alice she'd be back in twenty minutes and drove off.

As Alice walked toward me with a pink shoebox in her hands, I noticed how grown-up she had become. Her body was curved in all the right places, and her bare legs were long and shapely.

She stopped at the porch steps and smiled up at me. "Feeling better?"

"Much."

Silence.

"Want to sit on the swing?" I asked. "I just cleaned it." Alice set the shoebox on the porch and sat beside me.

The chain creaked as we swung back and forth. "Guess you heard, we're moving to Kansas City," I said. "Tomorrow."

"Mother told me." Her hip slid next to mine. She didn't move away.

"We're moving, too," Alice said quietly.

"*What?* Where? When?"

"Not so fast," she laughed. "As you probably know, father lost his job when the new owners took over. Mother talked grandfather into making him assistant ambassador or something, so we're moving to Paris."

"Wow! When?"

"A couple weeks."

She looked so achingly beautiful, I was tongue-tied.

Alice looked down and patted my leg. "You should always wear shorts. Your legs are gorgeous."

I blushed.

She dropped her eyes shyly. "I'll really miss you."

"Not as much as I'll miss you."

"Really?"

I crossed my heart.

I heard a tiny whimper. "What was that?" I asked.

"What?" Alice looked puzzled.

"Huh," I said, looking around. "Must be hearing things."

She placed her hand on top of mine. The hair on the back of my neck stood up.

"Remember what I said at the hospital?"

"I'll never forget it."

"Well, it's true."

"Well, I do, too."

"You do *what*?" she prodded.

"I love you, too."

"Oh, Donny." Alice burst out bawling and buried her face in my chest. I dragged the swing to a stop and wrapped my arms around her.

"Don't cry," I whispered, stroking her hair. It was soft as golden corn silk.

"It hurts so much," she sniffed.

I leaned back and lifted her chin. "Maybe I can come see you in Paris.

Or you could visit me in Kansas City."

She perked up and wiped her eyes on the sleeve of my T-shirt. "Yes! I'll make sure Father gets your address. And I'll send you ours as soon as we have one."

We gazed at each other in silence, searching for things to say. A question flickered across her face. "What's that around your neck?"

"Oh," I muttered, fingering my silver chain self-consciously. "Something Sister Celia gave me when I left the hospital."

"Let me see."

Tentatively, I pulled out the silver cross. "Think it's too sissy?"

Alice touched it as though it were holy. "Not at all. It's very manly."

A delicious warmth rose inside me. I let the cross hang outside my shirt.

A loud squeal interrupted us.

I sat up straight. "There, you must have heard that," I said.

Alice's lips formed a secretive smile. She reached down, picked up the shoebox and handed it to me.

Two things surprised me.

One, her fingernails weren't stumps any more. They even ended in small white curves.

Two, the top of the shoebox was punctured with a bunch of tiny holes.

I lifted the lid, and was greeted by two timid black eyes, a shiny black nose and a tiny pink tongue.

"Coco!" I exclaimed. "She had her babies!"

Alice nodded and pointed to the puppy. "I chose the best one for you."

I hugged Alice tentatively, careful not to crush the puppy between us. "I may have to clear it with Mom. What with us moving and all."

"No, you don't," Alice replied confidently. "Mother called this morning and your mom said it would be fine. She thought it was time you had another dog."

"You think of everything."

Alice lowered her eyes demurely. "I call her Alice Too. But you'll probably want to give her your own name."

I lifted her chin and looked at her ardently. "Not for all the world."

"She's just been weaned. And I put a note in the box that tells you what to feed her."

I lifted the pup to my face and nuzzled her. "She's wonderful," I whispered. "Just like you."

Mrs. Cody roared up to the curb and honked. Alice glanced at her mother, then turned to me with a mournful expression. I slipped the puppy into the shoebox and pulled Alice close. Our eyes closed. Our lips touched—tentatively at first-then urgently.

HONK!

Reluctantly, we separated.

Alice wiped her eyes and eased out of the swing. "I'll think about you every day. Every single minute."

"Me, too." I held up the puppy. "She'll remind me."

Alice ran down the walk and jumped into her mother's car without looking back.

I closed my eyes and raised Alice Too up to my face. She licked the salty tears that crawled down my cheek. I held my breath as I watched the Cody car get smaller and smaller and finally curve out of sight.

Eric's voice came back to me. *"Have you ever felt happy and sad all at same time?"*

Now I knew what he meant. So much had changed in such a short time. Not only was I leaving, but David, Miss Morris, Eric, Pete, and Alice were, too. My idea of a perfect place to live—where everything stayed the same—was all wet. It just didn't exist. And even if it did, it would be the most boring place on earth.

I nestled the pup in my lap, leaned back, fingered the chain around my neck, and stared up at the sky. A fragrant spring breeze and the swaying of the swing lulled me into a sweet half sleep. I reminisced about my short time in Farmington. Except for Chaplin's death, it had been the happiest time in my life. I might never experience anything like it again.

Still, I realized that a necessary part of growing up was letting go and moving on. And for the first time in my life, I rather welcomed what came next.

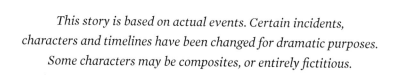

This story is based on actual events. Certain incidents,
characters and timelines have been changed for dramatic purposes.
Some characters may be composites, or entirely fictitious.

RON PHILLIPS

A former Senior Creative Director at international advertising agencies N.W. Ayer and Campbell-Ewald, Ron Phillips has helmed campaigns for megabrands ranging from AT&T to United Airlines. As a commercial director, he has won every major advertising award, including Gold and Silver Lions at Cannes. In addition to writing and directing the PG-rated motion picture *FunnyCar Summer*, Phillips has produced a number of CINE award-winning children's films. His written work has appeared in *Reader's Digest, TV Guide* and the *Detroit Free Press*, for which he was a features writer. Ron and his wife, Linda, currently reside in Ojai, California with their Goldendoodle, Max, and their one-eyed cat, Tux. An active supporter of several local arts organizations, Phillips is a board member of the Ojai Music Festival and the Ojai Film Society. *Donnyboy* is his first novel.

Made in the USA
San Bernardino, CA
29 April 2019